the Tutti-Frutti Collection

HarperCollins *Children's Books*

Skinny Melon and Me first published in Great Britain by Collins 1996
Becky Bananas: This is Your Life first published in Great Britain by Collins 1997
Fruit and Nutcase first published in Great Britain by Collins 1998

First published in this three-in-one edition by HarperCollins *Children's Books* 2005
HarperCollins *Children's Books* is a division of HarperCollins*Publishers* Ltd,
77-85 Fulham Palace Road, Hammersmith, London W6 8JB

The HarperCollins website address is
www.harpercollins.co.uk

5

ISBN-13 978 0 00 719862 7

Printed and bound in England by
Clays Ltd, St Ives plc

Skinny Melon and me

JEAN URE

Illustrated by
the equally masterful pens of
Chris Fisher and Peter Bailey

Monday

Skinny Melon and me have decided: we are going to keep diaries.

Skinny is going to start hers on Saturday when she has bought a special book to do it in. She says it is no use doing it in an ordinary pocket diary with spaces for each day as there will be times when we feel like writing a great deal and other times when we may not want to write anything at all, except perhaps what we had to eat for dinner. I agree with her but feel inspired to start immediately and so cannot wait to buy a special book but am using an old writing block with wide lines (I can't stand narrow ones).

I think when a person is writing a diary they ought to introduce themselves in case it is unearthed in a hundred years' time and nobody would know who has written it, so I will say straight away that this is the diary of me, Cherry Louise Waterton, aged eleven years and two months, and I am writing for posterity, in other words *the future*.

To begin with I suppose I must put down some facts, such as, for instance, that I am medium tall and neither fat nor thin but somewhere in between, have short brown hair and a fringe, and a face which is chubbyish (I think I have to be honest) and also round.

I know that it is round because I saw these charts in a magazine at the dentist showing all different shapes of faces, including heart-shaped, egg-shaped, diamond-shaped, turnip-shaped, square-shaped and round.

Mine is definitely round. Unfortunately. Round-faced people tend to have blobby noses, which is what I have got.

The school I go to is Ruskin Manor. It is not the school I would have chosen if I had had any choice. If I had had any choice I would have chosen a boarding school because I think a boarding school would be fun and also it would take me away from Slimey. Anything that took me away from Slimey would have to be a good thing. I did ask Mum if I could go to one but she just said, "Over my dead body". She was really pleased when I got to Ruskin because it's the one she wanted for me. She says all the others are rough.

Ruskin is OK, I suppose, though we have simply stacks of homework, which Mum needless to say approves of. On the other hand, I have only been there for three weeks so there is no telling how I might feel by the end of term. Anything could happen. Our class teacher, Mr Sherwood, who at the moment seems quite nice, could for instance suddenly grow fangs, or the Head Teacher turn out to be a werewolf.

Mr Sherwood   Head

I mean, you just never know. (The Head Teacher is called Mrs Hoad. What kind of name is Hoad? It sounds rather sinister to me.)

Skinny Melon

My best friend Melanie also goes to Ruskin. Her surname is Skinner and she is very tall and thin so I call her Skinny Melon, or Skinbag, or sometimes just Skin. John Lloyd, who is a boy in our class, said last week that we were the Long and the Short of it, but that is only because Skinny Melon is so tall, not because I am short.

This is me
standing by her →

Skin's face shape wasn't shown in the magazine. It's long and thin, the same as the rest of her. Sausage-shaped, I suppose you would call it. Like a Frankfurter.

Me and Skin have been best friends since Year 5 and we are going to go on being best friends "through thick and thin and come what may". We have made a pledge and signed it and buried it in a polythene food bag under an apple tree in my back garden. If ever we decide to stop being best friends we will have to dig up the pledge and solemnly burn it. This is what we have agreed on.

Where I live is 141 Arethusa Road, London W5. W5 is Ealing and it is right at the end of the red and green lines on the Underground.

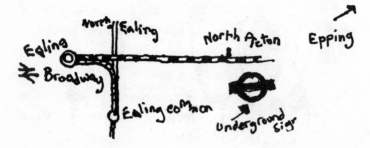

Skin and I once decided to go and see what Epping was like as we had heard there was some forest there, but we got on the wrong train and went to a place called Fairlop instead.

Ealing doesn't have any forests, just a bit of scrubby common which you can walk to from Arethusa Road. There is also a park where Skinny Melon and me take her dog Lulu to meet other dogs. I wish more than anything I could have a dog! Well almost more than anything.

What I would wish more than anything is alas impossible as it would mean turning the clock back, which is something you cannot do unless you happen to be living in a science fiction novel where people travel into the past and change things. I would like to travel into the past and change things. That is what I would like more than anything else. But after that the next thing that I would like is a dog.

Any sort of dog would do. Big dog, small dog, I wouldn't mind.

Why I am suddenly starting to write this diary is that Mrs James, who is our English teacher, said that it would be a good thing to do. She said there are several reasons for keeping a diary. These are some that I can remember:

a) It is good practice for when it comes to writing essays etc. for school.

b) It is a record of one's life and will be interesting to look back on when one is old.

c) It is a social document (for historical purposes, etc.).

d) It can help to clear out the cupboard.

When Mrs James said about clearing out the cupboard, we did not immediately understand what she meant and some people started giggling and pretending to open cupboard doors and take out cans of fruit and stuff and chuck it away, but Mrs James said the cupboard she was talking about was "the cupboard in your head". She said that sometimes the cupboard in your head gets all clogged up with bits and pieces that worry you or upset you or make you angry, and that writing them down in a diary helps to get rid of them. She said, "We've all got a lot of clutter that needs clearing out." She told us to go home and think about it – to look into our cupboards and see what was there.

Amanda Miles told me next day that she'd looked into her cupboard and as far as she could see it was pretty well empty, except for the grudge she still had against Mr Good at Juniors who made her go and stand in the front hall for throwing paint water at Andy Innes when it wasn't her. She said she didn't think that was enough to start writing a diary about.

"I mean, are you going to?" she said.

To which I just made mumbling noises, since there are some things you can't talk about to other people, and certainly not to Amanda Miles. The thing in my cupboard is one of them.

Slimey Roland is the thing in my cupboard.

I'd do anything to get rid of him. I wish he'd go and walk under a bus. I expect Mum would be sad for a bit, but she'd get over it. She can't really love him. Nobody could. He's a total and utter dweeb.

I nearly had a heart attack when Mum said she was going to marry him. I mean, I really just couldn't believe it. I thought she'd got better taste. I told her so and she slapped me and then burst into tears and said she was sorry but why did I have to be so selfish and unpleasant all the time?

I'm not selfish and unpleasant. I don't think I am. But it's enough to make you, when your mum goes and marries a total dweeb. And I had to go to their rotten grotty old wedding, which wasn't even a proper wedding, not the actual marrying part. Just Mum and Slime, and me and the Skinbag, who came to keep me company, and Aunt Jilly, who is Mum's sister, and this man who was doing it. Marrying them, I mean.

When he'd finished he said that now they could kiss

13

each other and they did and I looked at Skin and pulled this being-sick face (at which I am rather good) and Skin told me afterwards that I was horrid to do such a thing at my mum's wedding. It's all right for her. I know she hasn't got a dad, but who'd want Slimey?

One of the worst things about him is his name... Roland Butter. Can you imagine? I thought at first it was just one of his stupid jokes (he's always making stupid jokes, like: Where do pigs leave their cars? At porking meters. Ha ha ha, I *don't* think). Mum, however, said no, he really was called Roland Butter. He's an artist, sort of. He draws these yucky pictures of elves and teddy bears and stuff for little kids' books and he has this headed paper with a drawing of a roll and butter on it. Mum thinks it's brilliant but that's because she's besotted. If you ask me, it's utterly pathetic and I am certainly not going to change my name to Butter, which is what Mum would like me to do. Cherry Butter! I ask you! How could you get anywhere with a name like that?

Mum's name is Pat, and guess what? He calls her Butterpat. It's just so embarrassing.

Dad used to call her Patty. She was Patty and he was Gregg, unless they were having one of their rows and then they didn't call each other anything at all except names which I am not going to write in this diary in case it is ever published. It is true that Mum and Dad did have rows quite often, but what I can't understand is why they couldn't just kiss and make up like Skinny and I do?

We had this really awful row once, me and Skin, about a book I'd lent her which she'd gone and lost by leaving it on a bus and then refused to buy a new one because she said I'd never paid her back the money she'd lent me ages ago when we'd gone swimming and I'd left my purse behind, which definitely and positively was not true. We had this absolutely mega row and swore never to speak to each other again, but life wasn't the same without Skinny, and Skinny said it wasn't the same without me, and so after a bit, like about a week, we made it up and we've been best friends ever since. Why couldn't Mum and Dad do that?

Dad's living in Southampton now. It's near the New Forest and is really nice, but it takes forever to get there. I can't go out with him every weekend like I used to when he and Mum first split up and he was still living in London. Then, he'd come and pick me up and we'd do all sorts of things together – McDonald's, museums, the waxworks. It was really fun. After he got this job and moved to Southampton it meant I could only properly see him in school holidays.

I could have gone with him if I'd wanted. If I'd really wanted. I bet I could. I only stayed with Mum because I thought she'd be lonely. But then she went and met Slimey Roland at some stupid party and they went and got married and now she's totally loopy about him and I'm the one that's lonely, not Mum. So I could have gone with Dad.

Except that Dad's got a new wife called Rosemary, and he's totally loopy about *her*, so maybe he wouldn't want me either. Maybe nobody wants me. Mum says she does but how could she go and marry this creep if that was the case? He's really slimy. Look at him!

Ha! He's not the only one that can draw. There's nothing to it. That is exactly how he looks. Straggly hair and a beard and this long, droopy face like a damp dishcloth. And he's all freckled and gingery with white skin like a mushroom. Ugh! Whatever does Mum see in him?

She says that if I love her I'll try and love Slimey, for her sake. I've *tried*. But how can you love someone who has freckles and makes these awful jokes all the time? Another thing he does, he shoves these cards under the bedroom door while I'm asleep. It's really creepy. I find them lying there waiting for me when I wake up. They're all covered in these soppy drawings which I think are supposed to be messages. I don't bother to read them. I just chuck them straight into the waste-paper basket.

I know why he's doing it. He's so transparent it's pathetic. He's trying to impress me. Well, some hopes! I just think he's a total nerd.

Mum's best friend Carol that she was at school with and who is my godmother, but who has now gone to live in Austin, Texas, alas (though she has promised to send me a real American baseball bat for my Christmas present), told me that Mum and Dad had become very unhappy together on account of "developing in different directions", which meant they didn't really have anything in common any more – apart from me, that is, but it seems children don't count.

Carol said that it's lovely for Mum to be with Slimey because they are both in the same business, with Slimey being an illustrator of children's books and Mum being something called a copy editor, which means going through books that other people have written and making sure they've got their facts right and have put all the commas and fullstops in the right places and haven't called their heroine Anne Smith on one page and Anne Jones on another.

All I can say is that it may be lovely for Mum, but it isn't very lovely for me. And if writing a diary means clearing Slimey Roland out of the cupboard then I am ALL FOR IT.

Tuesday

He made another of his awful jokes this morning. He said, "What's a cannibal's favourite game?" To humour him and keep Mum happy I said, "What is a cannibal's favourite game?" though in fact I already knew the answer because it was a joke that was going round when I was in Year 5, for goodness' sake. So he beams into his beard, all jolly ho ho, and says, "Swallow my leader!" and Mum groans and rolls her eyes, but in a way that means she thinks it's really quite funny, and I just give this tight little smile and get on with my breakfast. It is extremely irritating when grown-ups behave in this infantile fashion. Doesn't he realise he's making a complete idiot of himself?

I have decided to record occasionally what I eat for dinner, because this school's canteen must I think be the secret weapon of someone who has a hate thing against children. Skinny asked Mr Sherwood the other day why he didn't eat there. She said, "Is it because you don't want to be poisoned?" Mr Sherwood said that at his age being poisoned was a distinct possibility. He said, "My digestive system is no longer geared to the hazards of a school canteen."

If that isn't an admission, what is???

I told Mum what Mr Sherwood said. I actually put it to her: "If you don't want to lose me, then maybe I ought to take sandwiches?" All she said was, "Oh, Cherry, don't be silly! What do you want sandwiches for? You're spoilt for choice, you people! In my day it was wet mash and soggy greens and that was that, like it or lump it. Now it's more like a five-star hotel."

I can only conclude that Mum has never been to a five-star hotel. I asked her to name one and she said,

"Oh, the Ritz! The Savoy!" I bet the Ritz and the Savoy don't dish up plates of disgusting white worms in congealed blood and call it spaghetti. That's what I had today, white worms in blood. Utterly foul.

Wednesday

Brown worms today. Brown worms in something-I-won't-put-a-name-to as it makes me feel sick. And anyway, I don't know how to spell it. Yeeeeeurgh!!!!!

Thursday

There are times when I hate Mum for the way she treats me. Skinny Melon couldn't walk home with me after school today because, guess what? Her mum was taking her to buy a bra! Skinny Melon who is as thin as a piece of thread! Not a bump to be seen. Not even the beginnings of a bump. I am practically a double-D cup compared to her. I mean, she doesn't even get on the chart! But her mum is so nice. It's like she went out and bought her brother a razor for his birthday even though he hadn't got anything to shave, hardly. So the Melon hasn't got anything to put in a bra, but still her mum takes her seriously.

She even takes the Blob seriously, for heaven's sake!

The Blob is Skin's sister and rather immature, as one tends to be at only eight years old. She is still at the stage of asking these dippy questions such as "Where do babies come from?" Skinny's mum never fobs her off with yucky stories about storks or gooseberry bushes but treats her like a real person and tells her the truth. That's how grown-ups ought to behave. It is very patronising and hurtful when they laugh at you behind your back, which is what Mum and Slimey do. I'm not saying they do it all the time but it is what they did tonight.

When I got back from school, Slimey was up in his studio (the back bedroom, which ought by rights to have been mine) and I took the opportunity to suggest to Mum in *strictest confidence* that maybe it was time I, too, started to wear a bra. I said, "If the Melon does and I don't, I shall get the most terrific inferiority complex… It could stunt the whole of my future sex-life." Mum said, "Oh, my goodness, we can't have that! But really why you all want to grow up so quickly I can't imagine."

I said, "Why? Isn't it any fun being grown-up?" and she said, "Sometimes it is, sometimes it isn't." So, as I said to her, where's the difference? She needn't think it's all fun being a child, because I can assure her it most definitely is not. Not when the parents go and split up and the child is just left like an old bit of baggage. "Who is going to take it? You or me?" And then they both go and get married again and probably wish there wasn't any child because really it is such a nuisance, always being so selfish and unpleasant. "Why did we ever have it in the first place?"

If Mum thinks that's fun, she must have a very strange sense of humour, that's all I can say.

Anyway, she agreed we could go in on Saturday maybe and buy me a bra, so that was all right. In fact I felt quite warm towards her and thought that in spite of divorcing Dad and marrying the Slime she was every bit as nice a Mum as Skinny's. I thought of what Carol had said about her and Dad growing apart and I thought that perhaps it was just one of those things that happened and that it wasn't really her fault. I even half made up my mind that in future I would try to be nicer to her and forgive her for what she'd done.

And THEN she had to go and blow it all. She went and betrayed me with *him*.

What happened, I'd gone upstairs to wash and she was in the back bedroom with Slimey and she'd left the door a bit open. I wasn't eavesdropping, but even if I had been, so what? I think one has a right to know what people are saying about one behind one's back. What I heard Mum say was, "Hasn't got anything there!" and then go off into these idiotic peals of laughter. I hate her for that. I shall never trust her again. I bet old Slimey thought it was *really* funny.

And anyway, I've got more than Skinny has!

Friday

There is a girl at school called Avril Roper whose dog has just had puppies. She said if anyone wants one they can have one free because the puppies were a mistake and her mum is only interested in them going to people who will love them, not in making money. I tore home like the wind and burst into the kitchen and yelled, "Mum, Mum, can we have a puppy? They're going free! And they're small ones, Mum!" I said this because last time I found some puppies, which was before she married Slimey, they were in a pet shop and cost £50 each and were some sort of mixture that was going to grow as tall as the kitchen table and eat us out of house and home. So naturally I thought as these were free, and were tiny, she'd say yes right away, no problem.

Instead she just laughed, sort of nervously, and said, "Puppies are always small, to my knowledge."

I said, "Yes, but these are going to stay small. Their mum is a Jack Russell and their dad was a Yorkshire terrier."

You can't get much smaller than a Yorkshire terrier. And anyway, she promised. As good as. After Dad left and Mum and me were on our own she said, "We'll get a dog to keep us company." But she never did. Now here was I offering her one free, so why didn't she jump at it?

Because of Slimey Roland, that's why. I said, "You promised!" and this shifty look came into her eyes and she didn't want to meet my gaze, which is a sure sign of guilt. She said, "I don't think I actually promised." I said, "You did! You promised!" Mum said, "I may have mentioned it as a possibility. That's all." I said, "Well, now it is a possibility! They're going for free!"

And then Mum sighed and said, "Cherry, I'd love a dog as much as you would, but how can we? You know Roly's allergic." I said, "Allergic to dogs?" How can anyone be allergic to dogs? I said, "I know he has hay fever." But hay fever is pollen. Mum said, "I'm afraid it's not just hay fever. The poor man's allergic to all kinds of things – dust, pollution, house mites…"

And dogs. He just would be, wouldn't he? He's that sort of person. All wimpy and sniffly and red-eyed. So Mum has to break her promise just because of him!

Saturday

That creep shoved another note under my door.
Something about a tortoise. I don't want a rotten tortoise!
I want a dog. Mum promised me.

This morning we went into the shops and I got a
couple of bras, one white and one pink. I suppose
they're all right, but it's all gone a bit sour now that I
know she and Slime have been sniggering about it. I
keep picturing them lying in bed together having this
good laugh.

I chucked his note into the waste-paper basket along
with all the others. If he doesn't stop doing it, it'll soon
be full to overflowing. Mum said today that we are going
to have a new regime. She said, "I looked into your
bedroom yesterday and it's like a pigsty," to which I
instantly retorted that as a matter of fact pigs left to
themselves are extremely clean and intelligent animals.
It's only horrible farmers that make them dirty by not

allowing them to lead natural lives. To which Mum said, thinking herself very clever, "Well in future I am going to leave you to yourself and we shall see how clean and intelligent you are. From here on in –" (that is a phrase she has picked up from Carol my godmother, who has picked it up in Austin, Texas) "– from here on in I wash my hands of your bedroom. You can take sole responsibility for it. Right?"

I just humped a shoulder, feeling generally disgruntled on account of Mum breaking her promise about the dog. Mum said again, "Right?" and I muttered "Right," and Slimey Roland did his best to catch my eye across the table and wink, but I refused to take any notice.

Later on, Avril Roper rang to find out if we were going to have one of the puppies. I didn't want to say no, so I said we hadn't yet decided, and she said me and Skinny could go round and see them sometime if I liked. She said, "They're so *sweet*. You won't be able to resist them. You can hold them in the palm of your hand!"

So then I rushed back to Mum and said, "Mum, they're so tiny you can hold them in the palm of your hand! Oh, Mum, can't we have one? Please?" thinking that if I really begged hard enough she wouldn't be able to say no, but she was obviously feeling in a mean mood because all she did was snap at me. She said, "I already told you, the answer is no! Roly's health happens to be of more importance to me than a dog. I'm sorry, but there it is."

I gave her this really venomous look as I slunk out of the room.

Sunday

It is after breakfast and I am writing this sitting on my bed. If Mum doesn't do my bedroom soon the waste-paper basket will be overflowing with notes from Slimey Roland. I am on strike. Mum *always* used to do my bedroom.

I used to help Dad clean the car but Slimey hasn't got one because he can't drive. And Mum can't have one because Slimey won't let her. He says they pollute the environment and we all have to walk or use bicycles. I am not going to help him clean his bicycle!!! He looks like a total idiot riding about with his helmet on and his soppy little cycling shorts. Like a stick insect with his head stuck in a goldfish bowl.

Anyway, I help with laying the table and putting things away and doing the wiping up. She won't let me do the washing up any more because she says I use too much washing-up liquid (Greencare, natch. Slimey won't have ordinary Fairy liquid in the house, you bet he won't. He's a complete nutter. He goes round reading all the labels and checking the lists of ingredients and spying on me and Mum to make sure we don't buy anything that might punch holes in the ozone layer).

Another reason Mum won't let me do the washing up is that she says I cause too many breakages. So now Slimey gets to do it and he does it ever so s-l-o-w-l-y and c-a-r-e-f-u-l-l-y and nearly drives me mad.

Dad never used to help in the kitchen, it was one of the things that he and Mum had rows about. But Dad used to go out to work all day. Slimey works at home (if it can be called work, just drawing pictures of elves). It's only fair that he should help.

It wouldn't have been fair if Dad had had to. I don't think it would. When I was little and Dad was in an office we were really really happy. He and Mum hardly ever had rows or shouted at each other. It was only when Dad got made redundant and couldn't find another job and had to go and do the mini-cabbing that it all became horrible. That was when the rows started, because of Dad having to go out and do something he didn't like while Mum just went on sitting at home and reading her books. Of course she was being paid money to do it but it wasn't the same as having to go mini-cabbing. That was what Dad said.

One thing about Slimey, he is interested in Mum's work. Sometimes he reads the books and they discuss them together. Also, he and Mum don't have rows. Yet. But they sit and hold hands and do a lot of kissing and I can't stand it! I hate to think of them holding hands and kissing all day while I'm at school. It makes me feel sick. Kissing with a *beard*. I hate beards.

It's eleven o'clock now and I'm going to go down the road and fetch their Sunday papers for them, which is another of the jobs I have to do that Mum doesn't take into consideration when she goes on about my bedroom. When I come back I might ring Skinny Melon and see if she's going to take Lulu up the park. Or I might ring Avril and find out how the puppies are. Imagine having a dog all of your own! I could have, if it weren't for Slimey. He's in the back bedroom at the moment, drawing elves, and Mum is downstairs on the word processor, writing to her friend, Carol in Austin, Texas. They write to each other every single week! It's almost unbelievable. What on earth do they find to say???

Sunday 27 September

My dear Carol,

Lovely to have all your news and so glad things are working out for you. Just forget all about Martin. He was a jerk and you are well rid of him. Some people are better apart. Take Gregg and me, for instance. We made each other utterly wretched, yet I couldn't be happier with Roly! I'm sure you'll soon meet someone else, though I confess I live in dread that it will turn out to be some big handsome Texan and that you'll settle down for good and all in the States! It's a long way to come and visit...

You ask how Cherry is getting on at her new school. Quite well, as far as I can make out, though she doesn't say very much. The thing she is most vociferous about is the food! She is becoming terribly faddy, but I suppose it's her age. I seem to recall when I was eleven going through a phase when I wanted to eat nothing but Mars Bars. Ah, those were the days! One Mars Bar, one KitKat, one Penguin biscuit, all gobbled up before the morning break and not a spare inch of flesh to be seen! Of course I wouldn't let Cherry eat stuff like that. Roly, fortunately, is educating me in the way to healthy living. No more junk food! No more snacks! In fact I think we shall all end up as veggies.

I wish I could say that Cherry's attitude towards Roland had changed for the better, but she is still very cold. It's so unfair, because he tries so hard. He keeps sending her these really charming little cards with coded messages in the form of pictures. Any other child would be delighted. But I see Cherry simply throws them in her waste-paper basket. It's so ungracious. As a result I am refusing to clean up her bedroom for her. She can jolly well do it herself!

She is a bit peeved at the moment because a girl at school has offered her a puppy and she has taken it into her head that I actually promised her she could have one. I'm sure I only said that I would think about it. Anyway, as it happens it's just not possible as poor Roly is seriously allergic. He's going to start digging a pond in the back garden so that we can have some fish. I think she'll like that.

Oh, I must tell you! It was so funny the other day. Cherry, as you may remember, has this friend called Melanie who is like a beanpole, and Melanie, my dear, was going out to buy a bra! So naturally Cherry decided that she wanted one, too, and we had to trundle out yesterday morning to get her a couple. But the joke is, she has nothing there! As flat as the proverbial pancake! Well, it probably makes her feel sophisticated and Roly says we mustn't laugh as one is very sensitive to these things when one is young.

Roly really is a most extraordinarily understanding sort of person. And sympathetic! Far more than I am when she starts playing up. She has really been trying my patience just recently. But Roly never loses his temper. He never allows himself to be goaded. That is why it makes me so angry, the way Cherry treats him. He could be such a wonderful dad to her! If only she would let him. I am hoping that the goldfish will do the trick...

Write soon! All love,

Patsy

Monday

Dad rang last night. He said his new job is keeping him really busy. He is having to work at weekends and that is why he can't come up to London to see me. But maybe I can go and stay with him at half-term. He is going to speak to Mum. She'd better say yes! It's the least she can do, now she's gone and broken her promise about letting me have a dog.

Old Slimey is digging up the back garden. He's trying to get me interested in goldfish and suchlike junk. Huh! He needn't think that will make up for not having one of Avril's puppies. How can you communicate with a fish?

Tuesday

Slime stew for dinner today. It had a cardboard lid which I thought they had forgotten to remove before heating but John Lloyd said it was pastry. All I can say is it didn't taste like it.

I told Skin about Slimey and his stupid goldfish and she said that as a matter of fact you can communicate with goldfish "in a sort of way". She said that they get used to you and will come to the surface for food. I said, "Oh, brilliant! Do they speak to you? Do they play games? Can you take them for walks?" Skinny told me not to be stupid. She said, "A fish is not a dog." I said, "I know that, thank you very much." She then informed me that I was just being horrible "because the fish were Roly's idea and nothing that he thinks of is ever right for you."

Cheek! What does she know about it?

On the way home from school we had a bit of an argument. Well, a bit of a quarrel really, I suppose. The Skinbag revealed to me that she thinks wearing a bra makes it look as if she has a real bust. Ho ho! What a laugh! I told her she was kidding herself and she got quite snappish and said, "Well, you needn't imagine you'd win any prizes! Two goose pimples is all you've got."

I thought that was uncalled for. I mean, that was a very personal sort of remark to make. You don't expect it from someone calling herself your best friend. We grouched at each other all the way home. Skinny said I was a midget, which isn't true because there are at least two people in our class that are shorter than me, and I said she didn't have any waist, which is true, and she can't deny it. She hasn't any shape at all. Then she said I had a nose like a squashed tomato, and I said she had a face like a Frankfurter, and by the time we got to her road we weren't talking any more, just stomping along in a simmering silence.

I went on simmering all through tea, because I think it's good to let people stew in their own juice for a bit otherwise they think you're crawling. I mean, I didn't see why I should be the one to ring when she was just as much to blame as I was. In fact she was the one who started it, going on about the goldfish. If she hadn't gone on about goldfish, I wouldn't have said that about her kidding herself over her bust. I know the goldfish were earlier, but it really maddened me her saying what she said. That is, about me being horrible to Slime. She ought to try living with him.

For instance, all the time I'm simmering he's sitting there at the table cracking his fingers, which is this thing that he does. Crack, crack, crack, going off like pistol shots. And then he starts making more of his stupid jokes like, "What do you get if you cross a witch with an ice cube? A cold spell," until I couldn't stand it any more so I went and tried ringing the Skinbag, only her number was engaged, but then seconds later she rang me and said she'd tried to get me before but *my* number was engaged, and I said, "That was me trying to get you," and she said, "Oh, right," and there was this awkward pause, and then we both spoke together in a rush.

I said, "I'm really sorry I said that about your face looking like a Frankfurter," and Skinny said, "I apologise for saying you were a midget." And so then we were friends again and started talking about our maths homework.

Why couldn't Mum and Dad be like that?

Wednesday

Scum and matter pie, and a dollop of cold sick. Well, that's what it looked like. Skinny and me have this theory about school dinners. We reckon they take all the stuff that's scraped off the plates and recycle it. Then they dish it back up as slime or slush or squidgy messes and give it fancy names such as Cheese and Onion Tart or Lentil Bake. No wonder the staff don't eat with us. Mrs James says it's to avoid the rabble (meaning us). She says, "We like a bit of peace and quiet."

I bet! They like a bit of proper food and not regurgitated yuck.

Thursday

Rat hot-pot. Slimey Roland wouldn't have touched it! He's a cranky vegetarian. He said to me yesterday, "You

wouldn't eat a puppy, would you? So why eat a lamb?"
He has a nerve, talking about puppies. If it weren't for
him I could have one. I'm going to see them tomorrow.

Friday

I saw them. They are gorgeous! They look like little
balls of fluff.

← Avril's puppies

But all of them have been spoken for except one. I
came rushing home to tell Mum and she said, "Oh,
Cherry, don't start that again!" in a pleading sort of
voice, which shows she's got a guilty conscience. I said,
"But Mum, they're so gorgeous!" and at that point
Slimey Roland came barging into the conversation. He
said, "Oh, Cherry Pie, I'm so sorry! It's all my fault.
Don't go on at your mum!"

I hope he isn't going to make a habit of calling me
Cherry Pie. It makes me want to throw up.

Saturday

Slime said to me at breakfast this morning, "By the way, little lambs are rather gorgeous, too."

What's that to do with anything? I'm not asking for a lamb!

141 Arethusa Road
London W5

Sunday 2 October

Dearest Carol,

Just a quickie as I have to go and help Roly with the pond. It's coming along apace! Cherry still refuses to have anything to do with it but she'll come round. When we actually get the fish she won't be able to resist it. She's still resentful of the fact that she can't have a dog, and I must say that I would rather like one myself, and so would Roly. He is not opposed to dogs, in fact he loves them, as he loves all small creatures (including cross-grained eleven year olds!) but we simply can't run the risk of setting off his allergy. I think left to himself he might weaken, but I'm not having him ruin his health just to keep Cherry happy. I know it was upsetting for her when Gregg and I separated; on the other hand she is extremely lucky to have a step-dad as warm and funny and caring as Roly.

He'll win her over in the end. I know he will!

Lots of love,

Patsy

PS I'm ashamed to say that I still haven't got around to telling Cherry about you-know-what. I'm terrified of breaking it to her in case she reacts badly. So far I've managed to keep it hidden by wearing baggy T-shirts but it's reached the point where not even the baggiest of T-shirts will hide the bulge! Fortunately, at the moment, she is so wrapped up in her own affairs that she probably wouldn't notice anyway. But I can't afford to leave it very much longer. As Roly says, it's not fair on her.

Monday

Janetta Barnes found a slug in her salad today. She's taken it home to show her mum. I'm hoping her mum will sue someone and then maybe we'll get to have better dinners.

Tuesday

We all had to line up in the hall at break while Mrs James and Miss Burgess walked up and down looking at us. They said they were looking for interesting faces for the Christmas play. I have been picked to be an angel! A *singing* angel.

I rushed home to tell Mum, thinking she'd be pleased, and all she did was laugh and say, "You? An angel?" I said, "Miss Burgess says I have an angelic face." Mum said, "Yes, you do! I'll grant you that. Isn't it strange how looks can be so deceiving?" I told her that it was a play and that I was going to be acting. I said, "And singing as well, as a matter of fact." Mum said, "*Singing?*" That really impressed her, I could tell. Mum never knew that I could sing. But I can!

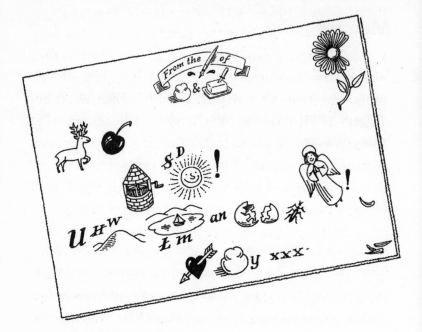

Wednesday

All the puppies have gone! Oh, and they were so beeeeeeauuuutiful! I hope they've been taken by people who will be kind to them and look after them. If I had a dog and it had puppies I would never give any of them away, ever, because you can't trust what people might be going to do with them. There are some people that are just so cruel it is unbelievable. Avril says her mum checked most carefully and they have all gone to good homes where they will be loved, but nobody could love them as much as I would have done!

Curried compost-heap for dinner today. I found what looked like the remains of a beetle in mine. Janetta says she showed the slug that she found to her mum and her mum said it wasn't a slug but a bit of oberjene (?) but Janetta is still sure it was a slug. She thinks what happened was it got squashed in her bag on the way home, on account of all the homework we have to lug about with us, and had therefore gone a bit flat. I think her mum just didn't want to admit that it was a slug. I've noticed that whenever you tell parents anything bad about school, like rotten school dinners or one of the teachers having a go at you for doing something when it wasn't you, they always take the teacher's side and say, "Well, you must have done *something*", or "You must be exaggerating". They hate to admit you could ever be right and a teacher might be wrong. I'm dead sure it was a beetle I found but it's no use taking it home as Mum would only say it was a mustard seed or something.

I forgot to record that Skinny was not picked to be anything in the Christmas play, I suppose because a long, thin face is perhaps not as interesting as a round, blobby one, but fortunately she doesn't mind as she has no wish to be an actress. She says even if they had picked her she wouldn't have wanted to be in it. It is a relief that she is not jealous, but I have to say that on the whole Skinny has a very nice nature. She has promised to come to one of the performances and cheer me on.

Thursday

Today I ate a plate of cold sick with dubious-looking objects floating in it. I had this vision of one of the cooks throwing up in the kitchen and someone running at her with a basin yelling, "Don't waste anything, don't waste anything! Recycle!" Skinny Melon says I am disgusting but I just happen to have this very vivid sort of imagination.

Skinny came back with me for tea after school and it was so embarrassing, I didn't know where to put myself. Slimey Roland was there, all covered in mud from digging this stupid pond he keeps on about. He looked such a sight! I could have died when he came and sat down with us at the table. I was so ashamed of him. And then he started making these awful jokes, the way he does, like, "What do you call two spiders who've just got married? Newly Webs!" and "What's full of sandwiches and hides in a bell tower? The Lunch Pack of Notre Dame!" I mean, they're just not funny. I don't think they are.

Skinny was really brilliant and kept groaning and giggling and making like she was amused. She was only doing it out of pity for me, I could tell. It was nice of her, but then he started to think he was some kind of big comedy star and just went on and on till I wanted to scream. Skinny actually choked at one point and I thought she was going to suffocate, she went so red. I expect the reason she choked was he was being so *ex-cru-cia-ting*.

I apologised to her afterwards. I said, "He's really grungy, isn't he?" I thought we could have a nice hate-Slimey session but Skinny wouldn't play. She has this thing about fathers, which is because hers went and died when she was really young so that she never properly knew him and as a result she thinks even a dad like Slime is better than no dad at all. I told her that a) he wasn't my dad. I already had a dad, thank you very much. Just because he isn't living with us doesn't make him not my dad any more and b) she'd change her mind quickly enough if Slimey Roland married *her* mum and went to live in *her* house.

I said, "Imagine listening to those yucky jokes every day!" Skinny said that she would be quite happy listening to yucky jokes. She agreed that they were yucky but said she thought that Slime was "an ace joke-teller". I said "Oh, do you?" and she said, yes, she did, so I said, "Well, I don't. I think he's pathetic." I said, "He's a wimp and a weed and he sniffles." To which Skinny retorted, "So what?" She then had the nerve to tell me that I wasn't being fair.

From the of
&

H R of YJ .... eggs-ercising,
eggs-spelled, eggs-it, eggs-acting
Silly, aren't they? y xxx.

Friday

The Skinbag must be mad. She said to me today that she thinks Slimey Roland is "really nice". She also said, "Is your mum going to have a baby?" which made me want to knock her head off. I said, "No, of course she isn't! What makes you think that?" and she said, " 'Cos she looks as if she is." So I said, "Oh?" raising both my eyebrows up into my fringe to show I was displeased. "What exactly is that supposed to mean?" She said, "Well she's all kind of bulgy round the middle."

I told her I'd poke her eyes out if she said anything like that about my mum again, so then she said, "Sorry, I'm sure," meaning she wasn't sorry at all, and went into a huff and shut up. We haven't talked all the rest of the day.

How dare she say Mum's bulgy round the middle? That would be like me saying her mum had sticking-out teeth, which she has.

← Skinny's Mum's gnashers

But I wouldn't ever say it because it would be rude. And anyway, what would Mum want a baby for? When she's already got me?

Saturday

I've been thinking about what Skinny said. I have a horrible feeling that it might be true. Mum *is* looking bulgy. I suddenly saw it when she was getting off the bus. And this morning after we'd done all the shopping and were going to go and have what Slimey calls "coffee and cakies". (He spends so much time drawing pictures of elves that his mind has gone completely infantile.) I couldn't help noticing that they spent ages standing outside a baby shop gorming at all the prams and potties and carry-cots. They didn't realise I was watching them. They thought I was too busy giving money to a person that was collecting for anti-vivisection, and I *was* giving them money, because I think that anyone that experiments on animals ought to be experimented on themselves, but at the same time I was watching Mum and Slimey. They had their arms round each other's waists! Pathetic, really. Mum is going to be thirty-six next year, and I know for a fact that Slime is even older. I don't think people of that age ought to go about in public with their arms round each other, I think it looks really naff. Especially when one of them is your own mother.

I don't think I could bear it if Mum was going to have another baby. But surely she would have told me? Maybe she is just suffering from middle-age spread.

While we were doing the shopping I looked at some aubergines (which is how it is spelt, not oberjenes as I originally thought) and they are not in the least like slugs, more like big purple eggs, so I really don't know what Janetta's mum was talking about.

After lunch Aunt Jilly and Uncle Ivo came and brought their new baby with them. It is a horrible thing, all sicky and stinky and does nothing but bawl.

Mum and Slimey both drooled over it. Slime kept giving it his bony old finger to hold and making these silly baby noises. I personally think you ought to talk to babies sensibly, in proper language, so that they can learn things. I don't see any point in filling their heads with all this gooey yuck. I mean, if they grow up thinking that stuff like "Doo doo doo" is how people communicate, for goodness' sake, it's just going to retard them. It stands to reason. They left me alone with it for a few

↑ Baby

minutes and I went up to it and said, "Good afternoon. How are you today?" and it actually looked at me quite intelligently. I don't expect it knew what I was saying, but I bet the words have gone into its head and I bet they'll be some of the first words it ever speaks. I bet they'll get a surprise one day when it sits up in its pram and says good afternoon to them.

"Good afternoon. How are you today?"

They won't know it's me they have to thank.

I'm getting more and more worried about Mum. She and Aunt Jilly went into the kitchen together to look at a plant that keeps shrivelling and they were there for simply ages so I went after them to find out what they were doing and as soon as she saw me, Mum gave Aunt Jilly this warning glance and they both stopped talking,

49

but not before I'd heard what they were saying. Well, what Mum was saying. She was saying, "Yes, I know, I'm really going to have to pluck up the courage and tell her."

It doesn't sound good.

9 October

Dear Carol,

Many thanks for your lovely long letter! I'm afraid
this is going to be another shortish one as we've been
out walking all day on Hampstead Heath and I am
whacked. Getting too old and fat!!!

The answer to your question, which I know you're
going to ask, is no... I haven't yet broken the news to
Cherry. Yes, yes, I accept that I'm a total coward, but I
am going to do it tomorrow afternoon when she gets
in from school. Roly has to go away for the night – he
is doing a talk to some mixed infants way up in the
north of England – and so it will be a good
opportunity. Just Cherry and me on our own. I think
she might take it better that way.

We all really enjoyed ourselves today. It was a
lovely family outing, the sort of thing we ought to do
more often. We took our food with us and had a good
old-fashioned picnic! It was Roly's idea, and he
prepared all the goodies. He was really imaginative –
and it was all vegetarian! Vegetable samosas, sausage
rolls made with vegebangers, vegetable kebabs, soya

desserts. I am quite being won over, and I think Cherry is, too. At any rate, she gobbled everything up. I don't believe she even realised that the sausage rolls weren't made with real sausages!

Altogether it was an absolutely super day. It gives me hope that Cherry is coming round at last. I am just keeping my fingers crossed that hearing about you-know-what doesn't set her back.

Jilly and Ivo came over yesterday with little Sammy, and at first Cherry was very cool, very aloof, refused even to look at him. But then we left them alone together for a few minutes, just to see what would happen, and she couldn't resist! Roly reports that she was nattering away nineteen to the dozen. So I think when she gets used to the idea she'll be fine.

She has been asked to take the part of an angel in the school nativity play, if you can believe it. An angel! Cherry! She is also going to sing. I don't know if you have ever heard your god-daughter sing? It is not an experience I would recommend! She has a voice rather like a hyena. I only hope they don't discover their error and give the part to someone else because she is terribly puffed up and looking forward to it. I wouldn't like her little bubble to be burst.

Her friend Melanie came to tea the other day. She is a nice child; steady and reliable. Cherry occasionally tries bossing her but fortunately Melanie can hold her own. I think that's why the friendship has lasted.

Melanie won't stand for any nonsense! Roly was there and kept everyone in stitches, clowning around and generally playing the fool. He is absolutely, instinctively marvellous with kids. I think Cherry was quite proud of him. She certainly ought to have been.

There! This letter hasn't turned out so short after all. Next time I will report how she takes the news about Mum's big secret…

All my love,

Patsy

Sunday

Today we all trailed half-way across London to go for a picnic on Hampstead Heath. On account of Slimey Roland refusing to pollute the environment, we had to go by tube. That meant taking the Central line to Tottenham Court Road, which is 13 stops, and then hanging about for ever waiting for a northern line to Hampstead, which was another seven. What a pathetic way to travel! We must have looked ridiculous. Slimey was wearing a T-shirt and shorts (shorts! With his legs!) and Mum was wearing a horrible sort of boiler suit and looking really dumpy. Definitely middle-age spread. In addition to the shorts, Slime was humping an enormous backpack. You'd have thought he was going on a round-the-world hike. I wore jeans and was the only one who looked half-way normal.

Them

←me

It was a really draggy sort of day because all we did was walk on the Heath and occasionally sit down and eat stuff and then get up again and do more walking and then sit down again to have a drink, and then they wanted to read their Sunday papers, which actually was the best bit because it meant I could go off on my own, which I did, and met this girl throwing sticks for her dog. She let me join in, which was fun. It was a really good dog, a German shepherd, which I would love, but some hopes.

Anyway, after all that we got on the tube and came home again, and what was supposed to be the point of it is what I want to know? If they wanted to go for a walk and sit on the grass and eat things why not just go up the road to the Common? Why trail all the way to Hampstead Heath? Mum says it's because Slimey used to live there before he married Mum and moved in with us and made my life a misery. Well, she didn't say that bit. I said that bit. I will never accept him as a second dad.

Dad was supposed to ring me this evening but he must have been too busy. Mum has said I can go and stay with him at half term. A whole week! Hooray!

The food today was pretty horrific, incidentally, for a true carnivore such as myself. Vegetarian sausages, for heaven's sake! I just munched in glum silence, not saying anything, as I could tell that Mum was really enjoying herself and I didn't want to spoil things for her, but she needn't think I didn't notice because I most certainly did. And if she thinks I am going to become a cranky veggie, she has another thing coming!

I'm really looking forward to tomorrow because HE is going to be away. He's going to go and bore some poor little kids at a school in Newcastle, showing them pictures of elves. That means Mum and I will be on our own! Double hooray!

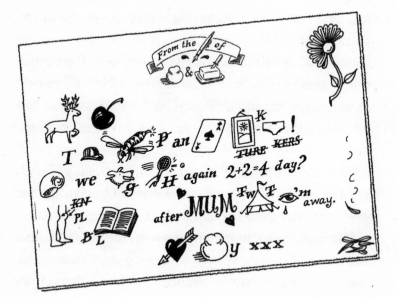

Monday

It's just as well I made things up with Skinny Melon today because it turns out she was 100% right. My worst fears have come true. Mum is going to have a baby.

She broke it to me after tea, just as I was thinking we could settle down to have a lovely evening all to ourselves like we used to before HE came. She said, "I know I should have told you months ago—" and then she didn't get any further because I said, "Months? You mean it's been going on for months?" and she admitted that it had. She said that she is going to have it, "Some time in the New Year... on or about St Valentine's Day." That is the 14th of February! No wonder she looks bulgy round the middle.

I hate Slimey Roland worse than ever now. Doing this to my mum! I bet it was his stupid idea. He's all gooey about babies. Mum would never have thought of it for herself. She and Dad were going to have another one once only she decided against it, so if she decided against it with Dad why would she go for it with Slime? She surely can't want to have a baby that's going to be all gingery and freckled and look like a fungus?

She kept trying to butter me up. Trying to make me feel better about it. She kept saying things like, "It'll make us a proper family", and "It'll be nice for you to have a brother or sister". I don't want a brother or sister! I hate babies! They mess themselves and yell all the time. They are totally disgusting. And its surname will be Butter and it'll belong to them, to Mum and him, and I'll be an outsider.

I'll never forgive him for this. Never!

Tuesday

I told Skinny Melon this morning that she was right, and she said, "Oh, you're so lucky! That is totally brilliant. I wish my mum would get married again so that we could have another baby."

There are times when I think that Skinny is not quite right in the head.

After school we had a rehearsal for the Christmas play and those of us that are angels were taught the angels' song. We each get to sing one verse on our own and then the chorus all together. Mr Freely came in while we were doing it and said, "My goodness, that is some voice Cherry has!" One or two of the others put their hands to their ears and complained that I was deafening them, but you have to sing loudly if people at the back are going to be able to hear you, and it is a rock nativity, after all. Not the wishy-washy churchy kind. That's why Miss Burgess chose me, because I have this big voice.

I really enjoy singing. It has made me wonder whether perhaps I ought to try and be a pop star when I'm older. I know it is an overcrowded profession and that last year I thought I might want to be a judge, but being a pop star would bring deep joy to a great many people's lives whereas quite often judges do the exact opposite.

This is me being a pop star

Oooh!!

This is me being a judge

Maybe I could be a judge after I've finished being a pop star as I don't think you can be a judge until you are quite old, by which time I would most likely be bored with the other. I once heard someone say that fame could become very wearisome.

Actually, the reason I would like to be a judge is so that I could say to children when their parents are trying to get divorced, "Do you want them to get divorced?" and if the children said no, then the parents wouldn't be able to do it.

I'd have said no. I didn't like Mum and Dad quarrelling but I hate having to live with Slimey Roland and Dad having another wife. What I'd have said is you've got to turn the house into flats, one upstairs and one downstairs, and Mum can live in one and Dad can live in the other and I could live in both of them and go upstairs or downstairs as I liked. That, I think, would be perfect.

Or else they could have sold the house and bought two littler ones next door to each other and knocked a hole through the middle. They could be in Southampton so that Dad could still do his new job. They could be in cottages with chimneys and little gardens.

And Dad could go off to work and Mum could stay at home and read her books and they wouldn't ever have to see each other if they didn't want, they could even go out with other people, I wouldn't mind, just so long as they came home at night and were always there.

I said all this to Skinny once and she said that if she had a dad she'd want him to live in the same house as her and her mum and her brother and sister and for them all to be together all of the time. This would be her idea of heaven.

I agree it would be mine if Dad could come back and he and Mum didn't quarrel.

There's a boy at school called Timothy Dunbar who lives with his mum during the week and his dad at weekends. He reckons it's brilliant as his dad spoils him rotten, giving him presents and taking him to places of interest, which he never did when he was at home. But it's all right for Timothy Dunbar. His dad only lives just a few streets away and his mum hasn't gone and got married again.

Slimey came back tonight. Worse luck. I was hoping he might have fallen through a crack in the paving stones.

Wednesday

Mouse droppings and jellied eyeballs. Or maybe it was frogspawn. Either way it was disgusting.

Now that Mum has told me about the baby she seems to think it's OK for her to keep on talking about it. She said to me at teatime, while Slime was upstairs with his elves, "What do you think we should call it? Think of some names!" I said, "There aren't many names that go with Butter." I said, "Barbara Butter, Brenda Butter, Belinda Butter," very heavily sarcastic, but that was the wrong thing as Mum immediately thought it meant that I was interested. She said, "Would you like it to be a girl?" Very quickly, and just as sarcastic, I said, "Bertram Butter, Bruce Butter, Bernard Butter." All Mum said was, "Bernard's nice! I like Bernard."

Bernard Butter? She has to be joking!

Slimey Roland brought me back a china figure from Newcastle. It is a Victorian lady with a crinoline and the crinoline is made of real lace.

My Victorian Lady →

Mum says it is valuable and that I must be careful not to break it. It is quite nice, I suppose. I have put it on the top shelf near my bed.

I would much rather have had a dog.

Thursday

I have found something new to worry about. Suppose Mum dies while she is having this baby? People do die. In olden times they were always dying in childbirth. Even today it could still happen. I couldn't sleep last night for thinking about it. It would be all Slimey's fault! Why couldn't he keep out of our lives? Why couldn't he leave Mum alone? We were perfectly happy without him!

Friday

I asked Mum two things when I got in from school and to both of them she said no.

First of all I asked her yet again if I could take sandwiches instead of having school dinner because today it was something quite unspeakable, I mean it looked as if it had been scraped up off the pavement. It is only a question of time before I get terminally poisoned. Mum said, "You can take sandwiches so long as you're prepared for them to be vegetarian" which as far as I'm concerned is the same as saying no because I am not going to change my eating habits just to please Slime. What's being veggie ever done for him? Made him look like a fungus. And anyway, it would mean he'd won and then he'd get all unbearable and triumphant.

So we had a bit of a dispute about it, with me saying why couldn't I have ham or chicken and Mum saying because it upsets Slime to see dead things in the fridge (and me thinking but not saying that it upsets me to see Slime in the house) and that if I choose to eat meat at school that's up to me but we're not going to have it at home, which means we shall all end up looking like fungus. Except by then I shall probably be dead of food poisoning so I suppose it really doesn't matter.

Anyhow, we then had tea and I said, "Oh, by the way, Gemma Parker has invited me to her sleep-over tomorrow. Is that OK?" and Mum tightened her lips and said, "Well, no, as a matter of fact I'm afraid I don't think it is. I think I'd rather that you stayed away from Gemma Parker."

I knew she'd say that. She has taken it into her head that Gemma is a bad influence all because last term she heard her say a four-letter word that she doesn't even know the meaning of. Gemma, that is. It was just something she'd heard her brother say. All the boys say it; all the older ones. Even Skinny's brother, who Mum thinks is such a "nice young man". They go round shouting it at each other. It doesn't mean anything. They think it makes them sound butch and grown-up.

I said to Mum, "Everybody else is going. I'll feel left out." She said, "Not everybody can be. There wouldn't be room for them." "Well, everyone who is anyone," I said. "The Melon, for instance. Her mum doesn't mind."

Mum likes the Melon. I thought it would sway her, but it didn't. After about ten minutes of arguing she said, "Look, I'm sorry, Cherry, but that is that. I do not want you going to the sleep-over." I shrieked "Why not? When the Melon is allowed to?" Mum said, "You don't have to shout at me. What Melanie's mother allows her to do is neither here nor there. She probably doesn't know that family as I do. I just don't trust them."

The only reason she says this is because Gemma's mum smokes cigarettes and she and Slimey think that anyone who smokes cigarettes is some kind of criminal and ought to be locked up, and also because Gemma's dad happens to work in a place called Franco's that once got raided by the police, which is hardly Gemma's dad's fault. He can't help where he works. What Mum doesn't understand is that Gemma is totally naive. She's like a six year old. Her mum won't even let her watch television without supervision in case she sees something she shouldn't.

I tried explaining this to Mum but she plainly didn't believe me. She said, "If you ask me, Gemma's mother is rather flighty."

What does she mean, flighty? Does she think she's a witch, or something?

Mum told me not to sulk. She said that to make up for not letting me go to the sleep-over, we'd all have a meal in the pizza place tomorrow night and then we'd go to the video shop and I could choose whatever video I wanted. That cheered me up a bit as I thought that I would get something really gross that they normally wouldn't let me have. But honestly, what does she think we do at sleep-overs? We don't do anything! Just sit and talk and try on each other's clothes and then tell scary stories in the dark. Gemma's such a baby she usually falls asleep.

I am going to get a really *gross* video.

The really gross video...

Saturday

I am seriously annoyed. They wouldn't let me have any of the videos I wanted. Mum said I was just picking them to be awkward, because of her not letting me go to the sleep-over. She said if I couldn't choose something sensible, then she would have to choose for me. When I pointed out that she had promised me, she said, "Oh, now, Cherry, act your age! You know perfectly well there are limits."

She never said anything about limits. She said I could choose whatever I wanted.

"Anything sensible," she said.

They cheat all the time, grown-ups do.

So while I'm mooching about looking for something sensible, and doing my best to find one they'd loathe, she and Slimey are wandering over to the kids' section and mooning about amongst the Walt Disneys. Suddenly I hear Slimey cry, "Oh, look, Butterpat!" (I nearly died. The girl behind the counter had to put her hand over her mouth to stop from sniggering.) "Look, Butterpat! Look at this... Snow White!"

And Mum squeaks, "Ohh! Snow White!" in a silly little girly voice, and claps her hands. "I haven't seen that since I was younger than Cherry!"

Slimey says, "Me neither. It used to be my favourite film when I was five years old." And Mum says, "Oh, we've got to have it! Cherry, it's all right, we've found one… we're going to watch *Snow White*!"

Which we did, whether I liked it or not. Which for the most part I did *not*. I mean, it's kids' stuff. Mum and Slimey sat there on the sofa together going oooh and aaah and "Oh, I remember this bit!" "That bit always terrified me!" Having a right nostalgia binge.

Afterwards I rang Gemma's number and spoke to Skinny. I asked her how the sleep-over was going and she said they were watching *When Harry Met Sally*, which actually I have already seen, though I wouldn't have minded seeing it again. At least it would have been better than *Snow Soppy White*. I said, "I'm surprised Gemma's mum lets her watch that," remembering certain bits which I felt sure she wouldn't think suitable. Gemma's mum is really strict, in spite of being flighty and going round on broomsticks. Skinny said, "She's sitting there with her finger on the fast forward button in case of dirty bits, but she can't always get there in time!" and we both giggled.

When I went back in the lounge Mum said, "It's good to hear you sounding so cheerful." I just frowned and didn't say anything. That is the second time Mum has broken her promise.

Sunday

Dad rang this morning. He said he and Rosemary are really looking forward to having me at half-term although it is unfortunate that I won't be able to stay with them for the whole week as they are both working and cannot get more than a few days off. He said they are very disappointed about this but they are not free agents like Mum and Slimey. They can't just take time off whenever they feel like it.

I said that I understood and that it would be lovely to get away even just for a few days. Dad said, "Why? Are you fed up? You're sounding a bit fed up." So I told him about Mum breaking her promises, not letting me have a dog or choose a video, and Dad said, "Breaking a promise to a child is one of the worst things you can do," which I must say I heartily agree with.

He said, "I can't offer you a dog, but when you come to us you can watch whatever video you like, and that is a PROMISE." I said, "You mean it? Any video I like?" and he said, "Any video except *Snow White* and those dratted Dwarves." And I hadn't even told him that that was what Mum and Slimey made me watch! He said they kept pushing it at him in his local video shop, trying to make him take it.

"Don't," I said. "It's really yucky."

Dad said, "I won't, don't worry! I was taken to see it as a kid and had nightmares for months afterwards."

Nightmares? What on earth could he have had nightmares about? Dad must have been an extremely sensitive little boy.

When I told Mum about him and Rosemary not being able to get time off she gave this sort of sneer, with her lip hooped up, and said, "You amaze me!"

"It's because they both go out and do proper work," I said. "They can't just go taking days off whenever they want, like you can."

"Of course they can't," said Mum, all sarky and snide.

"Well, they can't," I said. "They do very important jobs."

"I don't call being a computer programmer all that important," said Mum. "Nor being an office manager," she added.

It's Rosemary who's the office manager, Dad who's the computer programmer. They both work in the same office, which is probably quite nice for them.

I said, "If it wasn't important, nobody would care if they took time off," and to my surprise old Slimey jumped in and agreed with me. He said, "She's absolutely right!" and I saw him give Mum this funny little frown. I don't know what he did that for, but anyhow it stopped her trying to tell me that Dad isn't important, which I really resent. He said, "The way I see it, everyone is important in his own way." To which Mum snapped, "Her!" being a bit of a feminist which actually I am as well. So then old Slime says, "His or her. I stand corrected," and goes on to say that he personally doesn't see why a person that sweeps the road, for instance, should be considered any less important than a prime minister, which is just stupid. Anybody could sweep the road. Not anybody could be prime minister. And not anybody could be a computer programmer, either, so sucks to Mum! She certainly couldn't be.

141 Arethusa Road
London W5

18 October

My dear Carol,

Well, I've done it! My secret is out. On the whole
she has taken it very well; far better than I'd dared to
hope. To begin with I could see she was a bit stunned
– as she had every right to be – and a bit put out that
I hadn't told her sooner, but I apologised for that and
admitted that I was a coward, and I think she
understood.

I was dreading that she would feel resentful and
that we'd be in for an attack of the sulks, but the
other day she was even suggesting names to me and
was starting to sound enthusiastic! I realise now that I
was wrong to keep it from her – Roly said all along
that I was – but I'm hoping no real harm has been
done. I am making sure that we spend some part of
every day talking about the baby together, even if it's
just five minutes, so that she will be made to feel a
part of it and not left out in the cold.

I'm glad you've had a good week (meeting handsome
Texans! You just watch it!) because after a bumpy start
so have we. Roly went away to Newcastle for just one

night and I missed him more than I could have thought possible, but it gave me the opportunity I needed to talk to Cherry and make my confession, and when he came back the next day he'd brought her the most truly beautiful china ornament that he found in an antique shop. I told him that it's far too valuable to give to a child, especially one as clumsy as Cherry, but he insisted that he had bought it for her and that she must have it. She mumbled her thanks – not quite as ungraciously as usual – and seemed reasonably pleased with it. She has put it away very carefully on a high shelf, but it's only a matter of time before it gets smashed to smithereens.

I sometimes wonder whether Roly is trying too hard. Might it not be better if he gave her tit for tat and treated her with the same contempt as she treats him? Unfortunately – or fortunately – it's just not in his nature. He is a very gentle, caring person and I'm afraid that a child like Cherry rides rough-shod over him. I'm hoping that the baby may bring out the softer side of her nature. If she has one!

No, that's not fair. She has on the whole a very sunny personality, very bright and bubbly, and can be quite warm and loving when she chooses. I remember after Gregg and I first split up she was incredibly supportive. I couldn't have asked for a better daughter! It's just that at the moment events are rather conspiring to bring out the worst.

On Saturday she wanted to go to something she calls a sleep-over at a friend's house and we had a bit of a scene when I wouldn't let her. Roly says I should have taken the chance, but he hasn't seen the parents!!! The father works in a gambling den and the mother – well! The mother is something else. Huge peroxide beehive, mascara ten inches thick, mock leopardskin coat. Roly says what does it matter, but I don't want Cherry being led into bad ways and coming back here using foul language, which she is likely to do. The child swears like a trooper. Anyway, to make up for not letting her go we all went up the road for a pizza and then came back to watch a video. Guess what we saw? SNOW WHITE! Did you ever see it when you were a kid? I adored it – and still do! Cherry was inclined to be rather sniffy at first but afterwards she went out into the hall to telephone one of her friends and I heard her laughing, so she was obviously happy, which is something she hasn't always been just lately.

She's desperately looking forward to staying with Gregg for a few days at half-term. I just hope he doesn't let her down. Originally she was going to go for the whole week, but surprise, surprise! He can't get the time off. Funny he could spend a whole fortnight in Florida back in July and is going off skiing for another fortnight at Christmas, but can't spare just one week to be with his own daughter.

I know I mustn't run her dad down in front of her, but the temptation is sometimes very strong! Happily on this occasion, bless him, Roly stepped in before I could open my big mouth and say something which I might afterwards have regretted. I wouldn't want to poison Cherry's mind against her dad. I won't say she regards him as a god, exactly, but he is certainly far higher in the popularity stakes than my poor Roly. On the other hand, I do believe I have detected a slight softening in her attitude just recently. I am keeping my fingers crossed!

Please report on handsome Texans.

Love from

Patsy

Monday

He's still shoving these stupid cards under my door. I really hate the thought of him creeping about doing that while I'm asleep. I just keep chucking them in the waste-paper basket. I'm still on strike and so the basket is practically overflowing and everything is thick dust except for the crinoline lady on her shelf. I am too scared to dust her because she is so fragile and so I blow on her, ever so gently. Maybe if she gets too dirty I can give her a bubble bath and use the hair dryer.

Terrible row with Mum this morning when I arrived downstairs in T-shirt and leggings and my Doc Marten's. She screamed, "You can't wear that gear to school! You go back upstairs and change immediately!" I said, "Into what?" I said, "It may have escaped your memory, but we don't happen to have any school uniform at this school, we can wear whatever we like, and right now everybody is wearing T-shirt and tights and Doc Marten's."

Mum said not to take that tone with her. (What tone? What is she talking about?) She said she didn't care what other people were wearing, she wasn't having her daughter go to school looking like some kind of big-footed grotesque. I said, "That is very big-footist." And she snarled, "Never mind the smart mouth! I have spoken and that is flat and final. How can you expect to do any serious learning in that ridiculous get-up?"

Mum is incredibly hidebound. I said, "Well, if it comes to that, how can you expect to have any serious baby, wearing those ridiculous dungarees?" which is what she has taken to wearing now that her secret is out. I said, "I bet the Queen didn't wear dungarees when she was having babies." Mum started to get all red and hot, but old Slimey laughed and said, "She's got you there!" almost as if he were on my side against Mum. She still wouldn't budge.

I met the Skinbag at the school gates and asked her what the sleep-over was like. She said it was brilliant and that Harry meeting Sally was even better second time round and why wouldn't my mum let me go? I told her it

77

was because of Gemma's brother saying That Word and Mum thinking I might start saying it and the Melon agreed that mothers could be a real drag. She said that right at this moment hers was being even more of a drag than usual which I found hard to believe as the Melon's mum is really nice. She would for instance never make promises and then break them. Like if she said the Melon could have a dog, then she'd let her have a dog. I mean she's already got one, of course, but if she'd said she could have another, or choose a video or whatever, she would let her. So I said, "How is she being a drag?" but the Melon wouldn't tell me. She just said, "Behaving like a teenager."

I don't see anything particularly draggy about that.

When I got home from school, Mum started on about the baby again, wondering whether it was going to be a boy or a girl, trying to get me to say which I'd prefer. I wouldn't prefer either! I don't want to know about the beastly baby. I hope it never comes out. I hope it withers on the vine. I hate it!

Tuesday

Boiled organs and baked toenails for dinner. It was one of the boys that said they were organs. Male organs. He fished some out and made rude patterns with them on the table. Boys like doing that kind of thing. Skinny said she thought the toenails might in fact be potato skins, but who wants to eat potato skins? What happened to the insides of the potatoes? Skinny says we'll probably get to have those tomorrow, all lumpy and foul.

Got into trouble with Mrs James today because she said I was rude to her. I wasn't! She accused me of passing notes and I wasn't passing notes, it was John Lloyd and Steven Carter, I just happened to pick one up off the floor for them. Mrs James said, "There are other ways of letting me know that you have been falsely accused. There is no need to be aggressive."

I complained to Skinny Melon about it afterwards and Skinny said, "Well, you were aggressive. You always are, these days. People hardly dare open their mouths in case you jump on them."

I can't help it. I feel aggressive. I feel like screaming, sometimes. It's living with Mum and Slimey and this baby that Mum's carting around with her. That's what's doing it.

I keep remembering when Dad was here, before he and Mum started having rows. I was happy then. I haven't been happy ever since Mum and Dad split up. I hate them all!

Wednesday

Got into more trouble. Miss Bradley, this time. We were playing netball and she pulled me up for running with the ball when I wasn't. She just thought I was because someone barged into me. I explained this to her, as polite as could be. I said, "Excuse me, but you have made a mistake," and she instantly leapt down my throat and yelled that she was sick and tired of what she called my "attitude", and that if there was any more of it I would be suspended from the team. Why does everyone keep getting at me all the time? I can't wait till it's half-term and I can go and stay with Dad!

I was so disgruntled, what with Miss Bradley having a go at me and Skinny and me being a bit distant after her telling me yesterday I was aggressive, that I decided I wasn't going to stay in at lunch-time like we're supposed to. For one thing I couldn't stand the thought of having to eat the insides of yesterday's potatoes, and for another, I saw Skinny going off with Avril Roper and Uchenna Jackson, so I hopped out through the gates when no one was looking and went into town. I got some crisps and a bottle of Coke and walked up the road to the station, which is where the cab company is that Dad used to work for after he'd been made redundant.

Lots of the same drivers were there and they remembered me and asked me how I was doing and how Dad was liking his new job. They're ever so much more fun than the people Mum and Slimey know. All of Mum and Slimey's friends are either writers or publishers or something else to do with books. Books are all they ever talk about. They're always pushing them at me. "Here's a copy of my new book for you, Cherry." "Here's a copy of a book we've just published, Cherry." "Here's a copy of a book I thought you might like, Cherry."

And then I'm expected to sit down and read them and say what I think of them, which most of the time isn't much, only I'm not allowed to say so for fear of being thought rude or hurting their feelings. It's not that I don't like books, just that I don't like *their* books. The sort they push at me. They're all so babyish! I'm more into the hard stuff. Horror, and that. Mum and Slimey are horrified (ho ho!) but I say what's wrong with reading something a bit scary? They don't seem to realise that I've grown out of all this kiddy crud.

Anyway, when it was time to go back to school one of the drivers, who is called Ivy, said she'd take me in her cab. We talked a bit on the way and Ivy asked me how I was getting on with my mum's new husband. I was glad she didn't say "your new dad" as I can't stand it when people do that. So I pulled a face, and Ivy said, "Tough going?" And then she told me how it had happened to her when she was about my age and how she'd thought she'd never get used to her mum having a new bloke, "Never!" but how in the end she had and, "Now we're the best of friends."

I know Ivy was only trying to be helpful, but I am afraid it is not going to work out like that for me. I still have my real dad, even if he does live miles away. It was different for Ivy as her real dad was not really a very nice person. In fact Ivy said he was "a right *******". (I have to put stars as the word Ivy used is not the sort of word I wish to record in this diary.) I told her that my dad is the best dad in the world and that I am going to stay with him over half-term. I said that I am really looking forward to it. Ivy said, "Well, have a good time, but don't expect too much, will you?"

I don't know why she said that. I didn't have a chance to ask her as we had already reached the school gates. Skinny was mooning about nearby with Avril and Uchenna. You should have seen their faces when they realised who was in the cab!

Skinny   Avril   Uchenna

They couldn't have been more surprised if I'd stepped out of a Rolls Royce. Skinny shrieked, "Where have you been?" It was just my bad luck that Mrs James happened to be passing at that particular moment and also wanted to know where I had been. I told her I'd been visiting my dad's old work-mates and she said, "You do know you're not supposed to leave the premises at lunch time without permission?" and I said yes, which was a dumb thing to say. I should have said no, though I don't expect ignorance is any defence, and she said, "Very well, Cherry," all frozen and unsmiling like an ice lolly with the colour sucked out of it.

Mrs James looking like an ice lolly!

I am to go and see her tomorrow, first thing after assembly.

I know what that means. It means she's going to bawl me out and threaten to tell Mum. I don't care! It was worth it. I'm glad I went. I don't see what right they have to keep making all these rules and regulations anyway. Nobody ever asks us what we want. Grown-ups do just whatever they like. Get divorced. Marry creeps. Have babies. It isn't fair!

Thursday

Went to see Mrs James. Actually she was quite nice. She said that "this sort of behaviour" couldn't be allowed to go on but that she didn't want to have to write to Mum unless I absolutely forced her, and then she said, "Did you ever think about my suggestion for keeping a diary?" and I said yes, I was doing it, and she asked me if it was helping, but without prying into the reasons why I might need helping, which is what lots of teachers would have done. So to please her I said I thought perhaps it was, just a little bit, and she told me to keep on with it because it could only be a good thing.

I hope she's right. I do quite like putting things down in writing. I can say lots of stuff that I couldn't say to anyone else, not even the Melon – who is back being friends with me again, incidentally. It seems that we can't survive without each other. Avril and Uchenna are all right, but me and Skin have been together since Juniors.

I stayed in school at lunch-time and dutifully ate yuck in the canteen. It made me feel sick. I feel sick most of the time now, what with eating yuck and Mum and Slimey keeping on and on about this blessed baby. Even the names they have come up with are yuck. If it's a boy it's going to be Bernard... Bernard Butter. If it's a girl it's going to be Belinda. Mum says she likes what she calls the allitration.

Alliteration. (Just looked it up in the dictionary.) This

means having two letters the same. B and B. Like bed and breakfast. Or bread and butter.

I have just thought of a joke. If it's a girl they could call it Bredan, which is Brenda mixed up. Ha ha! That is a Slimey joke. I shall suggest it to them.

Friday

Dog's vomit and earwax, with crusty bits on top. I didn't ask anyone what it was supposed to be. I think it's better not to know. I just held my breath and swallowed. I am seriously thinking of taking up Mum's offer of vegetarian sandwiches. I would if it weren't for him. Old Slimey. I hate the thought of him crowing because he's won me over. If I decide to do it, it will be out of sheer desperation and a desire not to be poisoned. Nothing whatsoever to do with him.

When I got in at tea-time he was there, which I didn't expect him to be as he'd gone off to bore some more poor little kids, showing them how he draws elves. So I told them my idea for calling the baby Bredan and Mum (stupid) said, "Oh, you mean like Bredon Hill? But that's pronounced Breedon." Slime got it. He got it straightaway. He said, "Bredan Butter! Brilliant!" and promptly started to sketch a loaf of bread on the kitchen table with his felt-tip pen that he always keeps handy in case sudden inspiration comes to him. Mum said, "Oh! Yes. I see. Then we'd have a Roll and

Butter and a Bread and Butter. Clever!"

Slimey said, "Yes, and if we had another we could call it Toastan." I have been trying without success to think of other things that go with butter. All I can think of is T.K. Cann-Butter and Chris P. Bredan Butter. But they are not very good.

I suppose you could have Saul T. Butter. That is not bad.

A woman over the road who has just moved in has asked Mum if I'd like to go and have tea tomorrow with her daughter because her daughter is the same age as me and doesn't yet know anyone. Mum has gone and said that I will! It is terrible the way grown-ups just dispose of one's life for one. I don't particularly want to go and have tea with this person's daughter. She is called Sereena, which I know is not her fault, and her surname is Swaddle, which again I know she cannot be blamed for. Sereena Swaddle. That is alliteration. Mum says it is "unfortunate", but why she should think it's any more unfortunate than Belinda or Bernard Butter is beyond me.

Skinny rang later to know if I wanted to go swimming with her tomorrow afternoon and I had to say that I was having tea with this Sereena person. Skinny said "Who?" and I said, "Sereena Swaddle," and she said, "You're joking!" I said that I only wished I was. I went back to Mum and said, "Do I have to do this thing?" and she said, "Oh, Cherry, just once! It won't hurt you. She's a sweet little thing, I know you'll like her."

When Mum said, "sweet little thing" old Slime caught my eye and pulled a face. I'd gone and pulled one back before I could stop myself. I don't think I ought to do that. It's like him and me being ganged up together against Mum. Mum must have sensed it because she said, "You can laugh! It's nice to know there still are some sweet little things… they don't all clump around in bovver boots shouting four-letter words and watching ghastly horror movies."

I have just thought of something else that could go with butter. P. Nutt-Butter. That is a good one!

Saturday

Ha! So much for Mum not letting me go to Gemma's sleep-over in case she corrupted me. I went to have tea with the Sereena person this afternoon. The sweet little thing who doesn't swear or watch horror movies. I can see why Mum thought she was a sweet little thing. It is because she has a sweet little face. (Yuck!) She also has long blonde hair and rose-pink cheeks and eyes the size of satellite dishes and blue as whatever's blue. The sky. Forget-me-nots. Saffires. Rather revolting, really. At least, I think so. But it's what grown-ups like.

So anyway, we had tea and her mum was there and she's sort of… frothy. All fizzing and bubbling like Andrew's Fruit Salts that Dad used to take for his acid

Sereena ↑

indigestion. She kept giggling and saying things like,
"Oh, Reena." (That's what she calls her. Double yuck.)
"Oh, Reena, isn't this fun! You've found a friend
already!" But I don't know whether I want to be her
friend. I like to choose my own friends, and besides, I've
got Skinny.

Afterwards we went up to her room and she said,
"What do you want to do?" And I said, "Whatever you
want to do." And she said, "Would you like to see some
pictures of people having babies?"

I said, "I've seen pictures of people having babies.
We did all that in Juniors."

"All right," she says. "What about pictures of people
completely starkers?" I said, "Where would you get
pictures of people starkers?" and she said her best friend
Sharon where she used to live had torn them out of a
magazine and photocopied them for her. She said some
of them were really gross. Do you want to have a look?"

I was tempted to say yes as I thought it would pay

Mum out for not letting me go to Gemma's sleep-over, and also it would be a new experience and I do believe in having new experiences, but really to be honest I didn't fancy it, I mean that sort of thing could put you off for life and I would like to grow up to be reasonably normal.

Sereena said, "Oh, well, if you don't think you can take it, I'll tell you some jokes instead, shall I?" And before I can stop her she's telling me all these jokes that her friend Sharon had told her and which I shall not repeat in here as this is a diary and not a reseptikle for filth.

Pause while I look in the dictionary. That word is spelt receptacle. And saffire is spelt sapphire. I am very good at spelling, on the whole. Mrs James said to me the other day (before we had our little talk), "Your spelling and punctuation are excellent, Cherry." On the other hand I cannot understand figures, which is what Mr Fisher, who takes us for maths, calls "a decided drawback". Mum can't understand figures either, and nor can Slimey Roland, but it doesn't matter to them as they do the sort of jobs where figures are not important. Mr Fisher says that anyone who is not numerate, meaning anyone that can't add up or subtract, will have a hard time of it in the 21st century. He says we must come to terms with technology or perish.

Computers are technology and I'm not very good with computers, either. I don't know what I will end up

Me in → the future

doing. Sweeping the streets, I expect. I don't think I will be able to work with books like Mum, as I don't think there will be any books left, just CD Roms, or whatever they are. And I don't think there will be people drawing pictures of elves, either. It will all be done by computer and people such as myself will be left behind like old empty bottles on the beach.

I tried talking about this with Sereena, thinking I would find out what kind of things she is good at other than telling rude jokes, but you cannot have a proper conversation with her as you can with the Melon. All she can do is bat her satellite dishes and giggle. Of course the Melon is a bit of an intellectual, I mean, she has a real brain. Sereena's brain if she has one, is about the size of a pea.

When I got home Mum said, "There! That wasn't so bad, was it?" I told her it was "enlightening" and she said, "Why? What did you do?" I said, "Read porno mags and told dirty jokes." Mum laughed. She thought it really funny. "No, seriously," she said.

I said that seriously we had discussed what we thought would happen in the 21st century and I had come to the melancholy conclusion that far from being a pop star or a judge I would most likely end up living in a cardboard box as I was not numerate and couldn't make friends with computers the way some people could. Skinny, for example, and Sereena. Mum told me not to be so pessimistic. She said, "You're like me, you're into words." I said yes, but there won't be any words. Just computerspeak. Mum said, "Oh, what a bleak picture!" I said, "Yes, it is, but I think one has to face facts."

Mum doesn't want to face them. She says that if it's going to be a world without books and pictures then she'd sooner not be here. Slimey didn't play any part in this conversation as he was upstairs finishing some more elves to meet what is called "a deadline", meaning (I think) that his publishers will sue him for vast sums of money if he hasn't drawn the right number by a certain date.

It was nice being on my own with Mum, even if our conversation was rather doom-laden. At least she didn't mention the baby, which is now sticking out in front of her like a huge horrible sack of potatoes.

She asked me the other day if I'd like to feel it but I said no, thank you very much. Catch me!

Tomorrow I am going to stay with Dad. Hooray hooray hooray! Three whole days without Slimey Roland! No more stupid jokes, no more stupid cards! I can go to bed at night and know that nobody is going to come creeping along the passage and shoving stuff under my door while I'm asleep, which is something I really hate.

Dad is picking me up in the car. He is driving all the way from Southampton and is arriving at about 9 o'clock, so I must be sure and be up early. I am going to set my alarm. Fortunately I have already packed my case, I did it this morning with Mum's help. She kept saying things like, "Well, you won't need all that much, now it's only for a few days." She just refuses to accept that Dad is an important person and cannot simply please himself. This is because he is in an office. All Mum and Slimey ever do is sit at home reading books and drawing elves. But with Dad, there is a great deal depending on him and he has to be prepared to work long hours. It is not his fault. I do wish Mum could see this.

I am going to take my diary with me just in case, but I expect I shall be too busy to write anything in it. The next three days are going to be ACTION PACKED!!!

Dearest Carol,

I cannot believe it! A Texan called <u>Dwayn</u>? Is this a real name??? He sure does sound hunky, hon!

No, no, no, I'm only joking! In all seriousness, I'm really glad you've found someone to have fun with. You deserve it. Enjoy! But full reports, please. I am consumed with vulgar curiosity.

Cherry has suggested that if the baby is a girl we should call her Bredan...get it? Oh, ho ho! She is picking up this sort of humour from Roly. But I was so pleased that she feels able to make jokes about it. It shows she's been thinking.

Yesterday she went over the road to have tea with a new little girl who has just moved into our neighbourhood. I call her a little girl because although she is the same age as Cherry she is most delightfully quaint and old-fashioned! She actually wears a big red bow in her hair and shiny shoes with ankle straps. It takes me right back! Cherry by contrast is into all this heavy grunge gear and walks around looking like something that's crawled out of a garbage heap. I feel it would do her good to make friends with someone like little Sereena.

At the moment she is not here as she has gone off to spend a few days with Gregg. There are times when I could cheerfully strangle that man! He had arranged to pick her up at about nine o'clock and she was all ready and waiting, down in the hall with her suitcase, wearing her best clothes (ie, the grungiest ones she could find) and by 10.30 when he still hadn't arrived I rang Southampton and got this bimbo he's shacked up with and she says, "Oh, yah, he's just left about ten minutes ago." Of course by then the roads were busy which meant he didn't get here until lunch-time.

It really is too bad. Poor little Cherry sitting there waiting like some faithful hound, and this selfish irresponsible oaf not even bothering to call and let us know! Cherry was almost in tears. When he finally turned up she went catapulting into his arms and it was all kissy kissy huggy huggy. I expect I ought to have found it touching but the truth is I was too cross. Also, I suppose, if I am to be honest, I was a bit hurt at her being so obviously eager to get away from us. Roly says, "Come on, it's her dad! She hasn't seen him for six months," and I know that I mustn't be jealous but it seems so unfair! He comes breezing in, three hours late, and she's all over him with never so much as a backward glance for me and Roly. I offered the fool a cup of coffee (I wasn't going to offer him lunch!) but I could tell that Cherry just wanted to be off.

Oh, aren't I sour and crabby! But I do dread her returning home full of discontent, telling me how wonderful it is at her dad's and how horrible it is here. They're bound to spoil her rotten, it's only to be expected. And it will never occur to her that they've only had her for three days while we have her all the rest of the year! She's a bright child, but not always the easiest, which I know is partly my fault. My fault and Gregg's. Our getting divorced has been difficult for her. I keep telling myself that I must make allowances.

Oh, but she can be so ungracious! Roly felt that he would like to give her something as a going-away present. A little something to take with her. He said would she like a book and I said yes, I thought a book would be an excellent idea, because one thing she does do is read, even if it is mostly schlock horror just at present. He went to such pains to find one that she would like! She is writing this diary at the moment (it is supposed to be a secret, but she lets slip these little remarks from time to time) and we suddenly remembered that wonderful book which you and I read when we were Cherry's age. *I Capture the Castle*. Do you remember it? Cassandra Morton sitting on the draining board writing her journal with her feet in the sink? How we wallowed in it! So Roly combed through half the secondhand bookshops in London until he found an actual original copy and he slipped it into her bedroom while she was asleep, with one of his lovely funny little notes all done in pictures, telling her to take it with her to read while she was away, and what do you think? I've just been in there (it looks like a bomb site but I am not going to clear it) and she has just left the book lying on the floor! I haven't dared to tell Roly, he would be so hurt.

I really do begin to despair. It sometimes seems to me that the harder Roly tries the worse she treats him. And I have this horrible feeling that she is going to be even more impossible when she comes back from Gregg's.

Children! Think twice before embarking, no matter how handsome your Texan may be!

Eagerly await news of developments from your end. Will report back from mine.

Love from

Patsy

PS We are going to take the opportunity to re-decorate the spare bedroom ready for the baby while Cherry is away. We are also going to go and buy all the necessary paraphernalia – prams, potties, nappies! I thought I'd finished with all that. Roly is really excited. I only wish Cherry were, so that we could share it. I could really look forward to the event if I thought that she were happy.

Monday

No time to write in here yesterday so I am doing it now while Rosemary has her bath and gets ready to go out. She takes a long time to get ready, at least she did yesterday when we went for a pizza. We are going to go out every single day that I am here! This is because Rosemary doesn't like cooking, which is all right by me. I like to go out.

Tonight we are going for an Indian meal and tomorrow we are going for a Chinese one. To think that at home we only go out about once every six months! But Dad and Rosemary both do proper jobs and so I expect they earn a lot more money than Mum and Slimey, which is only right. Just sitting about reading books and drawing elves can't be classed as proper jobs. I don't think so.

I have only met Rosemary two times before so that I do not really know her very well. The times that I have met her are once before she got married to Dad (they did it in a love temple in the Seychelles. Incredibly r-r-r-romantic!) and once after, when they came back. That was almost a year ago. Since then I have only seen Dad in London except once when I came to Southampton just for the day and Rosemary was not there.

She is quite pretty and wears lots of make-up and really smart clothes. She is younger than Mum and of course much slimmer. Even if Mum weren't having this baby she would still be much slimmer. She and Dad go jogging every morning and Rosemary also does aerobics. Dad has started to play squash and is not anywhere near as pudgy as when he was driving the cab.

It is I must say a great relief to be in a house – well, a flat actually – where everything isn't being got ready for a baby. There are no signs of a baby in this place, thank goodness!

It was strange at first being in a flat after being used to a house but now I think that I prefer it. I think it would be sensible if everyone lived in flats because then there would be a lot more land where you could grow grass and trees. I think probably it is almost antisocial for people to live in houses. I am going to say this to Slimey next time he starts on about the environment and how we are ruining it. Dad and Rosemary aren't taking up half the space that he and Mum take up! Also I enjoy everything being on one level so that you don't have to keep rushing up and down the stairs all the time. Also there is a lift, in which you can meet people and talk. I shall live in a flat when I am grown-up – if I am not living in a cardboard box, that is.

I told Dad about the cardboard box and he said that he will buy me a personal computer for my Christmas present. He said, "I cannot have a daughter of mine being computer-illiterate, but of course your mother has always had a tendency to be a bit of a Luddite." I said what was a Luddite and he said they were people who went round smashing machinery. I said that I didn't think Mum smashed it on purpose, she just wasn't very good with it, like for instance last week she broke the handle off the washing machine and put the vacuum bag in the wrong way so that all the dust came flying out into the house.

Dad said, "Typical! And I suppose he's not much better?" I said, "Slimey? He's even worse!" which isn't strictly speaking true since it was Slimey who fixed the handle of the washing machine with superglue and changed the bag in the vacuum cleaner. But it's true that neither of them knows the first thing about computers. Mum just uses her word processor like an ordinary typewriter, which was a thing that used to drive Dad mad when he was living with us. He was always trying to teach her different things that she could do with it and she wouldn't listen. She used to say, "Oh, I can't be bothered with all that!" Deliberate stupidity, Dad said it was.

The journey from London to Southampton in Dad's car was brilliant except that half-way here I started to feel sick, which Dad said was probably because I'd got out of the habit of travelling by car. I said yes, Slimey always insisted on going everywhere by bus or bicycle and Dad said the man was an idiot. He said, "Like it or not, the car is here to stay," and, "You can't put the clock back." Anyway, we had to stop a couple of times so that I could get some air and then I felt all right again. But I have never felt car sick before. It is all Slimey's fault.

Today we went for a drive to the New Forest (I didn't get sick this time) and had lunch in a pub, in the garden, and then drove to a place called Lymington, which is at the sea, but it was too cold to go swimming and so we just looked at it and came home again. Tomorrow Dad has to go into the office in the morning because there is a problem which only he can sort out, so Rosemary and I are going to meet him for lunch and then go round Southampton where there are some things to be seen, such as an old museum and an ancient wall. Also of course the docks. I am looking forward to it.

I rang Mum last night to tell her that we had arrived safely as she worries about accidents, and she said, "So how are you getting on? I suppose everything is lovely?" I said that it was and that so far I was really enjoying myself (though in fact we hadn't done very much at that stage). I said, "Dad's told me I can stay till Friday if I want." He told me in the car. It was one of the first things he said. He said, "Rosemary's managed to wangle an extra two days and I'll take off what time I can."

"That's good, isn't it?" I said to Mum. I thought she would be pleased but she didn't sound very pleased. She just grunted and said, "If that's what you want."

"Well, I thought I might as well," I said. "Now that I'm here."

"That's right," said Mum. "Make the most of it. It doesn't happen that often."

Then there was a pause and she said, "You left your

book behind." I couldn't think what she was talking about. I said, "What book?" She said, "Roly's book. The one he bought specially for you." I knew from the tone of her voice that she was mad at me. I forgot all about his stupid book! I wouldn't have brought it anyway. What do I want a book for, when I'm with Dad?

Mum said, "You're not worth giving things to, are you?" I am if they're the right things, but anyway she needn't go getting all wound up about it because I am also pretty wound up, if she wants to know. What I am wound up about is the thought of him actually opening my door and creeping into my room while I'm asleep. I don't think he has any right to do that. He's not my dad. But if I'd said so to Mum she'd only have got all defensive, like she always does where Slimey is concerned, and I didn't want to quarrel with her over the telephone. So I just said, "Look, I'm sorry, I forgot," and she said, "Yes, of course, you left in such a rush!" I think she was being sarcastic. It was the way she used to get with Dad when they were having words. I hope she's not going to start on at me. It's ever so nice and peaceful here. I don't want Mum ringing up and making trouble.

Tuesday

The museum was very interesting. It is called The Wool House and is all full of relics from Napoleonic days.

102

French prisoners were kept there and you can still see their initials where they'd carved them into the wooden beams. It gave me a strange feeling to think of them doing that all those years ago and me standing here today looking at them. It made me wonder if people in two hundred years' time would stand and look at something I'd done, like for instance I once carved my initials on a tree and put the date. I imagined a girl like me finding it and wondering who I was and what had become of me. It was a bit creepy but at the same time comforting, to know that you have made your mark and will leave something behind you.

Tomorrow we are going to Portsmouth to see the *Victory*, which is the ship that Nelson sailed in.

Wednesday

We couldn't go to Portsmouth today because Dad was needed at the office again. Well, Rosemary and I could have gone but it wouldn't have been the same without Dad. She said we could go if I liked, but I said I'd rather wait for him and she said she would, too. She said as a matter of fact there were things she had to do, like finishing off an evening dress she is making for herself for a very posh dinner party that she and Dad are going to on Friday night. She said would I mind terribly if she stayed in and did that?

Of course I said no and she said I could do whatever I wanted, watch the television or go for a walk. She said there was a park just up the road, so I went up there but it wasn't very interesting, no dogs to play with and nothing really to do, so I came back again and watched for a bit as she used her sewing machine and wondered why Mum couldn't make her own clothes. Mum is absolutely useless, she can't even sew on buttons properly. I also wondered why Mum couldn't wear the sort of clothes that Rosemary wears. Her evening dress, for instance, is completely incredible, off the shoulder and showing lots of bosom.

← Rosemary in her dress

I have never ever seen Mum wearing anything like that.

We were supposed to be meeting Dad again for lunch but he rang to say he wasn't going to be able to make it (some very important Americans have come over and he has to be with them). I could see that Rosemary was a bit put out by this. I think she didn't quite know what to do with me. She said, "I guess we'd better find some way of amusing you. There's a zoo over on the Common. Would you like to go to the zoo?" I said that I was very sorry but I didn't believe in zoos, I think it is cruel keeping animals locked up in small spaces, and she said, "Oh, you're one of those, are you? I'm surprised you're not a veggie." I said, "I probably am going to be, soon," and she pulled a face as if I'd announced that I was going to have all my teeth pulled out or my hands chopped off.

Since I wouldn't go to the zoo she suggested the cinema. She said, "There's bound to be something suitable for children, seeing as it's half-term." I told her that I didn't normally watch things that were suitable for children. She said, "Well, I'm not taking you to some ghastly horror movie, if that's what you're after." I said she didn't need to take me anywhere, I am quite accustomed to entertaining myself, and so we ate some soup and a tin of peaches in the kitchen and she went back to her evening dress and I came in here to write this diary.

It's now three o'clock and Dad still isn't back. Rosemary thinks probably he won't be back until about seven, when we can all go out for a meal. It's difficult thinking what to do until then. I don't really want to watch television because it's in the same room where she's doing her sewing and she's got the radio on. I've looked for some books but there don't seem to be any. I should have brought the one that Slimey got for me, but how was I to know that Dad would have to work?

Maybe I could go into Southampton and buy something.

Thursday

I don't think Rosemary will ever have a baby. I don't think she likes children very much. I said to her yesterday that I was going to go into Southampton to look round the shops and she said, "You can't go by yourself, you'll get lost." And then she heaved this big irritable sort of sigh and said, "I suppose I shall have to come with you." We couldn't go by car because Dad had taken it and so we had to go by bus, which is a thing I am quite used to on account of Slimey not driving but which I don't think she is as she kept tapping her foot and looking at her watch and trying to find out from the timetable when the next one was due. It made me feel guilty, as if I ought to have stayed quietly indoors, but it's just as well I didn't as Dad didn't get home until almost nine o'clock, by which time I had read two horror books (*Scream and You're Dead* and *House of Horror*) and was absolutely starving.

Today was better as we went to Portsmouth to see the *Victory*. Dad and I went; Rosemary didn't come. The *Victory* was very interesting and it was nice being with Dad on my own. He was more like I remember him from the old days. When he is with Rosemary he is different. It is hard to describe it but he is not like my dad. He is more like one of those men that drive round in fast cars with pony tails and telephones. What Mum and Slimey call yuppies.

When we got back from Portsmouth, Dad said I could go to the video shop and make my choice, as he had promised me. I was tempted to choose a horror film, just to show Rosemary that if I wanted to watch it I could, but then I thought maybe if I chose that Dad would be like Mum and break his promise and so I chose instead a film called *Strictly Ballroom* which is all about ballroom dancing which to be honest I am not really into but Skinny Melon had told me it had this really gorgeous-looking boy in it, and she was right, it did! He's heaven. I am now seriously thinking of asking Mum if I can learn ballroom dancing. Imagine meeting a boy like that! (Some hopes!)

Dad and Rosemary, unfortunately, got bored. Rosemary went and sat over the other side of the room and switched on a light and did her sewing, and Dad went off to have a bath, so that I was left on my own. I didn't really mind, I suppose, though it is nicer when other people enjoy what you enjoy. I think Mum would enjoy it. It is her sort of thing. Next time we get a video I shall tell her to get that one.

Tomorrow I am going home. I am trying to remember the things that I have seen and done so that I can tell Mum. I have been to the New Forest. I have been to the sea. I have been in the museum. I have seen the *Victory*. I have seen *Strictly Ballroom*. I have eaten: one Italian meal, one Indian meal, one Chinese meal, one French meal, and one American meal (hamburgers, only I had a vegeburger thinking of Slimey and dead things in the fridge). I suppose that is quite a lot of things to have seen and done in five days.

Later

Dad and Rosemary have just had a bit of an argument about which of them is going to drive me back tomorrow. I heard them when I went to the bathroom. (I have noticed, in a flat, you can quite often hear people talking. It is not as private as in a house.) I heard Rosemary say, "She's your daughter!" and then Dad said something that I couldn't catch but I think it was something about needing to go into the office again, and Rosemary said, "I am not driving her all the way to London and that is that!"

I'm glad she isn't driving me. I don't think I could bear it, and I don't expect she could, either.

Friday

Now I am back home. I had to come by train because of Rosemary refusing to drive me and Dad having to go into the office. It is a bit of a drawback in some ways having a father who is so important. I mean, I am glad of course that he is important, but I would have liked it better if he had been there more of the time as it was not so much fun when he wasn't. I don't feel very comfortable with Rosemary. I think she would rather I hadn't come.

I rang Mum before we left, to tell her what time my train was getting in. She was furious, I could tell. She said, "Train? All by yourself?" And I said yes, because Dad had to work. "Oh, does he?" she said. "Where is he? Let me speak to him!" I didn't want her to but she started to shout. She shouted, "You put him on the telephone!" It was so loud that Dad heard it and came and took the receiver off me. He said, "Hallo? Pat?" quite pleasantly, I thought, but it soon developed into one of their rows.

I think Mum must have asked him why I couldn't stay till Saturday and come back by car because Dad sort of twisted his lips in a way which said, "I am being very patient but do not try me too far," and informed her that, "Rosemary and I happen to have a very important dinner party that we have to go to this evening. It is not something we can get out of, nor would we wish to. All right?"

I don't know what Mum said after that because I couldn't bear to listen any more. Why does everything always get so horrible when Mum and Dad talk to each other? I wish they hadn't! It ruined the end of my holiday.

Dad and Rosemary both came to the station with me. I would rather it had just been Dad, but at least

Rosemary stayed in the car which meant I was able to say goodbye to Dad on my own. He said, "We've had fun this week, haven't we? We must do it again – and not leave it so long next time." I said that maybe I could come at Christmas but Dad said unfortunately that wouldn't be possible as he and Rosemary had already arranged to go with some friends to Austria and do some skiing. I didn't like to suggest that maybe I could go with them as I don't think Rosemary would be happy. I don't think she likes me very much. So then I had a bright idea and said, "Parents' Evening! You could come to Parents' Evening!" Dad said he thought that was an excellent suggestion and if I let him know when it was, he would definitely be there. He said, "That's a promise!"

We had a bit of time to wait so we went over to the bookstall and Dad bought me some magazines and another horror book. Unlike Mum and Slimey, he didn't go "tut tut" about me reading horrors but said they looked jolly good and really exciting and ought to keep me on the edge of my seat all the way to London. As it happens I cannot read very well on trains as they jerk up and down and make my eyes go funny but I didn't say so to Dad. Instead I said that I would find out the date of Parents' Evening and let him know. He said, "Make sure you do!" and then it was time to say goodbye and for me to get on the train.

This was the first time that I have ever been on a long

train journey by myself. I kept worrying how I would know when we reached London, which was stupid because London is where the train stops. It doesn't go anywhere else. And then I worried about leaving my seat to go to the toilet in case I couldn't find my way back or someone stole my things. And then when I absolutely had to go because otherwise I would have to burst it was one of those ones where you have to press buttons to get in and more buttons to close the door and I was terrified I wouldn't be able to get out again, but of course I did. I expect if I got used to travelling on my own it would be all right.

Another thing I worried about was what I would do if I got to London and couldn't see Mum or Slimey, but Slimey was there, waiting for me, looking all Slimey-ish in an anorak and joggers and tatty old trainers.

↑ Roly at the station

He gave me a big hug and a kiss and I let him, which normally I wouldn't have done because normally it would revolt me, but I was just so relieved to see him. He said, "I'm sorry Butterpat couldn't come, but she has an appointment at the clinic." (Meaning the ante-natal clinic, where all the pregnant women go to make sure they are having proper babies and not babies that have things wrong with them.) He said he knew that he was second best but, "Hopefully better than nothing."

I felt sort of sorry for him when he said this. I also felt a bit mean about leaving his book behind, especially as I was clutching my horror book. I explained that Dad had bought me the book and that I hadn't left his one behind on purpose, I'd simply forgotten to pack it, like I'd also forgotten to pack my tooth brush (this was a fib but I said it to make him feel better). I said that I wished I had taken his book as I'd had to go out and buy myself some, and I promised that I would read his next. Slimey said, "I'm afraid you won't find it very exciting after your diet of horror. I probably made a mistake in choosing it." He sounded really sad, as if it mattered to him that I mightn't find his book exciting. I said that I would definitely read it and let him know.

When we got home Mum was there. I'd forgotten how enormous she looks after Rosemary. She asked me if I'd had a good time and I said, "Brilliant," because it would have been disloyal to Dad to have said anything else. Mum said, "Well, there's nothing very brilliant on offer at this end, but we can go up to the video shop and get a video, if you like." I said, "Can I choose?" and Mum said, "Yes, but you know the rules." So I chose *Strictly Ballroom* and I was right, Mum loved it! So did Slime. Mum said it was a "good old-fashioned movie with no sex and no violence" and Slime surprised everyone – well, he surprised me, but I think Mum as well – by saying that he used to be a champion tango dancer, and to prove it he jumped up and pulled me into the middle of the room and taught me how to do it! He was really good. And so now I know how to tango!

me and Roly tango!

Saturday

He's still shoving cards under my door and I still don't like it but I suppose he is only doing it to try and be friendly. It is rather pathetic, really. Imagine being so desperate to be liked!

After breakfast I rang the Melon and we arranged to meet at the top of my road and go round the shops together. She wanted to know what it was like at Dad's so I said the same as I said to Mum, that it was brilliant. I told her all the things I'd done and then asked her what she'd done.

Skinny said she hadn't done anything at all. She sounded a bit down in the dumps so I asked her what the matter was and at first she said nothing was the matter but then she said that her mum had met this man at the place where she works and he was called Melvyn and he was dire. I was going to say that he couldn't possibly be any more dire than Slime but then for some reason I didn't. I don't know why. I said, "Maybe she just has bad taste in men but it doesn't really matter so long as she's not going to marry him." Skinny said rather fiercely that of course she wasn't going to marry him, he was just a boyfriend. I said, "So what's the problem?" and she said there wasn't one except that she couldn't stand the sight of him. Then she cheered up and said she wanted to go and buy a new pair of leggings with some money that he'd given her. I said, "Dire Melvyn?" and she giggled and said, "He's trying to worm his way into my good books!"

I really don't know what she's got to complain about.

When I got home I found that Slime had finished the pond. I have to say that it is quite nice. It will be very pretty in summer, with water lilies and bullrushes. It is not quite ready for the fish but next week we are going to go and buy some. I am refusing to be too enthusiastic because if I am it will make Mum think I have forgiven her for breaking her promise about the dog, which I most certainly have not.

I would still like a dog more than anything else in the world. Far more than a personal computer, though naturally I wouldn't say this to Dad. A computer will help me not to end up living in a cardboard box (maybe – maybe not) but a dog would bring immense cheer and comfort into my gloomy life. I could play with it and take it for walks and feed it and brush it and cuddle it and talk to it and it could even sleep in bed with me. Oh, why can't I have one? Trust Slimey Roland to go and suffer from stupid allergies!

30 October

My dear Carol,

Your Texan sounds more divine every time you write! Photo, please. I picture him as being a sort of cross between Steve McQueen and the Incredible Hulk…my poor Roly cannot even begin to compete but I don't care! I love him to death!

Well, Cherry has come back from Southampton and just as I feared, they have spoilt her rotten. She informs me that, "Dad took me out to dinner every single night." Dad took her to have an Indian meal, Dad took her to have a Chinese meal, Dad took her to have a pizza, Dad took her to have oysters and champagne (so she says), Dad took her to see the *Victory*, Dad took her to the New Forest. I swear I shall scream if she tells me once more of the wonderful time she had with Dad!

Dad is a rat. He obviously had a guilty conscience because when she got there he informed her that she could stay on till Friday, but then I got a call early Friday morning saying that he was sending her home by train as he had to go into the office. When I asked why she couldn't stay over until Saturday he had the nerve to tell me that he and this bimbo he's married are going to a dinner party – a dinner party, my dear! – which they certainly didn't intend to cancel just on Cherry's behalf. So she ended up being bundled on to the train like an unwanted parcel and shunted back to us. Of course that isn't the way she sees it. She just thinks that Gregg is enormously important and that the office can't function without him. All he is is a computer programmer!

According to Cherry he has promised to buy her a personal computer for Christmas, but I shall believe that when I see it.

I suppose it's being over-protective to worry about an eleven-year-old girl travelling on a train all by herself from Southampton to Waterloo, but I kept having these horrific visions of all the things that could possibly happen to her. A mother's mind is like a museum of horrors... I had to send Roly off to meet her as I was due at the clinic. He tells me she was quite jaunty, in fact her normal ebullient self, so she obviously didn't suffer. I was the one to do that!

I asked after the bimbo, hoping to hear how ugly/stupid/fat/useless/generally disagreeable she was but it appears that she's thin as a rake, ravishingly beautiful, dresses like a fashion model, makes all her own clothes, and is a hard-headed career woman. This, at least, is what I gather. What Cherry actually said, in scathing tones, was, "She's never likely to have a baby," which is simply a not very subtle way of having a go at me. I suppose she blames the baby for me not going to meet her off the train. It wouldn't occur to her to blame Gregg for putting her on the train in the first place!

Oh, what a moaning minnie I have become! I don't mean to be but there's only three months to go and she still shows no real signs of any softening in her attitude. I tried to show her what we'd done in the spare bedroom, but she made it very plain she didn't want to know. She is so full of "Dad" and what it's like at Dad's place – she even had a go at Roly today for living in a house and not a flat! It seems it is now environmentally irresponsible to live in a house. Dad could live in one if he wanted, he is so rich and important he could live anywhere, but he chooses to live in a flat so as not to waste land.

If you believe that, you'll believe anything! I don't know how Roly puts up with her. He has the patience of a saint.

Lots of love from your harassed,

Patsy

Sunday

Mum showed me today what they've done to the spare bedroom while I've been away. I was quite surprised! The walls are dead white with little figures running all the way round and in the middle lots of teddy bears and beach balls and space rockets have been painted. Oh, and elves, of course! Elves all over the place.

Roly's soppy paintings

Mum said, "What do you think?" and I said, "I don't remember having this when I was a baby," meaning it was really nice and the sort of thing that a baby would like, but Mum took it the wrong way and snapped, "That's because you weren't lucky enough to have Roly for a father!"

She is really touchy these days. I can't seem to do anything right.

Monday

I said to Skinny Melon today that I didn't think my system could stand much more poisoning from school dinners. She said she didn't think hers could, either. She said she was absolutely positive that the other day she'd found a bit of worm on her plate. She'd shown it to Mrs James (this was the day I bunked off and came back to school by cab) and Mrs James had looked at it and told her not to be silly, it was "just a bit of grissle." (Gristle?) But as Skinny said, even if you believe her – which she personally did not – you don't pay out good dinner money just to be given bits of gristle. (I think this is the way it's spelt.) And as I said, it's not very nice to think you're chewing on pieces of dead animal anyway, whether it's pieces of worm or pieces of lamb.

Skinny didn't seem quite so sure about this until I pointed out to her that she wouldn't want to eat Lulu, would she, and she went a bit pale and said no of course she wouldn't. Whereupon I said so where was the difference between eating Lulu and eating a lamb, and she said she thought there was one but she couldn't think what it was.

We talked about it for a bit and in the end she agreed that if she saw a lamb in a field she wouldn't want to go and kill it, and it was only the fact that it came ready wrapped and not looking like a lamb that made her able to eat it. I said, "I bet if someone gave you a whole raw lamb to cook you wouldn't ever eat lamb again," and she really didn't have any arguments left.

So then I said that I was seriously thinking of becoming a vegetarian, and Skinny said that she was,

121

too. I said, "When shall we do it?" and she thought about it a bit and said, "Next term?" I said, "Why next term and not this?" and she said because of Christmas. She said they always have roast turkey at Christmas and she didn't think she could live without roast turkey. Not this Christmas. Maybe next Christmas when her taste buds had changed. (It was me who told her her taste buds would change. I don't know if it is true, but it's what Slimey said to Mum so I hope it is.)

We have agreed, therefore, and made a solemn pact, that next term we shall become veggies. I of course could become one immediately, since we shan't be having roast turkey on account of dead things in the fridge, but it seems better to keep the Skinbag company and start at the same time so that we can encourage each other when our spirits flag or our carnal appetites threaten to get the better of us. Also I don't want Mum crowing. I will tell her the good news after Christmas and not before. This evening it is Hallowe'en and some kids are roaming the streets dressed up as ghouls and ghosts and skeletons. Slimey said, "Don't you go and trick-or-treat?" But that is something I have never done. I don't know why; I just haven't. Skinny doesn't either. Slimey said that next year we must make a Big Thing of it and have fun. He likes to make Big Things of things. On Saturday it is Guy Fawkes night and he is taking me and Mum and Skin to a firework display. I suppose I am quite looking forward to it, really.

Tuesday

I am reading Slimey's book. It is called *I Capture the Castle* by a person with the very strange name of Dodie Smith. What kind of name is Dodie? A strange one! But the book is brilliant. Very funny and yet r-r-r-romantic!

It is all about a girl called Cassandra who wants to be a writer and is keeping a diary, just like me, except that she lives in an old ruined castle and her family don't have very much money, in fact they don't have any money at all on account of her father, who is also a writer, sitting up in the turret reading books all day and not doing any work. It is so cold that Cassandra has to sit on the draining board wrapped up in a blanket with her feet in the sink to write her diary. She has a beautiful older sister called Rose and a weird but equally beautiful stepmother called Topaz, who used to be an artist's model. The romance comes in when two Americans, Neil and Simon, arrive on the scene. Simon is a bit old and has a beard but Neil is gorgeous. This is as far as I have got. I think that probably Rose will marry Simon and that Cassandra, maybe, will fall in love with Neil.

Oh, I nearly forgot. There is also a nice-looking but rather dopey boy called Steven. Steven loves Cassandra and Cassandra is very fond of him but not in the way that he would like. The family owe Steven a great deal as he works for them for nothing and also goes out and earns money which he gives them. Without him they would not survive.

I have never read a book quite like this before and I can't wait to get back to it! I thought after horrors it would be slow and boring but it is not at all. Skinny is going to read it when I have finished.

Thursday

I forgot to write in here yesterday.

Friday

Stewed sewage and gunge. Thank goodness we have decided to go veggie!

Saturday

This morning we went to buy some fish for the pond. Fish, I feel, are basically uninteresting. All they do is swim up and down and gobble with their mouths.

I kept pointing out ones I thought we should have but these, it seems, all the ones I wanted, are warm water fish and not suited to outdoor life. They wouldn't be, would they? Mum said, "Oh, for goodness' sake, Cherry, stop being so awkward! You know perfectly well this is a pond, not an aquarium." I said, "If we'd had an aquarium we could have had some of the pretty ones." At least you could sit and look at them and get a bit of pleasure that way. Mum snapped (she is always snapping these days), "If it weren't for Roly you wouldn't have anything!"

I beg her pardon. If it weren't for Roly I could have my dog.

Now the pool is full of boring old fish that half the time you can't even see. If we had a dog he could get in there and chase them.

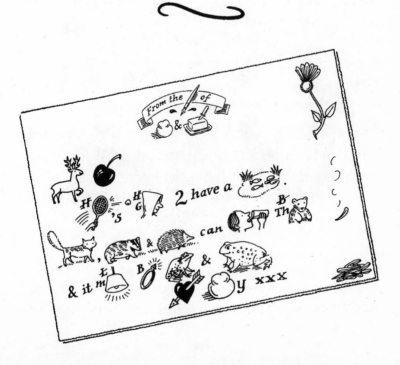

I nearly forgot to mention that this evening we all went to the fireworks display. It was up in the park and it was really good. Skinny doesn't like the bangers, but I do! The louder the better is what I say. (Mum and Slimey like the pretty ones. Wouldn't you know it?)

Sunday

Oh ho ho! Something has eaten the fish. They think it might be a heron. I am sorry for the fish but herons need to eat and if stupid human beings will go digging ponds in their back gardens and filling them with food, what do they expect? They might just as well write a big sign saying:

Mum says I am cruel and heartless but I am not. It is in a heron's nature to eat fish. They are programmed to eat fish. They can't do anything else. It is what the fish expect. And anyway Mum still eats prawns, she says it's her "one weakness". What are prawns if not fish? I told her this and she snapped (again), "That is not the point!"

So if that is not the point, what is?

6 November

Dear Carol,

I am too cross to be civil. I am almost too cross to
write. Cherry is trying my patience beyond the limits!

Yesterday we stocked the pond with fish and this
morning when we woke up almost all of them had
gone (a heron, we think). Roly was devastated. He had
already begun to personalise them. There was
Goldilocks and the Cheeky Chappie and Bright Eyes.
Bright Eyes is still with us, but Goldilocks and the
Cheeky Chappie have both gone. Two of his favourites!
That wretched child thought it was funny. She actually
laughed. She made some joke about putting up a sign
saying "Breakfast this Way". Then she said, quite rudely,
that I still ate prawns so what was I so upset about?

I tell you, I could have hit her! She simply tramples
over all Roly's emotions. She is too young to realise
what a rare and precious thing it is to find a man who
has feelings and isn't afraid of showing them. I suppose
she takes it as some kind of weakness and like a
typical bully can't resist putting the boot in.

Roly, as usual, speaks up in her defence. He says

that you can't really bond with a fish and that she is quite right, herons have to eat. She could still try to be at least a little sympathetic! Roly has slaved over that pond in an attempt to please her. How far do you have to go to try and keep your children happy?

To the ends of the earth, says Roly, if that is what it takes. We bring them into this world, he says; they do not ask to be born. I retort that he played no part in bringing this particular little horror into the world but he says that he has gatecrashed her living space and hijacked her mother and that she has every right to show her displeasure.

I don't think she has! You couldn't find a better man than Roly.

Lots of love,

Patsy

PS Forgive self-pity and bad manners, I know I'm a rotten correspondent. But Cherry is so trying!

PPS Don't forget I want a photograph!

Monday

I wish I hadn't laughed about his stupid old fish. He spent ages picking them out, choosing the ones with personalities. Well, he said they had personalities. Perhaps he really thinks they do. It is true he wouldn't have had time to get attached to them, I don't think, but I can see that it was a bit upsetting for him. He is quite soft about animals and as a matter of fact so am I, which is why I am glad I have decided after Christmas to give up eating them. Mum is giving up because of Slimey but I am giving up because of principles. Also because of not wishing to be poisoned, but that is really only a small part of it.

I am not sure why Skinny is doing it. Maybe just because of me. She does like animals, but I don't think she truly appreciates how lucky she is to have a dog. Sometimes she grumbles about having to take Lulu for her walks. I would never do that. If I had a dog I would take it out happily and gladly every single day.

my dream

I thought of telling Slimey that I was sorry I laughed about his fish, but if I did Mum would think it was because of her getting mad at me. He would be bound to tell her. They tell each other everything. When I am married I will still want to have secrets. *If* I am married. It might be difficult, living in a cardboard box.

Tuesday

Found out about Parents' Evening and rang Dad. He said, "Right! Got it. It's going in my diary. Have you told your mother?" So I went and told Mum and she wailed, "Oh, Cherry! Did you have to?" I said, "Have to what?" and she said, "Invite your father!" I said, "It is *Parents' Evening.*" And Dad is my parent.

There wasn't very much she could say to that.

I know why she doesn't want him there. It's because she wants to drag Slimey along with us. Well, it's *my* school and Dad's *my* parent and he's going to come whether Mum likes it or not!

Wednesday

Told Skinny about Dad coming to Parents' Evening. She said, "What about Roly?" I said, "What about him? He's not my dad!" Skinny said she knew that, but wouldn't he be hurt?

Why should he be hurt? He can go to Bernard Butter's rotten Parents' Evening. He's not coming to mine!

Friday

Forgot to write in here yesterday. I keep forgetting to write. I forgot last week, as well, only then it was Wednesday. And all I wrote on Thursday was just one line. Partly this is because of the enormous gigantic amount of homework they give us at this school and partly it is because of having to stay late for rehearsals and partly it is because of wanting to get back to my book. The *I Capture the Castle* book. I am nearly at the end of it and am getting worried about what is going to happen. I couldn't bear it if Rose got Neil!

Saturday

She did! She got him! And Cassandra ended up with boring old Simon. If it hadn't been for that it would have been one of the very best books I have ever read. Well, it still is one of the best books I have read but I think she got the ending wrong, that is all. I am going to write a note to Slimey and tell him so. And then I am going to put the note under the door of the back room where he does his elves.

I have written the note. It is a nice one to make up for laughing about his fish.

What I have said is this:

Dear Roly,

I have read I Capture the Castle by Dodie Smith and I think if she had got the ending right it would have been an extremely good book. Unfortunately she got it wrong by letting Rose go off with Neil and leaving Cassandra with Simon who is too old and boring and has a beard. Apart from that I thought it was a very good and interesting book which I enjoyed reading. Now I am going to lend it to my friend the Melon and see what she thinks. But I think she will agree with me about Simon.

xxx Cherry.

I put the xxx bit just to be polite.

Sunday

Sereena came over for tea. It was Mum's idea. I kept waiting eagerly for her to start telling some of her dirty jokes but she just sat there looking like she's made of marshmallow, all soft and sweet and gooey.

Marshmallow Sereena

Double YUCK!

It was repulsive! Specially as I happen to know what she's really like. I told her about Slimey's book that he gave me and she said it sounded as though it would be a bit too grown-up for her. How two-faced can you get? She said, "I'm still reading Judy Blume." "Oh, you mean like *Forever*?" I said, kicking at her ankle underneath the table. Her satellite dishes went huge as flying saucers. She said, "That's a rude one, isn't it? My mum wouldn't like it if I read that."

Mum said, "Three cheers for your mum!" which was a totally meaningless remark considering she hasn't the faintest idea what *Forever* is about. At least, I don't think she has. It was also hypocritical, since she has never stopped me reading anything I wanted. She was just sucking up to Sereena.

I was really disappointed in that girl. Talk about playacting! Now of course Mum is convinced she's the sweetest thing there ever was and is trying to talk Mrs Swaddle into sending her to Ruskin Manor next term. She thinks she would be a good influence on me. Ha!

13 November

Dear Carol,

Things go from bad to worse. Now she won't even talk to Roly but simply puts notes under his door! Well, one note. Ungracious as usual. She says she liked *I Capture the Castle* but thought the ending was wrong. She says Cassandra should have had Neil, as Simon is too old and has a beard. I pointed out rather tartly that as a matter of fact, if she had read the book properly, she would have noticed that he shaved it off, but she said she had read it properly and she knows he shaved it off but it didn't make any difference, she still thought of him as having a beard. She said that he was "a beardy sort of person" and that Rose going off with Neil ruined the entire story. How perverse can you get?

Roly says she is simply exercising her critical faculty. He also says that her note is in return for his cards and it shows she is willing at last to start a dialogue. Some dialogue! Ungrateful little beast.

The little girl over the road came to tea this afternoon. Sereena. I personally find her quite delightful – quite refreshingly innocent – and would be only too happy if she and Cherry became friends but Cherry is being her usual churlish self. Whenever I mention her name she either sniggers, as if I've said something secretly amusing, or else she rolls her eyes and groans, as if I've said something incredibly moronic. Roly, surprisingly enough, has not taken to her. Sereena, I mean. He said there is something that doesn't quite ring true but he cannot put his finger on it. I told him that he has lived with my ghastly daughter for too long and has forgotten what normal, nice children are like!

Who'd be a mother? Tell your gorgeous Hunk that you intend to preserve your sanity and remain childless!

All my love,

Patsy

Monday

When I got home from school today there was a parcel waiting for me from America! I tore it open and inside was a box which said "Armadillo Droppings" with a picture of an armadillo. An armadillo looks like this:

Armadillo droppings look like this:

They are round and squidgy and treacle-coloured and you can eat them! Of course they are toffees in fact, but very realistic. Mum said, "Trust Texans!" and shuddered when I offered her one. She said, "They'll stick your teeth up." Slimey on the other hand ate two and said they were "yummy" (which is the sort of word he likes to use). For once I have to agree with him! They are incredibly, scrumptiously yummy! I ate four, one after another, until Mum told me to stop being piglike, which is unfair to pigs who are actually not greedy animals left to themselves, but anyway I thought I had better stop or I would have eaten them all and I want to take them in to school tomorrow and see people's faces when I say, "Have an armadillo turd!"

Now I suppose I must write and say thank you. It is much easier to pick up the telephone, even all the way to Texas, but Mum would have a fit so I'd better not.

Tuesday

I took the armadillo droppings to school and everyone thought it was hilarious except for Mrs James who said, "What on earth have you got there, Cherry?" and when I showed her she pulled a face and said, "That is what I call bad taste." I don't call it bad taste! I call it scrummy! She should have tried one, but she wouldn't. Some people just have no sense of humour.

I went over to Sereena's place when I got in from school

and showed her the box (which now alas was empty). I waited till we were in her bedroom as I didn't think her mother would like it. All Sereena said was, "I bet they didn't look anything like the real thing!" I said, "They did. They looked just like it." She said, "How do you know? Have you ever seen an armadillo dropping?" I had to admit that I hadn't. Then she told me something really gross.

She told me that the brother of her best friend Sharon where she used to live works as a camera man for a TV crew and one day they went into this prison to make a film and they wanted to show the prisoners emptying their buckets that they'd done things into during the night and she said, "They didn't want to use the real thing 'cos that would be horrid and smelly so they made up this yellow mixture with lemonade powder and then they got some brown *playdo* and rolled it in porridge oats and dropped it into the lemonade water with bits of toilet paper and you couldn't tell the difference." She said, "That's the sort of thing they do when they make films."

Ugh! I think that's far nastier than armadillo droppings. And that was in *England*.

Wednesday

When I got in from school Mum told me that there had been a telephone call from Dad saying that unfortunately he wouldn't be able to get to Parents' Evening after all as he had a meeting to attend and wouldn't be finished in time. Mum said, "I'm sorry, sweetheart. I know you really wanted him to come."

It isn't very often that Mum calls me things like sweetheart. I knew it was because she was feeling sorry for me, and not wanting to gloat (on account of she'd said all along that Dad wouldn't turn up, or if he did it would only be to annoy her).

"It is quite a long way for him to travel," she said, trying, I suppose, to make things seem better.

I said, "He promised!" But what do grown-ups' promises mean? Mum promised me a dog, Dad promised to come to Parents' Evening. Neither of them did what they said.

I tried ringing Skinny Melon, thinking it would be nice to have a bit of a laugh about something – anything, really – but all the Melon wanted to do was moan about our maths homework which she said she couldn't understand. If the Melon can't understand it I certainly won't be able to. I'm not going to bother with it. Why should I?

Thursday

Tomorrow is Parents' Evening, which a few days ago I was looking forward to. Now I just think it's a drag. Last year when I was at Juniors, Mum went on her own.

This year she's making me go with her. She's also taking Slime, which is what she wanted all along.

I said, "Why do I have to come?" She said, "Because you're the one it's all about." So then I said, "Why does he have to come?" and she said, "If you're referring to Roly, it's because he's just as interested in your welfare as I am." Then she added, "Though sometimes I wonder why he bothers."

I haven't asked him to bother. I don't want him to come. Trying to get round me, Mum said, "Surely it will be nicer for you to have both of us there?" I said, "Why?" And she said, "Well, it's more normal to have two parents, isn't it?" I said, "Not really. Not these days. There's lots of kids with only one." To which she snapped, "So what have you been making all the fuss about?"

What fuss? I never made any fuss.

She said, "If there are all these other kids whose parents have got divorced, what's so special about you?"

I never said there was anything special. And just because I'm not the only one whose mum and dad have split up doesn't make it any better. It's my dad I care about.

I didn't say any of this to Mum. We don't ever really talk about things like that. We just get mad at each other and she snaps and tells me I'm selfish and ungracious, which is what she did now.

It's true I was in quite a bad mood tonight. I don't know why. Sometimes I just am.

Friday

As we were about to set off for school to go to Parents' Evening, Slimey suddenly said, "Cherry, do you mind me coming along? I won't if you'd rather I didn't."

It made me feel terrible. He'd got dressed up specially in his best clothes. He looks all funny and peculiar in them, like a sort of long floppy beanstalk inside a suit. His trousers bag at the back because he hasn't got any bum and his pockets sag because he keeps things in them. Pens and pencils and little notebooks for drawing. I wanted to say that as far as I was concerned I'd rather he didn't come anywhere near the place, but I couldn't bring myself. I just mumbled something like, "That's all right, I don't mind." His face went into this big happy beam and that was that. I was stuck with him. It wouldn't have been so bad if they hadn't looked so odd, but what with Mum being all fat with the baby and Slimey being all bean-stalky and thin, they made a right weird couple.

We were the *only people* who didn't turn up in a car. At least, I should think we were. Amanda Miles said to me the other day, "Can't your dad afford a car?" I don't know how she knew he hadn't got one, but anyway as I pointed out he's not my dad. And as I also pointed out, he could probably afford half a dozen cars if he wanted them. The number of elves he draws, he ought to be able to. I said, "It's a matter of principle. He happens to care about this earth and the creatures that live on it." She said, "What are you talking about?" I said, "Pollution. Cars ought to be done away with," and she said, "Oh, that's just nutty!"

I used to think it was but now I'm not so sure. Slimey pointed out the other day that all the fir trees up and down our road have gone brown and died. All of them. Mum says maybe it's a tree disease, but Slimey and I think it's acid rain.

Parents' Evening was quite embarrassing, actually. I knew it would be. I had to stand there while Mum and Slimey slunk about talking to all the teachers and I could just feel that people like Amanda Miles were looking at Slimey and sniggering. And then old Slimey keeps making these pathetic jokes all the time and some of the teachers are polite and pretend to think it's funny while some of them – Miss Milsom, for instance, she's really sour – just pinch their lips together and make their nostrils go all thin and you can tell they're thinking, "What an idiot!"

As a matter of fact I felt a bit sorry for him. I mean, he's completely ludicrous-looking, with his silly scraggly beard and this huge Adam's apple that keeps bobbing up and down every time he swallows and these enormous hands and feet that go clump, clump, clump, everywhere. He's really clumsy. But he does try ever so hard to be liked and I guess it's not his fault he keeps doing it all wrong. He just doesn't know any better. I didn't like the thought of Amanda sniggering at him. I felt like telling her that at least old Slimey doesn't go round eating animals or poisoning the planet with noxious fumes like I bet her dad does. Drawing elves might strike some people as a pretty drippy thing to do but no one can deny that it's harmless. And I suppose if you were only four years old it might bring pleasure to your little infantile life. I expect if I am to be truthful I probably quite liked elves when I was four years old.

Actually as a matter of fact I am not being fair to Slimey. He doesn't only draw elves. He doesn't really draw elves at all. Just in this one particular book that he did for tinies. Mostly what he draws are animals and people. Funny animals and people. Even his elves were funny elves.

I wish I could draw like he can!

↑my elves

144

Saturday

Sereena wanted to know whether I would go and have tea with her again, but I said I couldn't as I was going swimming with Skinny Melon. Mum got a bit cross when she heard. She said, "Why couldn't Sereena go with you?" It's hard to explain that Skinny and I don't want anyone with us. We are a pair. We like being just us. Mum ought to understand since she seems to like being on her own with Slimey.

I told this to Skinny and she said that Mum probably likes being with Slimey because he makes her laugh. She said, "He's really funny, he ought to be on telly."

Slimey? Maybe there is more to him that I thought!

Dad rang up tonight. He said he was very sorry he hadn't been able to get to Parents' Evening. "But you know how it is... meetings that go on for ever." I said that it was all right. I added that he hadn't really missed much. He said, "No, but I do feel bad about it."

I was going to suggest that maybe he could come to the school play instead, and hear me sing, but before I could do so he was called away by Rosemary. I could hear her voice yelling at him up the hall. "Gregg, are you coming?" Dad said, "Oops, got to go! I'll ring you back tomorrow."

I have decided that I hate Rosemary.

Sunday

Wonders will never cease! Slimey has shaved off his beard!!! Unfortunately he looks even more peculiar without it. He has these rabbit teeth and not very much chin.

Spot the difference

Oh, what does Mum see in him?

I know what she sees in him. It is what Skinny says; she thinks he is funny. And also he doesn't keep shouting or losing his temper. I have never heard him shout. He has quite a quiet sort of voice altogether, really. And he does these silly nice things like the other day for instance when we were walking up the road and he saw this worm in the middle of the pavement. Instantly he stopped and broke a bit of twig off someone's hedge so that he could pick it up and put it in a garden. He said it would dry out if it were left where it was.

There aren't many people that would care about a mere worm. I wouldn't have done before. Dad used to go into the back garden and tread on snails. Not purposely, but simply because they happened to be there and got in his way. Slimey never does that. He steps over them. Whenever you go into the garden early in the morning he says, "Watch out for snails!" It used to madden me but I've kind of got used to it. I suppose you can get used to most things.

The only thing I will never get used to is Mum breaking her promise about my dog. How could she do that to me?

20 November

My dear Carol,

So very many thanks for the armadillo droppings (a great success with my crude daughter!) and for the mug-shot of your DHT (Divinely Handsome Texan!) What is he doing working for a bank??? Why isn't he in the movies? On second thoughts, keep him in the bank! He's safer there.

I must tell you that Roly has shaved off his beard. I feel a bit guilty about it. He grew that beard when he was a boy of twenty to cover up the fact that he doesn't have much chin. He doesn't, poor love! And I honestly think he looks far better with a beard. But Cherry hated it – not that she ever actually said so, but she has ways of making her feelings obvious – and as you know he will go to almost any lengths in his efforts to please her.

This all came about, this beard thing, because on Friday it was Parents' Night at Cherry's school and Roly was keen to come along and "be a proper parent" as he put it, but he was scared that Cherry might not want him to. He asked her if she minded and for a wonder she was quite polite and said no, which made Roly really happy, but later that evening, after she was in bed, he suddenly said, "She was ashamed of me, wasn't she?" Of course I indignantly said no – what right has that little miss to be ashamed of a man like Roly? – but nothing would shift his conviction.

He jumped up and went over to the mirror and said, "Look at me! I'm just a mess! If I want her to be proud of having me for a father, I'm going to have to get my act together."

So now he has shaved off his beard and oh, Carol, it is such a mistake! With the beard he looked what he was – an artist. Now he looks like a – a chinless wonder! Only I haven't the heart to tell him. He is absolutely convinced that Cherry will prefer him like this. I don't think I could bear it if she made some hurtful comment. It is truly frightening, the power that children have.

Remember! Stick to your guns with the DHT... you are a career woman!

All my love,

Patsy

Monday

Amanda Miles said to me today, "Was that your stepfather that was with you on Friday?" I couldn't think who she was talking about for a moment as I don't think of Slimey as being my stepfather but I suppose he is. So I said, "Yes. Why?" And she gave this silly smirk and said, "Oh, I just wondered." I felt like hitting her.

Tuesday

Nothing very much happened today.

Wednesday

Nor today.

Thursday

Nothing seems to be happening at all in my life right now.

Friday

Dad never rang me last Sunday, like he promised. Maybe he will this Sunday. If that woman lets him.

Skinny came back with me after school and we watched a video but she couldn't stay the night as she has to go and visit her gran over the weekend. She said, "Dire Melvyn's going to drive us there in his posh car." I said, "What's he got? A Merc?" Skinny didn't know. "Something big and shiny," is all she knows. She's useless at things like that.

"I think we ought to go by train," she said. "Otherwise we're polluting the atmosphere."

She picked that up from Slimey. She'd never have thought of it for herself.

Saturday

I don't know how much longer I can go on writing this diary. It is very difficult when one's life is completely empty. I know it is good practice if one day I want to be a writer but if books are still around when I grow up I think I would rather draw the pictures that go inside them than have to write the words. I think actually I am quite good at drawing. This, for instance, is Slimey before and after:

Sunday

It rained all day. Dad still didn't ring.

27 November

Dear Carol,

I just got yours in which you remind me that when we were young and read *I Capture the Castle* we held exactly the same view as Cherry regarding men with beards.

You say, "I couldn't bear the thought of Cassandra being stuck with Simon. To an eleven year old he seemed practically senile!" Yes, you're quite right. One forgets, perhaps, what it is like to be eleven years old.

And I have been thinking, too, about what I wrote last week. That bit where I said what power children wield. They don't, of course, compared with adults. We're the ones who decide their lives for them – what they're going to be called, where they're going to school, where they're going to live – who they're going to live with. It wasn't Cherry's decision that Gregg and I should split up. The only power she's exercising is the power to hit back. I just wish she wouldn't pick on Roly! But children instinctively go for one's weakest spot. She knows very well that by hurting Roly she hurts me.

I'm feeling a bit down at the moment. Beginning to doubt if things will ever come right. Cherry is obviously never going to forgive me for splitting with Gregg and that means she is never going to accept Roly. What a mess!

But life at least is beginning to work for you. You've been through the dark days and come through them. And I don't ever remember you moaning and groaning the way I do!

All love from your wimpish

Patsy

Monday

Asked the Melon if she'd found out what car Dire Melvyn drives and she said she'd forgotten to look. She said she's not interested in his car. She's not interested in him. She wishes her mum had never met him. She is sick and tired of him always being there.

I said I knew how she felt because it was exactly what I'd felt when Mum started going out with Slimey Roland. I thought this was the sort of thing she would like to hear, but all she did was snap at me. She said, "That was totally different!"

How? That is what I should like to know. The Melon is really becoming very grumpy these days.

No card from Slimey for ages. Perhaps he's got the message at last?

Tuesday

I hope Mum hasn't gone and told old Slime that I chuck his cards in the waste-paper basket. It's just the mean sort of thing she'd do. I think I'll go and take them out and put them somewhere she can't see them.

I've taken them out. I've put them in a box under the bed. Now I suppose she'll think that I've stopped being on strike and am going to start tidying the rest of the room.

If that's what she thinks then she is wrong. I have only done it not to hurt Slime's feelings.

Wednesday

Dad rang. He said he's been very "tied up" at the office. He also said that he hasn't forgotten his promise to buy me a personal computer for Christmas. I expect when I've got used to it I will find it quite interesting. At the moment I'm more into drawing and painting. A big parcel of books arrived for Slimey today. They were all the same book, from his publishers. It is one of his *Freddy the Frog* ones. Freddy the Frog looks like this:

Well, something like that. I can't quite draw it as well as Slimey does, but he's had lots more practice than me. I bet I could if I kept at it.

I meant to ask Dad about coming to see me in the school play but I forgot. I don't expect it matters. I don't expect he'd have been able to come. He'd probably have a meeting or be going out to an important dinner party. I do see that it is difficult for him, being so busy and living so far away. Also I don't expect that woman would have let him.

Thursday

Twenty-four days to go until Christmas! I wonder what Mum will buy me?

Friday

I asked Slimey Roland at tea-time whether he was a crusty roll and butter or a soft roll and butter. I thought that was quite a good joke. So did Roly. I mean Slimey. He laughed. Mum didn't. I don't think Mum has much sense of humour. She never appreciates my jokes. She said, "He's a great big softie, as you well know, and you do anything to take advantage!"

She's always accusing me of these things. I don't know what she means.

I've been drawing frogs all day long and can now do them almost as well as Slimey.

Saturday

He pushed another card under my door last night. He is not so bad really, I suppose. It's just that he is not my dad!

Sunday

Today I took out all Slimey's cards and read them, which I never really bothered to do before. Once you get used to it, it is quite easy. At first you have to puzzle a bit but then you learn the symbols, like he always draws a 🐝 for words like he or we. And a 🗝 for not. I'm going to write out what they say and practise doing it myself. It would be fun to write picture messages in Christmas cards!

I'm sorry that dogs and cats make me sneeze. What about a tortoise?

I'm sorry,
I'm sorry!
What about a bird?
Or a fish?
I will dig a pond
if you like.

We can have
goldfish, snails,
bullrushes and
water lilies.
It will be fun!

Please don't
eat us!

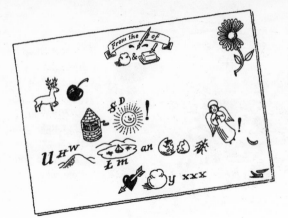

Well done!
You will make
an excellent
angel!

Here are four
examples of
egg jokes.
Exercising,
expelled,
exit, exacting.

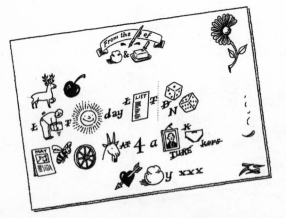

If Sunday is
nice maybe
we'll go for
a picnic.

That was an
ace picnic!
Shall we do it
again some day?
Please look after
Mum when
I'm away.

It's ace to be back!
I miss you and Mum
when I'm not here.

PS Here is
something for
you. I hope you
like her!

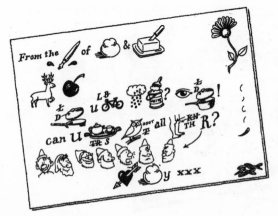

Did you like
Snow White?
I did!
Can you say who
all these are?

I hope you are
happy about the
baby? I'm very
happy! I think
a baby will
be fun!

Have you read a book
called "I Capture the
Castle"? It's good.
Take it with you to
read on holiday.

Welcome home!
Good to have you
back. We miss
you when you
are not here.

It's good to have
a pond. Foxes,
badgers and
hedgehogs can
drink there
and it might bring
frogs and toads.

I'm happy that
you like the
book but sad
you didn't like
poor Simon
and his beard.
Maybe he
looked OK
when he
shaved it off?

I hope you like
me better now
that I have no
beard!

I'm crusty when I'm cross and soft when I'm not cross. Today I'm not cross. Today I'm happy! It will soon be Christmas!

I have just realised what the little symbols are down the sides.

She loves me,
she loves me not...
And he always does these
little pictures of a flower.

There aren't many petals left now. I wonder what he'll do when he gets to the end???

I'm not sure yet that I love him, but he's not as bad as I used to think.

Monday

Tuesday

Today we had cowpats and cardboard slices for dinner. Well, that is what I had. Skinny Melon had what looked like armadillo droppings in greasy washing-up water. We both suffered stomach pains, dizziness and a feeling of total norseea. Norsea?

I have not been recording school meals just lately. This is not because they have been good, but simply because I have had too many other things to think about. Like, for instance, the end of term play! Old Roland the Rat and Mum are both going to come, though Mum says she is thinking of bringing ear plugs in case my loud untuneful voice frightens the baby, which she says it well could, even though it is still in the woom. I told her it will give it a feeling for music but Mum only laughed. Mum is very rude about my singing. All I can say is, she is in for a Big Surprise!

One of the seniors who is in the play, called Davina Walters, stayed for an angel rehearsal the other day. When I had finished my solo she cried, "That's it, Cherry baby! Sock it to 'em!" And Miss Burgess told Amanda, who is another angel, that she ought to "take a leaf out of Cherry's book". She said, "Her voice may not always be quite in tune but at least it can be heard."

She only said about it not being in tune because she didn't want to make Amanda jealous. Amanda has a voice like a sick cow.

I have given up the idea of asking Dad to come. If he said yes and then at the last minute found he was too busy I would be disappointed and hurt so I think it is best not to raise false hopes.

Wednesday

I looked those words up. It is nausea and womb. Why is womb pronounced woom and comb pronounced coam?

I sent a picture message to Skinny Melon in class today and now we are going to do it all the time but not with Mrs James or Miss Milsom as they can be mean.

Thursday

Green grollies in sicky sauce. Yeeeurgh!

Friday

Horse dropping tart. I just don't believe they were mushrooms. They were brown. Whoever heard of brown mushrooms?

Dad just rang! He said, "I haven't got anything special to talk about but I thought I'd call and say hallo and find out how you're getting on." I said I was getting on OK except for maths and computers and CDT and also home ec. where Mrs Marshall despairs of me. I know this for a fact because she said so. She said, "Cherry Waterton, I despair of you." This was because I sewed a hem all wrong and she had to unpick it and start again, and when she gave it back to me I said, "I'm left-handed, does it matter?" And of course it did because I sew from a different direction.

I told this to Dad and he laughed and said, "All the best people are left-handed." I wonder if this is true? I have just realised that old Ratty is, though I didn't say this to Dad.

So anyway we talked for a bit and then Dad said he had to go but that we must "see each other again very soon", so before I could stop myself I said why didn't he come to the school play and hear me sing, but he said unfortunately he couldn't do that as he is so busy. All these Americans keep coming over and Dad is the only person who can deal with them.

At least it is better to know now than to think he is coming and then he doesn't.

Saturday

Went shopping with Mum and Roland Rat and saw brown mushrooms! I never noticed them before. But the ones they dished up at school were all soft and squashy so I still think they were horse droppings. I expect they get them cheap by the bucketful.

Sunday

Sereena came over and I taught her how to do picture messages. That girl has a mind like a sewer. All she could think to do was giggle and draw pictures of lavatories and bums.

That's have and bump. Geddit? Roly Rat is far cleverer than that.

What he would do is:

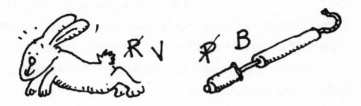

But Roly is a real artist. Sereena is just stupid. She has a one-track mind. Also she said something which annoyed me so much that I shouted at her. I was showing her some of Roly's picture messages and she said that personally she thought they were somewhat childish. I snapped, "Oh do you? Well, for your information that is just where you're wrong. My stepdad happens to be a totally brilliant picture book artist who has had books published in every country in the world. Even in Russia. Even in Japan."

That shut her up.

Monday

I told the Skinbag about Sereena and Skin said that she sounded like a very obnoxious kind of person. I said that she is and that I hoped now I had snubbed her she would stay away from me. I think she had some nerve saying that about poor old Roly Rat's drawings. The Melon agrees. She thinks Roly is the cat's whiskers. She said today that she wished her mum could meet someone like him.

Tuesday

Only 12 days to go till Christmas! Mum asked me this evening what I wanted as my Christmas present and I said, "You know what I want! I want a dog." She sighed and said, "Oh, Cherry, we've been into all this! Roly can't help being allergic. Don't be so selfish all the time."

I don't call it selfish wanting someone to keep their promise that they made you. I said, "If I can't have what I want then I don't want anything," which Mum said was just cutting off my nose to spite my face. Whatever that is supposed to mean.

nose →

I think what it means is that I'm not going to get a dog anyway, so I might as well accept it and find something else. But I can't think of anything else! Not anything big. I told Mum this and she said that I must be a very contented person to have so few wants. I would be contented, if I could have my dog. I would even be contented living with Slime.

Wednesday

11 days! I am marking them off on the calendar. It is a pity the baby is going to miss Christmas. February seems a long time to wait.

Thursday

10 days!

We had the dress rehearsal for the play this afternoon, which meant we were let off lessons, hooray! I hate Thursday afternoons as it is double maths and Mr Fisher says I am the only person he knows who can take one away from two and make it come to three. I said that was because I am a naturally creative person and he told me not to be cheeky but his eyes sort of crinkled as he said it so I don't think he will report me.

The dress rehearsal went really well. At least, it did for me. Amanda Miles and some of the others forgot their words and had to be prompted, but I was word perfect. A few of the teachers came and sat at the back of the hall and watched and at the end, one of them I don't know said, "I like the angels." Miss Burgess said, "Could you hear them all right?" And he said, "All except the little redhead," (meaning Amanda, who is carroty) and then he pointed at me and said, "The police could use that one as a siren." Miss Burgess said, "Oh, yes, we never have any problems with Cherry." Amanda hated me for it, you could tell.

Friday

Last night old Roly Rat pushed another card under my door. It was quite a nice one, he made it look like a telegram, so I took it to school with me and stuck it on the wall of our dressing room (which is only one of the classrooms by the side of the hall). Everyone wanted to know what it said, so I translated it for them and they all thought it was really good except for Amanda who said she'd sooner have a proper telegram, but nobody agreed with her.

Miss Burgess told me that I ought to keep it as it might be valuable one day. She said, "It's an original drawing, and your stepfather is quite famous."

Is he? I never thought of Roly Rat as being famous! I didn't tell Miss Burgess I had a whole stack of his drawings at home. But I'm glad now that they weren't thrown out with the rubbish, which is what would have happened if I hadn't gone on strike. Mum would simply have emptied my waste-paper basket into the dustbin. I like Ratty's cards and I'm going to keep them to show my own children, if I ever have any (if I am not living in a cardboard box). Not because they might be valuable but because they are funny and interesting.

My performance tonight was quite good I think. At the end all the angels had to go in front of the curtain to be clapped and afterwards I was taken home by Skinny Melon's mum and her boyfriend, Dire Melvyn, in Dire Melvyn's car (which is a BMW! Dead posh), as Mum and Ratty are not coming until tomorrow. Dire Melvyn said, "Well, at least we had no trouble hearing you." and her mum told me that I was a very confident performer. Skinny giggled and said, "She was the Foghorn Angel!" but I don't mind Skinny giggling as she doesn't do it nastily.

I didn't want Mum and Roly Rat coming to the first night in case I had stage fright, but they will be there tomorrow. They are looking forward to it.

Saturday

I was even better tonight! I felt I was really getting into it. I am thinking again about maybe becoming a singer. I know I have the voice for it because that is what everyone says. A vicar came up to me afterwards and said, "Aha! The Angel of the Clarion Call!" Even Mum was impressed, I could tell. And a man from the local paper came to take our photograph and he took one of the angels, and he said, "Where's the little one with the big voice? (Meaning me.) "Let's have her in the middle." Amanda was cross as crabs! She really fancies herself.

Instead of waiting for a bus we all went home by taxi because Ratty said, "It's the only way for a star to travel." Mum said, "Well! I suppose we shall have to pay to speak to you now."

This is us being photographed

Monday

Skinny came to school this morning looking dead miserable. I asked her what the matter was and she said, "Nothing." So then I said, "What did you do on Sunday?" and she said, "Nothing." I said, "I didn't do anything, either. We could have got together if I'd known. But I thought you were going out with Dire Melvyn?" She said, "We did." I said, "So how can you say that you did nothing? You must have done something. Even if you just drove somewhere, that's doing something. You can't call driving somewhere not doing anything. Unless you mean you were just sitting

175

there in a great useless lump suffering from brain death. Maybe that's what you mean?"

She was in a very strange mood. She told me in decidedly huffish tones to just shut up and stop getting on her nerves. Then she didn't speak to me again until break.

Weird. She is all right now, though.

Tuesday

Hooray! We have broken up. Mrs James said our reports will arrive after Christmas. I am not sure whether this is a good thing or a bad thing. Skinny says it's bad as they will be hanging over us but on the other hand it avoids any unpleasantness before Christmas. I expect mine will be foul. Skinny expects hers will be foul too though I don't know why as Skinny on the whole is very quiet and well behaved. I am the one who is always getting told off.

Tomorrow we are going to go out together and buy our presents, both for each other and for other people. We have a rule that we will spend £2 on each other and no more. I think this is a good rule as it stops one from worrying. For instance, if I only bought Skinny a calendar with pictures of dogs (which is what I'm going to do) and she bought me a new pair of Doc Marten's, then I would feel mean and guilty. Not that she is very likely to buy me a new pair of Doc Marten's as she wants a pair herself.

Wednesday

I have bought:

A calendar for Skinny Melon, some leggings for Mum, some aftershave from the Body Shop for Roly Rat and a teddy bear for the baby.

It was very difficult knowing what to get for Roly Rat but in the end I thought if I got something from the Body Shop it would demonstrate that I care about the environment and about things not being tested on animals. That will please him.

I bought the leggings for Mum because I am tired of seeing her in those horrible dungaree things and think it will be good for her to wear something bright and pretty when she no longer has the baby inside her and is back to normal. They are a lovely orange colour with swirly patterns in yellow and purple. She will look really great in them. She has nice legs when they are not hidden in dungarees.

I bought something for the baby because although I know it is not going to be here until February I think it should have some presents waiting for it. I thought that a bear would be suitable. There were all different coloured ones, pink ones, yellow ones, blue ones, browny ones, so in the end I got a browny one as we don't know whether the baby is going to be a boy or a girl.

I have been wondering which I would rather have, a brother or a sister, and I think on the whole I would rather have a brother as it would be something different. I am quite looking forward to it, I suppose, now that I have got used to the idea. Skinny wants to come and look at it when it's born. She says that she likes babies. I can't imagine why, since as far as I can see they don't actually do anything except eat and sleep. Well, they also mess their nappies and sick up their milk and cry a lot and sometimes scream. They also dribble. All of which I think is pretty revolting.

Skinny says this just goes to show how little I know about them. She says that all these things may be true but that when they are not messing or dribbling or sicking things up they are nice and cuddly and what she calls "fun". She says as well that it is very exciting when they give their first smile and say their first word and grow their first teeth. Hm! We shall see.

Thursday

Today the Skinbag came round and stayed for tea. I asked her if she would like to watch a video of Laurel and Hardy which belongs to Ratty, who has dozens of them, and she said all right so I put it on and it was really funny. I was giving myself a pain from laughing so much, and all the time the Melon is just sitting there glum and gloomy with a face like a wet washing-rag, until in the end she starts to get on my nerves and I switch the video off and snarl, "What's the matter with you? Has your sense of humour gone?" In reply to which she instantly bursts into tears and informs me that life as she has known it is over.

Well! I am completely taken aback because one thing Skinny is not and that is a watering pot (as Mum calls it). So naturally I ask her why life as she has known it is over, and it all comes pouring out, about Dire Melvyn and her mum and how her mum has just broken it to her that they are thinking of getting married.

My immediate instinct is to remark sarcastically on her sudden change of attitude. Funny that when I used to carry on about old Ratty, the Skinbag could think of nothing better to say than how lucky I was and how any dad is better than no dad and how she wished that her mum would get married again. However, because I am her friend I very nobly suppress my instinct and croon in syrupy fashion that I know just how she's feeling as I've been through it all myself.

"It's not the same," she says; "Roly's nice. Anyone would be glad to have Roly for a dad." And then she goes into these really loud sobs and says that nobody in their right mind would want Dire Melvyn.

So while I'm sitting there wondering what to say next, Mum comes in to tell us that tea's ready, and of course she sees the Melon in floods and wants to know what's wrong so I explain the situation and Mum goes all soft and mumsy (she's never like that with me) and puts an arm round the Melon's shoulders and coaxes her out into the kitchen, where Ratty is, and before I know it the Melon's weeping all over Ratty and saying how Dire Melvyn is the pits and life as she has known it is over.

After a bit, when she's finished blubbing and has blown her nose on Ratty's hanky (I wouldn't! It's all covered in paint), Ratty asks her what exactly is so dire about poor old Melv. I say, "There isn't anything dire. He drives a BMW and he gives her money." But the Melon glowers at me and says he's got this big fat belly and grey hairs growing out of his nostrils and hands like damp fungus and he treats her as if she's about six years old. She says it's all right for Matthew (that's her brother); he's hardly ever at home. And it's all right for the Blob (that's her sister) because she's only eight and doesn't seem to mind if she's treated like an infant.

"But I can't stand it!" wails the Melon.

And then old Ratty says something which surprises me. He says, "The poor man's probably terrified of you. You young girls frighten the lives out of us poor, plain middle-aged men." I said, "*Do* we?"

"You'd better believe it!" said Roly.

The Melon hiccuped and said she didn't see any reason why Dire Melvyn should be terrified of her.

"Because he's desperate to make a good impression," said Roly. "He's desperate for you to approve of him and it makes him nervous." And then he told her to try being kind to him and to laugh at his jokes and maybe even ask his advice about something, because that would make him feel that he was wanted. He promised that if she did, it would work miracles.

I could see that the Melon was doubtful, but at least it shut her up and stopped her dripping all over the place. When her mum came to collect her (in her old VW) I went out to the car with her and reminded her, in what I hoped were comforting tones, that when Mum first got married to Roly I thought he was the biggest creep around. "And now," I said, "I quite like him." I said that what happened was, you sort of grew used to them.

The Melon just gave me this dying duck look and clunked her seat belt. She really is making a big production of it. I suppose she wants to be the centre of attention. Pathetic, really. I didn't make anywhere near this amount of fuss.

Incidentally, I have discovered what Mum has bought me for Christmas! It is on top of the wardrobe as usual. She always puts my presents up there. She thinks I don't know but I found out years ago. It is not cheating to look, as it is only the lesser ones. My big ones she hides somewhere else that I have not yet discovered.

I only took a very quick peek. Some of the things are in bags and when they are in bags I don't look. That is one of the rules. But I saw a couple of CDs which I really want, so that is good. There are also what I suspect may be books (flat and hard) and some that I think are clothes (soft when you poke them). That is good, too!

Friday

Horrors! Today I had a fright. I went in with Mum to do some last-minute shopping (Roly Rat stayed behind to draw some last-minute elves) and we walked through the tights and leggings department and Mum suddenly said, "Maybe I shall splash out and buy myself a pair of leggings. What do you think?" and she headed straight for the very pair that I had bought for her! Very quickly I said, "You don't want those. What about these ones?" pointing to some drab and boring ones in plain colours. To my great relief she said, "Yes, I suppose those are rather more suited to a middle-aged woman, aren't they?" It was a tense moment!

I have wrapped up all my presents in Christmas wrapping paper and put little gift tags on them with picture messages.

Roly's says:

Mum's says:

I am going to tidy my room for Christmas.

Saturday

Today I felt the baby move! Mum said, "Oh! He's kicking me." "Or she," I said. "It might be a she." Mum agreed that it might be.

I don't mind which it is. I just want it to get here!

The Melon rang up in the evening to wish me a Happy Christmas. She said that Dire Melvyn was going to be with them for three whole days but that it was "all right" as she had done what Roly said and asked his advice about something. She had asked him what sort of plant she could grow in a really dark and boggy part of the garden (old Skin is quite into gardening), and he had come up with some really brilliant suggestions. It seems he knows about plants and boggy patches, so now she doesn't mind so much about the fungussy hands and grey nose hairs and the big fat belly. What she actually said was, "He's not absolutely as dire as I thought."

Thank goodness for that! It means I can enjoy Christmas without having to worry about her. After all, she is my best friend – my *very* best friend – and I wouldn't have liked to think of her being unhappy.

24 December

My dear Carol,

I am writing this on Christmas Eve. Haven't had a chance until now, what with one thing and another.

Last Saturday we went to see Cherry doing her singing angel bit in the school play. Oh, dear! What can one say? They obviously chose her because she looked right – very pretty and cheeky. Very impish. But she cannot sing! Of course we told her she was the greatest, or at any rate Roly did, and as a result she has been blasting our eardrums ever since. I wish she would take up something quiet, such as painting.

Roly has bought her a whole range of pens, paints, crayons, drawing blocks, etc., for Christmas, but as it's from him she'll probably just look at it with that terrible expression of condescension and contempt that girls of eleven can have. Do you know what I mean? Cold and cutting and oh, so knowing and superior! Were we ever like that when we were eleven?

In fairness to her I have to say that she has been quite sweet and considerate these last few days (apart from the ear-blasting). It was very funny the other day!

I was going to splash out and buy myself a pair of leggings and Cherry practically tied herself in knots trying to guide me away from a pair in glaring orange that she has quite obviously bought me for Christmas!!! I shall have to feign utter astonishment when I undo the parcel, just as Cherry will feign utter astonishment when she undoes some of hers. Not very much is a secret in this house. She always climbs up to look on top of the wardrobe because she knows that's where I keep all her "pillow case" presents. She's been doing it for years. It's a sort of game we play, except that she doesn't know that I know she does it! (Don't worry, I have hidden your baseball bat! I spirited it away the minute it arrived.)

I'm a bit worried in case she hasn't bought anything for Roly. I've kept dropping hints but the only kind of hint she understands is the kind that you apply with a sledge-hammer! She is incredibly thick-skinned. So I've got some after-shave from the Body Shop and gift-wrapped it, just to be on the safe side. He would be so terribly hurt if she forgot him.

Meanwhile, we have a real surprise for her! I won't tell you what it is. See if you can guess!

A few weeks ago, in the middle of the night, Roly suddenly shot bolt upright in bed and cried, "I've got it!" When I asked him, "Got what?" he said, "The solution... I'm allergic to fur, not skin. We'll get her a hairless one!"

So we hunted high and low – and incidentally, paid

the earth, though Roly assures me it will be worth it for the pleasure it will bring – and all I will say is that it is HAIRLESS, that it comes originally from CHINA, and that right at this moment it is over the road being looked after by Mrs Swaddle (the mother of Sereena).

Have you guessed???

Roly is going to go over and collect it tomorrow immediately before breakfast. I can't wait to see Cherry's face!

Gregg, incidentally, has kept his word for once and sent her the personal computer, it was delivered last week while she was at school. I'm sure it will come in very useful but I can tell you here and now that between a hairless Chinese wotnot and a personal computer there will be no competition!

I do hope you and your Dwayn have the most wonderful Christmas ever. If I could only rid myself of fears that a) Cherry will have forgotten to buy something for Roly and that b) she is going to resent the baby, I would be the happiest soul on earth! I will keep my fingers crossed. Maybe I am misjudging her.

All my fondest love,

Patsy

Christmas Day

Dear Roly,

Charlie Chan is the best present I've ever had. He makes me very happy. I adore him already! Thank you, thank you, thank you!

Love Cherry XXX

Boxing Day

Now that I have my beautiful Charlie, I won't be keeping this diary any more. I'll be far too busy, taking him for walks! So this is where I am going to end. It has been quite fun and it has done what Mrs James said it would do, it has cleaned out the cupboard, but I feel that from now on I am going to be concentrating more on drawing than on writing. I have decided… when I am grown up I am going to be an <u>artist!</u>

Becky Bananas

JEAN URE

Illustrated by Mick Brownfield
and Stephen Player

*For Ann-Janine, with love and gratitude
and in the hope that we may be able to work
together again one of these days*

The story that follows was taken from Becky's thoughts, and hopes, and dreams as she recorded them over the last few months; also from the conversations that she had with her family and friends, and especially Sarah and Zoë.

"It's always sad having to say goodbye to someone you love. But I wouldn't have missed knowing someone like Becky for the world!"

Jean Ure

1. "This is Your Life!"

Becky Bananas, this is your life!

Yes, it is. It is *my* life! And I have lived it for eleven and three-quarter years.

Eleven years nine months and three days, to be precise.

Eleven years nine months three days and fourteen hours, to be even more precise.

I can work it out, because I know when I was born. I was born at ten past two in the morning. Mum's told me about it heaps of times.

"You arrived all of a sudden, in this terrible rush. It took everyone by surprise, including me!"

I can never understand how it can have taken Mum by surprise. You'd think if you had a great enormous thing like a baby kicking and battering inside you, you'd feel when it was starting to come out. I should think it would be really painful.

I've asked Mum about this. She says, "It was painful, but it was worth it. Every second of it!"

But she still doesn't explain how it took her by surprise.

I said, "Didn't you feel it was happening?" and she said, "I felt *something* was happening but I wasn't quite sure what. Not until someone said 'Push!' and you came bursting out, all red and angry without any hair."

Ugh! What a yukky sight.

It seems a very odd way of carrying on if you ask me. You'd think things could have been arranged a bit better. Like with worms. Or amoebas. When amoebas want babies, they just split in half so that there are two of them.

Ever so much easier. I don't expect it hurts at all, hardly.

Not that I would want to be an amoeba. They are plain, blobby-looking creatures without any brain and they don't really seem to do anything, as far as I can see, save flop about in the bottom of pools and suchlike. But I suppose they are happy.

Can you be happy, if you haven't any brain?

At least you wouldn't be *un*happy, I shouldn't think. Or scared. Or cross or lonely or saying to yourself that things aren't fair. But then you wouldn't be able to dance or laugh or read books, either. So on the whole I wouldn't want to be one.

How could you cuddle a baby amoeba?

There are lots of pictures of Mum cuddling me. There's also a picture of me completely naked, waving my arms about on a blanket.

I've always found that really embarrassing. If I grow up and have babies, I will never take those sorts of pictures of them.

Sometimes when my friends come round, Mum pulls out the photograph albums and shows them. She says, "Look!" and she giggles. "There's Becky when she was only a few weeks old… like a little pink slug!"

Mum thinks it's funny, but I can see that other people are just as embarrassed as I am. Sarah once said, "Isn't it frightful, the way your parents come out with these terrible things?"

She meant her parents as well as Mum. Everyone's parents. *All* parents. But I don't think Mum means to say terrible things. She just can't stop herself. It's what comes of being an extrovert, which is a word I learned from Mrs

Rowe. She said it to me last Parents' Day. She said, "Your mother is quite an extrovert, Rebecca, isn't she?"

I didn't know what it meant. I asked Sarah and she said it meant that you laugh a lot and are friendly.

Deanne Warburton said it meant *noisy*.

It is true that Mum does laugh more than most people and also I suppose her voice is quite loud. But she can't help it! It's just the way she is. That's why she's in show business.

I love my mum. She is beautiful and funny and I am really proud of her. I don't mind her being loud! I wouldn't want her any different. But I do wish she wouldn't keep showing people the picture of me as a little pink slug! I won't ever do that to my children, if I have any. Which most probably I won't, I don't expect.

On the other hand, I might. You never can tell. But if I do, I won't embarrass them.

Another of the things Mum says about me is that I was a bonny bouncing baby. "Oh, you were *such* a bonny bouncing baby!"

She's got this story about how one time I bounced so high I almost managed to bounce right out of my playpen.

She says, "I used to think you'd end up being a pole vaulter in the Olympics!"

If ever they decide to do one of those *This is Your Life* programmes about me, like for instance when I am a famous dancer, Mum will be able to come on and tell all the people that are watching about me bouncing out of my playpen. She'd like that.

I'm not sure that I would. I think I might find it a bit embarrassing. But I suppose if you are on *This is Your Life* you can't always choose what people say about you. More's the pity!

2. My Goal

Oh, she was such a bonny bouncing baby!

Poor Mum. Sometimes when I'm tempted to feel sorry for myself, I start thinking about Mum and feel sorry for her, instead. All that pain when I was being born, and what was the point of it? Just a waste of effort, really. That's what I would think.

I've made her cry, I know I have. I've heard her crying, when she doesn't know I was there. I can't bear for Mum to be unhappy! But when I've tried talking to her about it, like one time I said about it being a waste of effort, it made her really upset. She said, "Becky, you must never, ever think like that! What a dreadful thing to say! It was the most wonderful day of my life, the day I had you."

She didn't know how things were going to turn out. People don't, when you have babies.

Like Violet, Gran's best friend, who used to teach me dancing and who had this son called Bobby that was Down's syndrome. I remember once I was at

Gran's and Gran and Violet were talking, and Violet suddenly burst out, "I wouldn't change my Bobby for the world!"

I suppose if you have a baby, you love it no matter what. Even if it's got two heads or is brain-damaged. It's still your baby. But it would be ever so much better if things didn't happen like brain damage and Down's syndrome and such. Not till you're really old, and then perhaps it wouldn't matter quite so much. I think God should have arranged it so that everyone is allowed to live to be at least forty. I don't think you would mind so much then.

I am going to live to be a hundred. Ha! That will surprise them. Except that nobody will be here by then. Only Danny. And he will be ninety-three!!!

this is my
Little Brother

What will the date be when I am a hundred? It will be... 2086! And I will get a telegram from the Queen.

No, I won't, because the Queen won't still be alive. And I don't think Prince Charles will, either. I don't know how old he is but I think he must be older than Mum. So it won't be King Charles III. And it won't be William V, because Wills is sixteen and that would make him 103 and practically no one lives to be 103. And it won't be King Henry, I shouldn't think, because Harry would be 100 and I bet there's never been a king that's 100. But whoever it is, they will send me a telegram!

HIP HIP HOORAY! ·····ONE HUNDRED TODAY···HAVE FUN ON YOUR BIRTHDAY·· LOVE FROM THE QUEEN·

I wonder what they say when they send telegrams?

The only trouble is, you couldn't really have much fun if you were a hundred. You wouldn't be able to play games or go to parties or visit Wonderland. You'd just sit about in a chair all day wearing false teeth.

Yeeuch! I can't stand false teeth. There's this old woman I saw once that had taken hers out and put them in a glass of water by the side of her bed.

Ugh. It made me feel really sick. I don't ever want to have false teeth.

Maybe I won't live to be a hundred. Maybe I'll just live to about... forty. That's probably long enough.

I once heard Mum say to her friend Anna when they were speaking on the telephone that she was going to hold a big party when she was forty. She said it was going to be a special farewell party.

"Farewell to my lost youth... before I go into my zimmer frame."

Zimmer frames are what old people use to help them walk.

But you have to be *really* old for that. I can't imagine Mum being really old. I can't imagine her having grey hair and wrinkles.

Mum says that she can't, either, so I expect she will have a face-lift and dye her hair. That is what people in show business quite often do. They also, sometimes, have their noses altered or their boobs made bigger, to make themselves look more beautiful.

Gran used to say, "We didn't do that in my day," but Mum said, "Go on! I bet you wore falsies."

I thought she meant false teeth. It was ages before I discovered that falsies were special padded bras to make people think you had big boobs when in fact you only had small ones, though personally I can't think why anyone would want big boobs. I would think they must be quite heavy and get in the way, I mean if you're running or dancing, or anything. Surely they would wobble up and down? And if you were doing a pirouette, for instance, they would probably spin round faster than your head and unbalance you.

I wouldn't want to have big boobs. Sarah says it's men that like them and that's the reason women go and get them made huge. Just to please men.

Weird.

I bet in a hundred years' time people will be able to order bits of body from catalogues, like nowadays you can order clothes and things. They'll have these sections saying "Noses" or "Boobs" or "Ears", and all these different shapes and sizes.

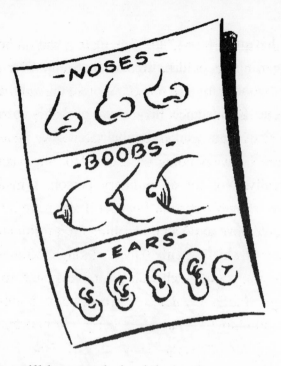

All you'll have to do is pick out the ones you think will suit you and fill in an order form saying how many you want and when you want them fitted. Only by then things will be so advanced that you won't have to have an operation and be cut open, they will be able to change your shape simply by pointing some sort of ray gun at you which will make your body go like gloop.

Some people will even be able to do it for themselves, I shouldn't be surprised. They will have their own personal ray guns. They will wake up in the morning and think, "I don't like this nose. I am sick of this nose. I think

I will make a new one." Or if they are going on holiday, for instance, they will be able to use the gun for taking away all the bits of flab round their tummies so that they can wear their nice new bikinis and be attractive to men. Just zap! with the gun and all the flab will be melted.

Mum is always going on about flab. She hasn't got any, really. Not for an ordinary person. I mean, an ordinary showbiz person. I expect if she were a dancer she would have to do a bit of toning up. I fortunately do not have problems with fatness, though Mum says I have now lost too much weight and must start to put it on again. She is threatening to feed me on nothing but pasta and chips!!! I have told her I will end up like a beach ball but she says, "That will be the day."

When it is the year 2086 – when I am a hundred! If I decide to be a hundred – people I should think will be able to pump themselves up with special pumps if they are too thin. The pumps will inject calories into them, as many as they want. And if they are too fat they will take the calories out. It will be a bit like the sludge-gulping machines that go round the gutters gulping sludge.

It is interesting to speculate how people will say it when it is 2086. Will they say, twenty eighty-six? Or just eighty-six? Or will they say it in full? The year two thousand and eighty-six?

If they are American they will probably say two thousand eighty-six without the "and". I have noticed that Americans do this. They shorten things. Like they say math instead of maths and wash-up liquid instead of washing-up. I expect they do it to save time, as they are always frantically rushing everywhere and talking very fast and being busy.

The way I know about this is because of Susie Smith, at school. You'd think she was American, the way she talks, but she isn't. It's just that she lived there for a year. So now she calls her Mum "Mom" and writes these essays about her little sister wearing diapers.

Mrs Rowe says, "*Diapers*, Suzanne? What are *diapers*?" making like she doesn't understand. She's ever so English, Mrs Rowe.

She doesn't mind people speaking American when they are American, but she can't stand what she calls "apeing". But it's difficult not to pick things up. Like when me and Sarah saw this film where people kept shouting "Way to go!" and it started us off saying it, so that whenever we met we used to yell it at each other. "Way to *go*!"

We didn't know what it meant, but it sounded good.

We were only little, then; we were still nine. I always wanted to be nine. I don't know why. It used to be my favourite age. And then when I got to be it, it didn't feel all that much different from being eight, and so I decided that the next thing I wanted to be was eleven.

I never specially wanted to be ten. Perhaps it was because ten reminded me of decimals. I hate decimals. I also hate adding and subtracting and multiplying and dividing and everything that has numbers in it, including telephone numbers because I can't ever remember them.

Gran once told me that before I was born we didn't have great long telephone numbers like we have now. Instead of being 020 7373, for instance, you'd be a name, like Bluebell, maybe, or Elgar. Those are the only two that I can remember, but there were lots of them. I think Bluebell and Elgar are really pretty. Much better than boring old numbers.

Maybe that's why I didn't specially want to be ten. Or maybe it was because eleven was like a sort of goal. Like eleven was a really Great Age and if I got to be eleven I would have achieved something. Except that now I'm here it doesn't seem like very much at all.

My present ambition is to be twelve. If I get to be twelve I am going to go to Wonderland. *In America.* Mum has promised.

Mum always keeps her promises; she's really good

about that. Sarah's mum forgets. She once told Sarah she could come swimming with me and then at the last minute she said she hadn't said it and that Sarah had to go and visit her aunt and uncle instead.

Mum isn't like that. She *always* keeps her promises. So I know I shall go to Wonderland. I've got to. I want to so much!

It said in a book I read that if you want something badly enough you'll get it, but only if you keep it in front of you the whole time, like a vision, and "work steadily towards it". That is what I am doing. I am keeping Wonderland in front of me and I am working towards it.

I told this to Uncle Eddy and he squeezed my hand and said, "That's my girl! Go for it!"

I am going for it. Definitely, absolutely, and without question. I AM GOING TO WONDERLAND. And maybe Sarah could come with us. That would be fun!

It would be lovely if Zoë could come as well, but I know her Mum couldn't afford it and I don't think she'd let us pay because she's what Mum calls "proud". That means she doesn't like accepting charity, even for Zoë. But I could always get Mum to ask. It would be brilliant if Zoë could come! She would be so excited and we could keep it in front of us together. That would be like double determination, and then we would be bound to go.

If only one of them could come, it would have to be Zoë, because although Sarah is my oldest friend, and my best friend, Zoë is my *special* friend. And Sarah could go to Wonderland any time she wanted, so for her it wouldn't be such a treat.

I think it is ever so unfair that some people are rich and some people are poor. Like it is unfair that some people are born ugly and some people are born beautiful, and some are born stupid while others are born clever.

I know what Uncle Eddy would say. He would say, "That's the way the cookie crumbles, kiddo."

He is always using these quaint and colourful expressions. Sometimes I try using them in essays, but Mrs Rowe just puts big exclamation marks by them.

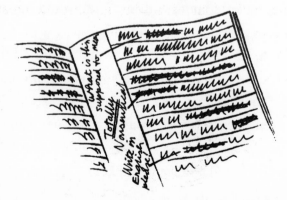

All I can say is that whoever crumbles the cookies doesn't make a very good job of it, what with big heaps here, and little heaps there, and even occasionally just crumbs.

Even sometimes nothing at all.

Being born, I must say, is a very strange and unsatisfactory experience. Why is it, for instance, that no one can ever remember it? You would think you would remember such an amazing event. For nine whole months you live in the dark, all warm and safe and tucked away, with nothing bad happening to you, and then quite suddenly you're pushed out into the world in really a very brutal rough fashion, like being squeezed headfirst out of a tube, gasping for breath and wondering whatever can be going on.

where am I?

I would think it must be quite frightening. Maybe that is why you don't remember it. Maybe it is so terrible that your brain seals it away in a little corner, never to be thought of again.

It is spooky, when you think about it. All these poor defenceless little babies being expelled from the womb with absolutely no idea what the future is going to hold. Some people, if they knew what was going to happen to them, might not want to be born at all.

If everyone was allowed to look into their future before they were born, then they could decide whether they liked it or not, and if they didn't then they wouldn't have to come, and that way perhaps there wouldn't be any more awful things such as illness and accidents and starvation.

Zoë told me that she believes everyone who dies is born again as someone else. She said, "You don't really die, because you always come back again." She told me that she read this somewhere and she most firmly believes it.

It is a nice thought but I don't understand how it can be, since the population of the world is getting bigger all the time. For example, there were probably only about – oh, I don't know! – about five hundred people, maybe, before the Stone Age, whereas now there are about five hundred million, I should think. Five hundred billion. Five hundred *trillion*. So where have all the extra people come from?

It doesn't really make any sense, though I suppose it would be a comfort to think that you weren't just going to disappear.

I asked Zoë, if you *did* come back, whether you would come as someone quite different or as just another version of yourself, and she said she'd thought about this and she reckoned you'd come back as another version of yourself. She said this would account for people sometimes claiming to remember being alive in another age.

That is true. People do make these claims. Like there was this woman who could remember being an

Egyptian slave and could even speak ancient Egyptian.

I think there may be *something* in it but that it is not quite as simple as Zoë makes out. On the other hand, if that is what she wants to believe, it would be unkind to spoil it for her by asking too many questions. We all have to find our own things to believe in. That is what Gran said and I think it is true.

What I believe is that even if I have been someone else before and am going to be someone different in the future, it is me as I am now that is important.

And me as I am now is going to go to Wonderland! That is my big, immediate goal. To be twelve years old and go to Wonderland.

I am really determined about it.

You were born Rebecca Banaras, but everyone calls you Becky Bananas.

It was Sarah started calling me that. The first day I was at Oakfield, out in the playground at break.

"Bananas?" she said. "Is that really your name?" And before I could tell her that it wasn't, she'd gone and shrieked, "Becky Bananas!" and got everyone giggling.

I didn't think then that I was going to like her very much. But now she's my best friend and we do everything together. Well, almost everything. There are some things I can only do with Zoë, and that's why Zoë is my *special* friend. But for school and home, it's me and Sarah. We get on really well.

She'll be one of the guests when I'm on *This is Your Life*!

I don't mind her calling me Becky Bananas. I've got used to it. Once I almost wrote it on an exam paper! I got as far as: *Becky Banan*

and I had to go back and change it: *Becky Bananas*

We didn't have Mrs Rowe then, which is just as well or she'd have made one of her remarks like "I see we nearly stumbled at the first hurdle, Rebecca!" She said that to Sarah once, when Sarah wrote the date wrong. She can be ever so sarcastic.

And she *always* always calls us by our full names: Rebecca, Joanna, Suzanne. It's like she's scared of being too friendly. She says, "You do not shorten my name. Why should I shorten yours?"

It's hard to think how you could shorten Rowe. Sarah sometimes calls her Rosy, only not to her face. I don't think anyone would dare call her that to her face!

She's all right, really, Mrs Rowe. She's very fair. She doesn't pick on people or have favourites, like some teachers. I think she's one of those that Gran would have said their bark is worse than their bite. I wonder if she'd be one of the guests?

She might be! When I was off school last year she came to see me, which not everybody did. When I told Sarah, Sarah pulled a face and said that if she was off school a visit from Rosy was the last thing she'd want.

"Freeze the blood in your veins, that would!"

But she was really nice and not at all sarcastic. Also, she brought me a book of ballet photographs and a get-well card with a picture of Darcey Bussell on it. I wonder how she knew that Darcey is my ace favourite dancer???

Maybe she's seen the photos I've got pinned inside my locker! But she still must have gone out and bought it specially. Not everyone would have done that. So now I think that seeming to be cold and unfeeling is just her manner, like Sarah is always laughing and making jokes so that maybe you would think she doesn't care about things, but that would not be true. We wouldn't be best friends if she didn't care. For instance, she cried ever so when her favourite goldfish died.

He was called Golden Boy and it was particularly terrible and tragic as her little sister Tasha took him out of the tank when no one was looking and he squiggled through her hands and fell on the floor, and instead of putting him back she got scared and ran screaming for her mum. By the time her mum got there it was too late and he had expired (which is simply another way of saying died).

Sarah was really sad. She said that although goldfish don't have much in the way of personality it is very upsetting to think of them suffocating on the living-room carpet. I can see that it would be. Especially if it happens to be your favourite one.

We once wrote out long lists of all our favourite things, Sarah and me. We made scrapbooks and stuck them in there, with little drawings and pictures that we'd cut from magazines. Of course we were only young then. I expect if I looked at my list now I would cringe and think "How childish". I mean, for instance, when I was six years old my favourite food was – *jelly babies*!

I wonder if it would be fun to make up a new list, now that I am more mature? I think I will!

List of my Favourite Things

Favourite colour Blue. I don't know why, but it makes me happy. It is just one of those things.

Favourite book *Ballet Shoes* by Noel Streatfeild, even though it is old-fashioned. And my favourite character from *Ballet Shoes* is Posy, because she is the one who becomes a dancer!

Favourite ballet *Swan Lake*. Odette is what I want to dance more than anything else! My favourite part is where she is on point, leaning back against Prince Siegfried, and he has his arms round her.

I think that is so beautiful and romantic!

Favourite TV programme *Ask Auntie.* I have to say that because it is Mum's programme! I like it because I like to watch Mum. I suppose if Mum wasn't in it I might say... *General Practice.* I *really* like that.

Sarah says it's fuddy-duddy. That is an expression she recently read in a book and now she keeps repeating it like a parrot. Everything that she thinks dull and boring is fuddy-duddy. She says that *General Practice* is for old people. It is true that there are quite a lot of old people in it, but sometimes there are children and that is interesting. Zoë likes it, too. We have thought of writing an episode together and sending it to the BBC.

Favourite Film *Little Women.* I have seen it three times and would like to see it again, even though I always drench about ten hankies when Beth gets sick after holding poor Mrs Hummel's baby. This is because I know that she is going to die, though she doesn't actually do so in the film. (But I have read *Good Wives* and that is how I know.) Last time I watched it Mum got worried and said it was too upsetting for me. She would like it if I only watched things that made me laugh, not things that make me weep. I know she means well but you cannot cocoon people. "Wrap them in cotton wool" is what Gran used to say. I don't want to be wrapped in cotton wool. I want to watch *Little Women* again and again!

Jo of course is my favourite character. She is Sarah's too. I think she must be everyone's. The reason she is my favourite is because she is so full of life. And also because she is brave. Cutting off her hair and behaving like a boy at a time when girls were not supposed to behave like boys.

I wish I were as brave as Jo, but I don't think I am. If I were, I wouldn't choose blue as my favourite colour. I would choose… red!

I bet Jo would choose red. Red is bold and exciting. She would probably think blue is a bit boring. Uncle Eddy says it is the colour of peace and rest. That makes it sound like an old person's colour. Does it mean that *I* am like an old person?

No! It is simply that I like blue things. Blue sky. Blue sea. Blue flowers. Forget-me-nots and pansies. Harebells, bluebells. And the little trumpety things that Mum calls periwinkles.

Favourite flower My favourite of all flowers is sweet peas!

I love sweet peas because they are very dainty and fragile. Like butterflies. Gran used to grow them at the end of her garden. They grew up the fence that looked onto the railway line.

Sweet peas come in all beautiful colours. Pinks and mauves and whites and purples. Scarlets and lemons and even a sort of pale orange. But not, I think, blue. That is strange! Fancy having a favourite flower that doesn't come in my favourite colour.

When I was little I called them fairy flowers. I even made up a ballet for them.

I can't remember the steps now but I expect they were just skipping and hopping. I was only about four. I didn't know steps like *pas de chat* or *arabesque*.

Let me think of some more of my favourite things.

Favourite Animal The cat. Mum says cats are like liquid ornaments. She says she'd rather have a cat sitting on the mantelpiece than a Ming vase. I'm not quite sure what a Ming vase is, but I know that it is something very precious and expensive.

Siamese cats are *quite* expensive.

They are also very beautiful and intelligent, and also they talk all the time, in a yowling sort of way. Also, they have blue eyes!

Kitty had green ones. She was just an ordinary cat. Not like Bella and Bimbo. They are pedigrees. But she slept on my bed and she cuddled and purred. She was my very favourite cat of all.

I shall never forget Kitty.

I am still thinking of favourite things.

Favourite activity Dancing! When I was young we were too poor for me to go to a proper dancing school and so Gran's friend Violet taught me. Gran called her Vi but I called her Violet. Even when I was six years old, that is what I called her. She used to say, "I don't hold with all this formality, ducks."

Violet was younger than Gran but they'd been on tour together in the old days, when Violet was a dancer and Gran was part of a double act with Granddad. And then Violet had Bobby, who was Down's syndrome, and gave it all up to look after him. Only she would never say that she had given it up. She would say, "Gave it up? I didn't give *it* up, it gave me up!" And then she'd laugh this funny, crackling laugh and light another fag. She always called them her fags.

"Where are me fags? Pass me me fags!"

She used to smoke her fags even while she was teaching me.

I don't suppose, really, that Violet was ever a very good dancer. She never did proper ballet. I think what she did was called show dancing. But she taught me how to do *pliés* and positions of the feet, and *battements tendus* and *ronds de jambes*.

Later, when I went to the Russell, Miss Runcie said I'd had a good grounding, so Violet must have known what she was doing even if she did pronounce *ronds de jambes* as "rondy jombs".

I didn't know what Miss Runcie was talking about the first time she told us to do them. I said, "Oh, rondy jombs!" and everyone laughed and I couldn't understand why.

And then I realised and I went home and pretended to be Violet saying things wrong – rondy jombs and arabeskys and grond jetties – and Mum overheard me and told me off. She said, "Don't you *ever* let me catch you making fun of Violet again!"

Mum said that Violet was a good and genuine person who had had a great deal to cope with in life. So then I felt ashamed and regretted that I had mocked her. I wish I could tell Violet how sorry I am!

Maybe she will be one of my guests.

Then I will be able to tell her.

What are some more of my favourite things?

Favourite dancer Darcey Bussell! One Christmas Mum took me backstage to meet Darcey and she is really nice and friendly. She gave me a signed photograph and encouraged me to keep up with my dancing. She said that maybe one day it would be her coming backstage to see me!

I'd *really* want Darcey to be on the programme. If I was going to be anyone other than who I am then I would choose to be Darcey. She is everything that I dream of being.

What else is there?

Favourite season of the year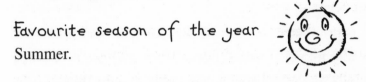
Summer.

Favourite sort of weather Sun! It is very sad and depressing, I think, in the winter, though Sarah doesn't agree. Sarah's favourite weather is snow! But that is because she likes to go skiing.

Favourite Food Just at the moment it is difficult to say as I am not terribly into food owing to my mouth being sore, but as a rule I would say it is… chocolate ice cream!

Favourite drink Pineapple milkshake. For sure!

Favourite place Covent Garden.

Favourite music *Swan Lake*! Because every time I hear it I can imagine that I am on stage, dancing!

Favourite group The Beatles. Me and Sarah are really into the Beatles. It was Mum who got us listening to them. John Lennon was her favourite Beatle. She says she cried when he got shot. My favourite is Paul. He is Sarah's, too. Imagine if he was a guest!

I think Paul is the *best* Beatle. He cares about animals, and I approve of that. I am going to stop eating animals as soon as I can. I wanted to do it when I was eleven but Mum wouldn't let me. She said it wasn't the time. Now she says, "Maybe in a year or two. We'll see."

I think I will ask her if I can do it when I'm twelve. I am going to do all sorts of things when I am twelve! Going to Wonderland is just one of them. Being twelve is my immediate goal. It is Zoë's, as well. But I will be twelve before she is! I will be twelve on 14th September. Zoë has to wait until the end of the year.

Sarah will be twelve before either of us as her birthday is next month. But to her it isn't anything particularly special. She just wants to go out with her Mum and buy a whole load of new clothes, and she could do that any time. Sarah's Mum is always buying her clothes. And she always gives her a good birthday party, too. One time she hired a bouncy castle and another time there was a conjuror. But Sarah says she wants to be more sophisticated now that she's going to be twelve.

I don't know whether I will have a party or not. I didn't last year. Not a proper one. Mum said it would be "too much". And this year I shall be in Wonderland!!! It might be greedy to ask for a party as well.

I have just thought of another favourite thing to add to my list.

Favourite person Uncle Eddy! After Mum and Danny, of course. Uncle Eddy will *definitely* be on my television programme.

4. "Here's Looking at You Kid!"

Here's looking at you, kid!

Uncle Eddy is Mum's brother. She calls him her *baby* brother because she was seven when he was born. That is exactly the same difference as between Danny and me!

Of course Danny is only actually my half-brother. This is because we had different dads. I told him this once, when I was in a really mean mood. I said, "You're only my half-brother! And that's as much as I want you to be!"

I only said it because I was feeling cross and self-pitying. It wasn't anything Danny had done. I told Uncle Eddy afterwards and he said that sometimes when we're feeling hurt we take it out on other people, just because they happen to be there. He said it's a bit like getting in the way if someone's running down the street. They don't necessarily *mean* to knock you over, but that's what happens.

I didn't mean to be horrid to Danny. I wish I hadn't been. He's only a little boy! He doesn't understand.

He clambered on to my bed the other day and put his arms round my neck and whispered, "I want to be your real *whole* brother, Becky." It made me cry, that did.

Danny is a truly sensitive little boy. I think he picks up on a whole lot more than people realise, even though he is only four years old. Uncle Eddy agrees with me.

We talk a lot together, me and Uncle Eddy. The reason I love him so much is that he is like an uncle and a dad and a big brother and a best friend, all rolled into one. He is also, quite simply, the most beautiful person I have ever seen. The most beautiful man, that is. (Darcey is the most beautiful woman. After Mum!)

Zoë agrees with me about Uncle Eddy. She says that her insides go "all tingly" just at the sight of him. Even Sarah admits that he is quite hunky, and Sarah is a very difficult person to impress.

But I would love him just as much if he had cross eyes and a hump back and horrible whiskers growing out of his nose! (Which is what some men have and which really puts me off.)

I wouldn't care what he looked like, he would still be my favourite person. After Mum and Danny.

One way I am lucky is that Uncle Eddy isn't married and therefore has no children of his own. If he had children of his own I wouldn't see him nearly as often, because why would he leave them to come and see boring old me? It wouldn't be fair.

I am glad he isn't married! I expect that is selfish, but I don't care. I don't want him ever to be!

Well, not for a *long* time in case his wife got cross and said, "Oh, you are surely not going off to visit that stupid, dim child again? I want you to spend more time with me!"

Sometimes people's wives are like that. Like Zoë's dad's wife. Zoë's dad got married again after he and Zoë's mum were divorced and now he lives in Yorkshire and Zoë hardly ever see him. Even once when she was really sick and her mum called him and he came down, he could only stay one night because of his wife.

"She can't manage on her own." That's what he said. So he went back off to Yorkshire and I don't know when was the last time that Zoë saw him. I feel really sorry for her. That's why I let her share Uncle Eddy. I wouldn't let just anyone. Mostly I would like to keep him all to myself.

If Uncle Eddy got married and had children I would probably be jealous of them. That is another reason I don't want him to do it. And maybe he won't because me and Sarah have discussed it and we think that perhaps he is gay. Elinor Hodges, at school, says we didn't ought to talk about things like that. Not at our age. But I don't see why we shouldn't, there's nothing wrong with it. Being gay, I mean. Mum has lots of friends who are.

I expect she'd tell me if I asked her, she's always told me everything, like about babies and everything, long before we did it at school, but I'm scared to ask in case she laughs and says "No! What on earth made you think that?" She might tell me that Uncle Eddy has a million beautiful girlfriends, scattered all over the globe, and then my dream would be shattered.

My dream is that when I grow up he will ask me if I would like to go and live with him in a flat overlooking Hyde Park. Of course I know it is not very likely to happen, but that is my secret dream.

What Uncle Eddy does is, he makes me feel brave. I think I am quite wimpish, actually. Not like Zoë. She is brave. I can't imagine Zoë ever being scared of anything.

Or Sarah, although Sarah as far as I know does not have anything to be scared of. She is lucky. Some people just are.

It is when I am on my own sometimes that I get frightened. I have these thoughts, and they scare me. But when Uncle Eddy is here, I feel like – like I could do anything! Like there is absolutely no reason to be frightened. Because while he is here you just know that nothing bad could ever happen. He is that sort of person.

They are my golden days, when Uncle Eddy is here. He comes whenever he can but quite often he is away on location. Being a TV cameraman means that he has to go all over the world, like at the moment he is in Africa.

I wish he was here! But I know that he can't be. When you are away filming you cannot simply drop everything and come running back home. It is not like an ordinary job where you can just say to your secretary, "Tell them that I am out of the office" or "I will deal with it later". If Uncle Eddy is not there, then there is nobody to work the camera and the programme cannot be made.

It is no good wishing that I could have golden days all the time. I am lucky to have any at all. I know this.

I probably shouldn't have thought of Uncle Eddy. It is silly thinking of things that upset you.

I will think of some more favourites.

No, I won't! I will think about when I was little.

5. Bow Bells

You were born in London, within the sound of Bow bells.

I am a true Cockney! Like Gran. The only way you can call yourself a Cockney is if you are born within the sound of the Bow bells.

Mum always tells people that she is one, but she isn't because she wasn't born there. She was born in Manchester, when Gran and Granddad were on tour. And Uncle Eddy was born on the Isle of Wight. I am the only one – apart from Gran – who is a real, true, actual Cockney!

I said this to Mum once and she laughed and told me not to be so pedantic. When I asked her what pedantic meant she said, "Boringly sticking to the absolute truth." Well! I thought that was what you were supposed to do. But Mum insists that "For all intents and purposes I am a Cockney", and that is what she tells people when they come to interview her for magazines, etc.

Uncle Eddy is more Cockney than Mum because he didn't go to drama school and get rid of his accent. He still talks what Mum calls "gorblimey". She is always mimicking him, and pulling his leg, but Uncle Eddy doesn't mind. I wish I could talk Cockney like he does! I probably would have done if Mum had let me, but she always used to keep on about how I had to speak properly.

I don't see that speaking like Mum does, is any more proper than the way Uncle Eddy speaks. Uncle Eddy thinks it's a joke.

"Gotta talk nice," he says; and then he winks at me behind Mum's back.

Uncle Eddy calls me his little Cockney sparrow (only the way he says it, it sounds more like "me liddle Cockney sparrer") and he's taught me all this rhyming slang. Sarah and me sometimes use it when we want to mystify people. Like Sarah might say, "I'll be on the dog, Saturday morning," and I'll know she's going to ring me. Or I might tell her that Mum's meeting me after school to go and buy me some Daisy Roots, and everyone will look at me as if I've gone mad, but Sarah will nod and say, "Doc Marten's?"

Oh, and one time when Mrs Rowe was collecting money for something, Sarah couldn't find her purse and she cried, "Some rotten tea leaf has gone and nicked it! All my bread has gone!"

It was really funny because Mrs Rowe didn't have the faintest idea what she was talking about. She doesn't understand *any* Cockney slang.

Once when we walked into the classroom there was this simply terrific stink coming from outside, and Sarah said, "Cor, wot a pen!" and Mrs Rowe said, "Please don't use expressions like that, Sarah. It's not very becoming." And Sarah said, "But there is a pen! It's horrible!" and Mrs Rowe looked all round and said, "Indeed? Point it out to me. I observe no pens of any description."

She thought Sarah was talking about fountain pens!

This is some of the Cockney slang that Uncle Eddy has taught me:

Pen and ink

Titfer tat

Daisy Roots

Currant bun

Bread and honey

Hampstead Heath

Jam jar

Mince pies

Boat race

North and south

Apples and pears

Mutt and Jeff

Dog and bone

Plates of meat

Rosie Lee

Tea leaf

When I was little and Gran used to talk about
having a nice cup of Rosie, I never knew why she

called it that. Like with titfer. She would say, "Nasty cold wind out there. Not going out without me titfer." So I always knew that Rosie was tea and titfer was hat, but it wasn't until Uncle Eddy explained that it was rhyming slang that I really understood.

There is another one he told me which is a naughty one. When Uncle Eddy needs to go to the toilet he says, "I gotta have a gypsy's." That is short for "gypsy's fiddle" and it means... piddle! I would love to say that to Mrs Rowe!!!

I wish I were bold enough. I don't have any bottle at all. But Sarah does! I think I shall suggest it to her. If I dared her, she would do it.

Bottle is also Cockney slang. It is short for bottle and glass. I don't know what it is supposed to rhyme with but when Uncle Eddy says that someone has no bottle he doesn't mean what I used to think he meant when I was small.

He means that they're not very brave. Like me. I hate myself sometimes for being so bottle-less. Like when I have to have injections and I cry. That is an example of not having any bottle.

Uncle Eddy says that he is scared of injections. He quite often has to have them when he goes abroad. He says, "They frighten the living daylights out of me!" But I think he is only saying it to be kind. I am such a crybaby!

I haven't always been. I remember Gran had to take me to the hospital once because I fell off my bike and cut my hand and had to have stitches, and all the time they were stitching me I just, like, ground my teeth and never made a sound. Gran was ever so proud of me! She said I was brave as ninepence (ninepence is to do with olden-times money) and that I deserved to have a special treat and "something nice for tea" so she bought this beautiful pink cake with pink icing and we ate it in the kitchen with Violet and Bobby.

I'll always remember Gran's cake with pink icing. Cakes with pink icing mean you have bottle. I wouldn't have any cakes with pink icing now. And I don't think Gran would call me brave as ninepence. Gran would be *ashamed* of me.

Gran had a really hard life. I know this because

Mum told me so. But Gran faced up to things. She wouldn't have cried just because people kept sticking needles in her. And I bet Uncle Eddy doesn't, either. He's not really frightened of injections. Uncle Eddy isn't frightened of anything! He just says it to make me feel better. And to try and make me be brave.

But I can't be brave! I've tried and tried and I can't. I hate it! My body is getting to be like a pincushion, all sore and covered in holes. If they keep on like this, my blood will start leaking!

I don't want to think about things like that.

I'm not going to think about things like that! I'm only going to think about things that make me happy.

6. My Gran

*For the first few years of your life you lived in
Samuel Street, in Bethnal Green.*

We lived with my Gran and Uncle Eddy in Gran's house where Mum and Uncle Eddy were brought up. The house was very little and old. It was squashed in the middle of a row of other little, old houses, all the same.

Gran's House

Downstairs there was a front room and a back room and a kitchen. Mum used to complain that it was dark and poky. Some people in the street had knocked down the wall between the front room and the back room to make one large room. Mum wanted Gran to do it in her house, but Gran wouldn't. She said, "Lose all me privacy that way."

She had a piano in the front room which she called "a Joanna". I don't know why she called it that. Maybe Joanna is also Cockney slang. If you called a piano a pianner then it would rhyme, so maybe that is it.

Gran said that the Joanna was mine and I could play on it, but I wasn't ever very good.

Later I went to Mrs Dearborn and did it properly, scales and things, but Mrs Dearborn said that although I was musical I would never make a pianist. But that was all right because I didn't want to be a pianist, I wanted to be a dancer. Ever since I was tiny I have wanted to be a dancer. Being twelve is my *immediate* goal, but being a dancer is my Big Ambition.

Sometimes people expect me to want to be an actress, because of Mum, but I don't think I would like that. For one thing I wouldn't like having to learn lines. Learning steps is different: you learn with your feet. When I have done a step once, I can remember it. With lines you have to go over and over them. Mum is always grumbling about it.

And then for another thing there is *resting*, which

means being out of work sometimes for months or even years. I think with dancing that wouldn't happen so much because if you were in a dance company you would be dancing all the time.

Of course I realise you might not be lucky enough to get into a dance company and then you would have to do something ordinary, like working in a shop or being a waitress, but that is what Mum would call "thinking negatively". Thinking negatively is a bad thing to do. So I am not going to do it. I am only going to think positive things, such as going to Wonderland.

Remembering is a positive thing. Mum couldn't say that was negative. She is always taking out the photograph albums and all her press cuttings. That is what I am doing, except that I am doing it in my mind. I am remembering Gran's house.

Upstairs there were three bedrooms and a teeny tiny

bathroom without any toilet. The toilet was downstairs in the yard. It was spooky going out there at night so when I was little I used to have something that Gran called a jerry, but which most people call a potty.

I asked Gran once why she called it a jerry and she said because that was what *her* gran had called

it, but then she stopped to think and she said it was probably because in the First World War people had referred to the Germans as "Jerries" and the German helmets had looked a bit like potties.

So now that is what I always call them. If I ever have a baby I will not put her on the potty, I will put her on the jerry. I think that potty is a silly and childish word. All it means is a little pot. It is baby talk!

Another word Gran used to use for it was "po", which I thought was rude until Mum explained that it was simply the French word for pot. The French pronounce pot as po! But I still think that po sounds vulgar.

It is strange how many different expressions there are for such a small and insignificant object.

Like all those words for lavatory. There is Ladies & Gents, with the little signs.

There is WC (which stands for water closet).

There is bog (which Uncle Eddy sometimes says).

There is karzy (which he also sometimes says and which I don't know how to spell).

There is loo, though this is really just the French word for water. *L'eau*. Loo is how it got to be said in this country. In Edinburgh, in the olden days, when people used to empty their chamber pots out of their bedroom windows, they used to shout "Gardy loo!" to warn the passers-by.

They really meant "*Gardez l'eau*". Watch out for the water! Mademoiselle LeClerq told us this at school.

Gran's toilet got a bit pongy sometimes, because of the damp and being outside. Also, it used to have spiders in there.

All the rooms in Gran's house were absolutely tiny, even the big back bedroom where Mum and me slept. Uncle Eddy used to sleep at the front and Gran had the littlest one of all. Gran's bedroom was like a cupboard but Gran said that she was old and didn't need much space.

"Not like a growing lad."

That was Uncle Eddy! It is odd to think that when I was born he was only –

I am not very good at sums. Mum is thirty-three. And I am eleven. That means that when I was born Mum was twenty-two. And Uncle Eddy is seven years younger than Mum, so he was...

Fifteen! I can hardly believe it. That is the same age as Sarah's brother.

I loved it at Gran's. Outside in the yard she had a row of giant toadstools that Granddad had made for her. I think they were made from cement. Or stone, or something. They were painted bright red with big white spots and I used to spend hours trying to jump from one to another without falling off.

Kitty used to jump with me.

At night when I went to bed she would come and sleep with me, all curled up on the pillow, right next to my head.

When the trains went past you could see the lights from the carriages flickering on the wall. I asked Mum where the trains were going and she said they were going to Stratford and Bow. I thought it sounded incredibly romantic. I was only very little, then. I didn't realise that Stratford and Bow were just up the road.

There was a sweet shop on the corner of Samuel Street. It was owned by a lady called Mrs Platt who had a big bosom. Once I went in there with Stacy Kitchin who lived next door and we stole things. I stole a bar of chocolate and Stacey stole a packet of crisps. We did it while Mrs Platt was serving someone. She never knew.

I don't think she did. She never said anything about it. But quite soon after that she put up this notice saying, "Only two school children in the shop at any one time", so maybe she did after all.

I feel really bad about it now.

Mrs Platt is someone else it would be nice if I could say sorry to.

I don't know why we stole things. I suppose we thought it would be exciting. It must have been Stacey's idea; she was always the one that had the ideas. I just followed. Mum never liked me playing with Stacey. She said she was a bad influence. She never liked having to live with Gran, either. She loved Gran, but she didn't like having to live with her.

It was because we didn't have enough money to buy a home of our own. Mum didn't work very much in those days. Not on television. Sometimes in the theatre, and sometimes she had to go away on tour and then she used to leave me with Gran. I didn't mind. I loved being with Gran! Mum said she spoilt me, but she didn't. She was quite strict. For example, she wouldn't ever let me use bad language or stay out late.

We used to play in the street, me and Stacey and some other kids that lived on the block. Once when Gran came to call me in I ran off and hid and she got really mad. She stood on the front doorstep and yelled, "Becky Banaras! You come here this instant or I'll tan your hide!"

I think to tan your hide means to wallop someone, but Gran never did that. She just used to slap my legs and tell me I was a "little bleeder".

When I am on *This is Your Life* it will be too late for Gran. But I will think about her! She said to me before she died, "When you have loved someone, they are with you always." And I do believe this to be true because sometimes I can feel Gran with me even now.

I hear her saying things to me, such as, "You just pull your finger out, my girl!" if I'm being lazy, for example. Or if I wake up in the night feeling a bit wimpish and scared she'll whisper, "Don't you worry, my lovey! You hang on in there. It'll all come right in the end." And that makes me feel stronger and gives me some bottle.

It is strange to reflect that if I had had a dad the same as other people, I might never have gone to live with Gran. I loved my Gran so much! I wish she hadn't died. I know that everybody has to, sooner or later, but when it happens it is so sad to know that you can never see the person again. Not until you die yourself, and then you will meet in the afterlife and it will be as if no time at all has passed, as if it was just yesterday.

This at least is what I believe.

7. Reflections

*Your parents got married when they were students,
but you never met your dad.*

I've never even met him. My own dad! He and Mum stopped being in love with each other before I was born. I think that is so sad, when people stop being in love with each other. Gran used to say, "I warned them, but they wouldn't listen."

The problem was that they got married when they were too young. That is what Gran used to say. They were students together at drama school and they were only nineteen. But Mum says she doesn't regret a moment of it. She says that it was wonderful while it lasted. She says that young love is the most passionate and the most romantic kind that there is. I wonder if I shall ever experience it???

Another thing Mum says, and she always smiles sort of sloppily as she says it, is that "Hari was very good-looking."

Hari was my dad. He was Indian. He came from Madras, which I have often looked at on the map.

Just in case one day I might bump into him in the street and not know who he was, though unfortunately I don't think this is very likely as he went back home to India and Mum thinks this is where he probably stayed. She says his mum and dad didn't like it when he came to England to be a drama student. Also they didn't like it when he married Mum. It wasn't because they didn't like English people, just that they would have liked it better if he had married an Indian lady.

I expect by now he probably has. I think she will be very beautiful and have a red spot in the middle of her forehead and wear a sari and that they will have four children.

I wish I could have met him just once! How lovely it would be if he woke up one day and said, "I think I will go and visit my daughter in England." And then he would turn up, all handsome, on the doorstep, and people would wonder, "Who is that gorgeous man?" and will not realise he is my dad!

Maybe when I am on television they will be able to find him and he will fly over specially to appear on the programme!

The name Banaras is a particularly special sort of name as it is another way of spelling Benares, which is the Holy City of the Hindus. Mum suggested once that I might like to change my name to something more English so that people wouldn't call me Bananas all the time. She said, "You could change to Danny's name, if you wanted." But Danny's name is Martin, and Martin is an *ordinary* name.

I like being called after a holy city! And Mum never changed her name. At least, she did for when she has to sign cheques or anything official. Then she's Marianne Martin. But when she's on TV or being interviewed she's Marianne Jacobs, the same as she always was. So I am going to stay as I am!

Violet used to have this dog that was a cross between a German sausage and a Yorkshire terrier.

I am a cross between Indian and English.

I am also a cross between Hindu and Jewish. My dad was Hindu and my mum is Jewish. I think that is interesting. The Hindu religion is very colourful, it has Lord Krishna and lots of gods with names such as Siva and Vishnu. It also has Diwali, which is the Festival of Lights. You can buy nice cards at Diwali and send them to your Hindu friends if you have any.

If I knew where my dad lived, I could send one to him. I would write in it, "Happy Diwali! With love from your daughter in England." And I would put my address in case he decided to come and see me.

The Jewish religion is in the Old Testament. It is full of ancient history and exciting stories, like the one about David and Goliath. It also has festivals. My favourite is Hanukkah because you get presents!

I could be whichever religion I choose. I could be Hindu or I could be Jewish. At the moment I am not either. Maybe I won't ever be. Maybe I'll just be me.

I'm not too sure about religion. God, and everything.

I expect there might be a god of some sort, because otherwise how did we get here? But I don't see how anybody can know. Not for certain. It seems a bit odd to me, going and worshipping someone that might not exist. And even if he did – though it might be a she – how do we know that it wants us to worship it, necessarily? And *why* would it want us to worship it?

I tried talking to Mrs Rowe about this, but she wasn't very helpful. She said, "Surely we are worshipping God in order to give thanks for our existence?"

I said, "But suppose it's a miserable existence like it is for people that are starving or paralysed after motor accidents?"

All she did was lift her shoulders and say, "We must all take our chance in this world."

Another time she told me that "You have some very strange ideas, Rebecca."

I don't see what's strange about my ideas. Neither does Uncle Eddy. When I talked to him about God he said he didn't think that a god that was worth worshipping would actually *want* to be worshipped. So then I asked him if he thought it was all right not to be religious but just to be yourself, and he said he didn't see why not. He said that some people feel the need for religion, and some don't. There are some people, for example, where religion gives meaning to their lives. (But my life already has meaning! I am going to be a dancer.) Then there are other people that religion is a comfort to, when they are ill, for instance, or afraid of dying.

I have done a lot of thinking about this. I have tried very hard to believe in God, because I think it would be nice and that it *would* be a comfort. But I can't. So I think I might as well give up trying.

What I believe is what Gran said. When Gran knew she was going to die she told me that it wasn't anything to be scared of. She said that when you were dead you got to meet up with all the people that had gone before you.

I said, "In heaven?" and she said, "You can call it heaven, if you like. It's only another name for what lies beyond."

Gran said she was looking forward to it. She was sorry she would have to say goodbye to me and Danny, and Mum and Uncle Eddy, but she knew she'd see us all again one day. She said, "In the meantime, darling, we must be patient." She said, "I've lived a long time and I'm tired." She said that life beyond was going to be lovely and peaceful "after all this strife". No more pain or misery. No more wars or cruelty or people starving.

I said that it sounded beautiful, but it made me so sad to think that Gran wouldn't be here any more. That was when she told me that if you've loved someone, they would be with you always. She said, "You might not be able to see me, but I'll be around. Never fear!" And she is, I know that she is.

She told me that she was really disappointed that she wouldn't get to see me grow up and become a famous dancer, but on the other hand she couldn't wait to be with Granddad again. So although I missed her terribly, I knew that she was happy and that it would be selfish to want her back.

Mum agreed. She said, "Your gran was in a lot of pain at the end. It was a blessing for her when she went."

I hadn't been thinking about the pain; I'd just been thinking of her being with Granddad. Gran loved Granddad ever so much. She kept a big photograph of him on her bedside table and she told me that she never went to sleep without saying goodnight to him, even though he'd been dead for years and years.

Granddad died before I was born. And I've never seen my Indian grandparents, so Gran was the only one I ever had. Sarah has *four*.

I've met one of Sarah's grans. She isn't like a gran at all. She wears these really trendy clothes, including short skirts that show all her legs.

And her eyes are all spikey with mascara, and she has these incredibly long nails, like claws, that she paints blood red.

I'm glad my gran wasn't like that!

My gran was a real gran. She was little and old and she had white hair.

I think this is how a gran should be. A gran shouldn't be glamorous, she should be soft and cuddly and comfortable. My gran was all of those things. I know she sometimes smacked my legs when I was naughty, but she always came and tucked me up at night and once when I had a really bad dream and Mum was away she let me go and sleep with her in her big old bed where she had slept with Granddad. I can't imagine Sarah's gran letting her do that.

Gran's bed was so big it took up almost the whole of her bedroom but she wouldn't ever get rid of it because of her memories of Granddad. That is how much she loved him.

My gran was born in Bethnal Green, just two streets away from Samuel Street. She lived there the whole of her life (except when she and Granddad were on tour). She spoke Cockney even better than Uncle Eddy does. Mum used to shake her head and say, "Honestly, Ma! I couldn't take you anywhere." She used to call her a denizen: Denizen Daise, on account of her name being Daisy.

I didn't know what a denizen was so I asked Violet and she said it was "sort of like an inhabitant… someone that lives somewhere."

It didn't make any sense to me. Why should Mum call Gran a person that lived somewhere?

Next time she said it, I asked her. I said, "Why are you calling Gran a person that lives somewhere?" and she said, "I'm not. I'm calling her a denizen," and I said, "Denizen means someone who lives somewhere," and Mum said, "Not when I use it. When I use it, it means low life." And she laughed as she said it.

Gran laughed, too, as if she didn't in the least bit mind being called low life, so that now I think perhaps it must have been some kind of joke between them.

Sometimes when Mum and Eddy talk about Gran, Mum still refers to her as "the poor old denizen", though not at all in a nasty way. I think she really loved her.

I like to hear Mum and Uncle Eddy remembering the old days, when they were young. Uncle Eddy says that Mum was the bane of Gran's life.

"A proper little madam!"

She was always getting into trouble, my mum. Uncle Eddy told me that one time when she'd given

Gran some really bad mouth and Gran had lost her temper, Mum had come galloping out of the kitchen and up the stairs with Gran chasing behind her "yelling blue murder and taking these swipes with a tea towel".

He said that Mum got to the top of the stairs, shouted "Ha ha! Missed me!" and dived into her bedroom before Gran could get her.

That sounds like Mum! She always has an answer for everything. "Smart mouth," Uncle Eddy says.

I wish I were a smart mouth! I would love to be able to think of clever things to say. But I can't, and even if I could I would be too afraid of getting into trouble. I hate it when people are cross. Mum just doesn't seem to care.

I don't think I take after Mum very much at all. I think I probably take after my dad, though of course it is hard to tell when I have never met him.

There can't be many people that have never met their dads. I should think it is quite unusual. You would have thought he would at least have stayed to see what I looked like, but Mum says he didn't want them to have a baby because a) he didn't think they could afford one and b) he was scared it might interfere with his career as an actor.

It is hard not to have feelings of rejection, knowing that your own dad didn't want you. Mostly I try not to think about it but just now and again it comes back to me and I get a little sad. Mum says she ought not to have told me and that she can't imagine why she did. She says, "My wretched tongue runs away with me! I always was a blabbermouth. You ask your Uncle Eddy… he'll tell you!"

But I expect it is only right that I should know about such things. I can understand my dad thinking they could not afford me as I am sure a baby is quite an expensive thing to run, what with nappies and prams and suchlike. It would have been nice, all the same, to have known him.

8. My Brother Danny

*When you were seven years old, your brother
Danny was born.*

I was really jealous of Danny when he was born. I didn't think it was fair that he should have a dad and I didn't, especially as he'd sort of, in a way, Danny's dad I mean, been my dad before Mum went and had Danny.

I'm sorry now that I was jealous. It wasn't Danny's fault. He couldn't help it. And he's never minded me sharing. Even after I was mean to him that time and told him he was only my half-brother, he still talked about "Daddy" as if he belonged to both of us. If he'd wanted to be mean back to me he could have started calling him "*My* daddy". But Danny isn't like that. He is a truly nice little boy. He's ever so quiet and gentle. Not like some of them that run around shouting and fighting all the time.

I wish I'd played with him more! His most favourite game of all is having a teddy bears' picnic with his soft toys. Danny has loads of soft toys. There's Bruin the

Bear and Winnie the Wallaby and a dirty old pink rabbit called Clyde that he used to suck when he was a baby. Then there's Roly Rat and Dolly the Donkey and Horace, the hand-knitted giraffe. And of course there's Teddy, who used to be Mum's and then was Uncle Eddy's and then was mine and now belongs to Danny. Teddy's been mended heaps of times. He's really old and moth-eaten, but if ever you ask Danny which one he likes best he always says "Teddy!"

I should have played with him. He loves it when I join in. I give all the animals different voices, like high and s-q-u-e-a-k-y for Roly Rat and dark and DEEP for Bruin the Bear. And "Ee-aw ee-aw!" for Dolly the Donkey. And "Bloop bloop" for Winnie and "Woffle woffle" for Clyde. Danny gets all giggly and bunches his hands into little fists and stuffs them in his mouth. He's so funny!

Mum took us to a special children's show last Christmas and afterwards she asked us if we'd enjoyed it and which our favourite bits were. Danny said, "I liked the bit where the man fell over." Mum said, "But that was an accident! The poor man caught his foot in something. It wasn't meant to happen!" Danny said, "That was the *funniest* bit. I liked that bit." And he chuckled away ever so happily. Mum shook her head and said, "I don't know!" But he's only four years old. Four is very young.

That's why I wish I'd been nicer to him and made more time for him. I wonder if everyone looks back on their life and has regrets or if it's only me?

When Danny comes on my programme I'll make it up to him! I'll give him an enormous great kiss and tell everyone that's watching that he is my real, *whole* brother. I will, I promise!

Danny's dad is called Alan Martin. He's quite a nice person, really. I wouldn't have minded if he'd stayed married to Mum. Mum brought him to our Open Day once and everyone went "Ooh" and "Aah" because they'd seen him acting with her on television.

He's in America now, making movies. Maybe when I'm on *This is Your Life* they could do a satellite link-up so that he could say "Hi!" They do that, sometimes, when people are living in another country and don't want to make long journeys.

I don't think he'd fly over specially. I shouldn't think he would. Not just for me. He sends me a present at Christmas and on my birthday, the same as he does Danny, but we don't ever see him. He's married to an American lady and they have a baby of their own called Emerald.

I think it must be sad for Danny, knowing his dad has another baby that he loves more than he loves him. If he didn't love her more, he'd come to England and visit us. He does speak sometimes on the phone, but it isn't the same. Sometimes the line is crackly and once we heard Emerald bawling in the background. And Danny is always tongue-tied and never knows what to say.

Maybe Mum will get married again. Actresses often do.

It was ever so posh, when she got married to Alan. "A really glitzy do" is what Uncle Eddy called it. Not like when Mum married my dad, when they didn't have any money and just went up the road to the local registry office.

Mum and Alan also got married in a registry office, because of both of them having been married before and not being allowed to do it in church, but their registry office was a smart one, in Kensington. We all got dressed up in our best clothes. I had a special new dress made, orange and rose-pink, with a bunch of flowers to carry and confetti to throw. And loads of photographers came to take photographs for the papers because now that Mum was in *Ask Auntie* she was famous.

It was very strange at first, Mum being famous. It meant that everyone knew who she was and recognised her in the street so we couldn't go anywhere without people coming up and asking her for her autograph.

Sometimes it was really funny, like when we were

shopping in Safeway and this woman came rushing across the store and peered up at Mum and shouted, "It's her! It is!" and this other woman that had been waiting immediately came flying over and asked Mum if she'd mind her looking in our trolley. She said, "I like to know what the stars are buying."

Mum and I giggled over that. For ages afterwards, whenever any of her friends came round, Mum used to act it out for them. She'd make me be her, pushing the trolley, and she'd be the two women. Everyone always went into shrieks of laughter.

But later on, when Mum and Alan decided they didn't love each other any more, it was horrible. There were all these headlines in the papers.

And then underneath they went on about how Mum and Alan weren't going to live together any more. They seemed to think it was amusing. Just because Mum played the part of an agony aunt on the telly.

I can see now why they call them agony aunts. When people write them letters all about their problems, I expect they probably are in agony. Especially if they are quite well known and everyone recognises them and they are being written about in the newspapers. It isn't very nice having to go into school and knowing that everyone knows all about what is happening in your life.

Elinor Hodges was ever so nasty about it. She said she thought it was disgusting the way people in television kept getting married and divorced all the time. She said she thought they were immoral and that marriage should be for ever.

It made me really upset, Elinor Hodges saying my mum was immoral. Sarah told me not to take any notice of her. She said, "Her mum and dad are religious nuts."

It is true that Elinor's parents are rather peculiar. They won't ever let her act in school plays and she always has to wear a scarf over her head, even though she is not a Muslim, but I think I sort of agree with her, just a little bit, about marriage being for ever.

I know people can't help falling out of love, any more than they can help falling in love. At least, I suppose they can't. It is difficult to be certain when I have never actually been in love myself, though I cannot imagine Darcey, for instance, ever not being my favourite dancer or Sarah not being my best friend.

But just because love cannot last for ever, I don't see that is any reason why people shouldn't go on living together. Lots of people live together that aren't in love. And then there wouldn't be all this horribleness that happens, with stories in the newspapers and people like Elinor Hodges telling you your mum is immoral.

I don't think Mum is immoral. I think that is a horrid thing to say. I think it is just that she is not very good at being married.

Elinor Hodges says lots of things are immoral. Music. Videos. Dancing. Kissing your boyfriend (if you have one). Sarah is right and I shouldn't take any notice of her.

I am not going to think about people like Elinor Hodges. I am trying to remember about the past.

And, of course, plan for the future!

9. My Cat Kitty

When your mum got married again, you left Bethnal Green and moved to a different part of London.

When Mum got married to Alan, we came to live in Kensington. "Out West," Uncle Eddy calls it.

It is nice out West and Alan was a nice dad (just for a short time). The house that we live in is a nice house. The garden is a nice garden. Everything is nice.

The house is very tall and thin, with attics that are real rooms that you can sleep in and a basement where there is a kitchen.

It has a garden with a wall round it, with spoke things stuck in the top so that the cats can't get out into the road and be run over.

There isn't any grass because it is not that sort of garden. Instead there are paving stones and lots of little trees, and plants growing in tubs.

I asked Mum if we could have Gran's toadstools when Gran died but Mum said there wasn't room for them. What she really meant was that she didn't like them. She never liked Gran's toadstools. She said they were as bad as garden gnomes.

I don't know what the matter is with garden gnomes! I think they are fun. I would like to have a pond with fish in it and gnomes sitting all around, smoking their little pipes and sitting in garden chairs underneath the toadstools. When I suggested this to Mum, she shuddered. She said, "Darling, don't be so vulgar!"

What is vulgar about it, I would like to know?

Mum says that Uncle Eddy is vulgar when he talks about needing a gypsy's or going to the bog. But Uncle Eddy just grins and makes a gesture with two of his fingers which is *really* vulgar. I know this for a fact because Sarah once did it to Elinor Hodges and Mrs Rowe saw her and nearly had a fit. I don't think Sarah realised that it is as terribly rude as it is.

It is funny how many things are rude that you don't know are rude until someone tells you off about them. Like once when I was little I saw this word written on a wall and I said it to Mum and she flew into the most furious rage and said that if ever she heard me say it again she would box my ears. She said that that was what came of having to live in Bethnal Green and let me mix with people like Stacey Kitchin.

That was ever so unfair. It wasn't Stacey's fault. She couldn't have said the word because she didn't even know how to read properly. She was still on her first reader when I was into real books. I wonder what has happened to Stacey?

She could be one of my guests!

I think nowadays that we have quite a lot of money. Mum has been in *Ask Auntie* for six years!!! It is shown in loads of other countries, including America, and when it is shown in other countries Mum gets a cheque. A *big* cheque if it's for America. When she gets a big cheque we go out and celebrate.

Last time she had one she took us to tea in a specially posh hotel in Piccadilly and I ate squishy cakes and buns with pink icing. Danny made a mess of everything as usual, dropping crumbs all over the floor. He is really too young to go to posh hotels. He doesn't know how to behave.

Mum said if he didn't learn better manners he wouldn't be able to come again.

It is nice having lots of money as it means we can buy clothes and go on holidays, which we never could before. It also means that I can have my own bedroom and can go to ballet classes with Miss Runcie. I adore Miss Runcie! When I am famous and on *This is Your*

Life I will tell everyone that it is because of her.

And also of course because of Violet.

We are very lucky to have so much money as it is much better than worrying all the time how the bills are to be paid. It is terrible, I think, to see people begging in the street because they have nowhere to live, especially if there is a child or a dog with them. I get upset when there is a child or a dog, thinking of them being cold and hungry. So I am very grateful that Mum is a success and I can go to Oakfield and learn ballet with Miss Runcie. I am definitely not complaining, but I still can't help remembering how it was when we lived with Gran.

I wish that Gran was here! I wish I could see her again, just once. I would far rather have Gran than new clothes and holidays. If I had a choice, that is. I would have my gran every time!

And Kitty.

I would have Kitty, as well. Bella and Bimbo are beautiful, but they are too superior to be cuddled. And they are Mum's cats. Kitty was mine. Well, she was Gran's really, but Gran always said she loved me best. I wanted to take her with us when we moved but Mum said it wouldn't be fair. She said that Kitty had lived with Gran all her life and she was too old to start again somewhere else.

She said, "She's seventeen, darling. It's a great age for a cat. She wouldn't be happy, in a new place."

I thought Mum was just making excuses. I thought she didn't want her because she had lost all her teeth and because she dribbled and sometimes bits of her fur came out. But Mum was right. When Gran died, Kitty missed her terribly. She came to live with us and she slept on my bed, but she pined. She wanted so much to be with Gran!

I hope Gran is right and that when you die you meet all the people who have gone before you. I would like to think of Kitty being with Gran again.

I cried oceans when Kitty died. Even more than when Gran did. I think it was because with Gran I knew that she wanted to go and be with Granddad, and so I knew that she was happy. But with Kitty, I couldn't be sure. Do animals meet up with their people or is it just for human beings? Heaven, I mean. If it's just for human beings, then where do the animals go?

I kept thinking of poor Kitty all on her own, without either me or Gran. I kept thinking how lost and lonely she would be, and I couldn't sleep for crying.

Mum got really worried. She said, "I knew we should have left her at the vet's instead of bringing her back home."

It was me that begged for Kitty to be brought home. I wanted her still to be with us. So Uncle Eddy came round and he took up one of the paving stones in the back garden and dug a hole and we made a proper little grave for her. Mum wrapped her in her favourite pink blanket and I kissed her goodbye and Uncle Eddy wrote "Kitty, a much loved cat. Aged 18 years 7 months" on the paving stone and painted some pawprints.

And then I cried and cried and couldn't stop, and that was when Mum went out and bought Bella and Bimbo, in the hope that they would comfort me.

I suppose they did, in a way. Kittens are very amusing and delightful, so that you cannot ignore them. Bimbo used to climb up the curtains, and Bella

ate Mum's house plants. It was really funny! You would pass her on the stairs carrying bits of plant in her mouth.

One year she climbed into the Christmas tree and tried to sit at the top of it as if she was a Christmas cat.

Mum was cross, because she fell off and ruined all the decorations. She said, "That cat! I'll have its guts for garters!"

But she didn't mean it. Mum loves her cats. I love them, too, but I still think about Kitty.

10. New School!

After you left Bethnal Green, you started at a new school.

It felt quite peculiar when I first went to Oakfield. Where I went in Bethnal Green, with Stacey Kitchin, there were boys. At Oakfield there are only girls. Mum said she thought this was a good thing. She said, "Boys would only distract you."

Uncle Eddy winks and says, "What she means is, boys distracted *her*!"

Mum had heaps of boyfriends when she was young. She was always having battles with Gran because Gran thought some of her boyfriends were unsuitable and because Mum used to defy her by staying out later than she should have done.

I wonder if I will ever have a boyfriend? Uncle Eddy says, "You bet you will! Dozens of 'em!" But sometimes I am not sure.

Sarah has one. Sort of. He is a friend of her brother Barney. He is fourteen and very handsome, or so Sarah says. I have never seen him. She has only met him twice, once at her brother's party and once when she went to their school's sports day with her mum. But at least it is a start.

I have never even met a boy. Not properly. Sarah says if I didn't spend so much time at ballet classes I could get out and about and do other things and that way, perhaps, I would extend my social life, but all I want is to become a dancer!

It is quite posh at Oakfield Manor. Lots of the people there have parents who are seriously rich. Mum and Uncle Eddy sometimes have arguments about it. Uncle Eddy says Mum is a class traitor and should be ashamed of herself. For sending me to a posh school, he means. He says it sort of jokingly, but at the same time I think he is a little bit serious.

Mum always retorts that she doesn't want a daughter of hers going to a dump like she had to go to, and then Uncle Eddy says that she hasn't done so badly for someone who went to a dump, and Mum says, "No, but I've had to fight every inch of the way. I want to give my kids all the advantages that I never had." She says that if Uncle Eddy had kids, he would feel the same.

I don't know whether he would. He is very fierce about that sort of thing. Politics, and that.

On the other hand, when he came to see me and Zoë one time, and afterwards I was telling him about Zoë's mum being really poor and how it didn't seem fair that some people had simply loads of money while others had none, he told me not to worry myself too much about it because it was "just the way of the world".

I said that I didn't worry all the time, only just now and again when I was with someone like Zoë and it made me think about things, and he said, "Don't think too much. Just concentrate on being happy." I said, "But *you* think." And then I asked him whether he really believed that it was wrong for me to go to Oakfield and be privileged, which is what he once told Mum that I was, and he looked sort of… stricken. I think that's the word. And he put both his arms round me and hugged me really hard and said, "Little Becky, you grab all the privileges you can."

So maybe it's all right. Even if it isn't, there is nothing I can do about it. You have to go to the schools that you are told to go to. And I would hate to leave Oakfield now!

This is partly because I am used to it and partly because of Sarah. We have been best friends almost since that first moment in the playground when she called me Becky Bananas. That is a long time! Other people quarrel and stop being friends, but Sarah and I don't like quarrelling. Sarah's mum and dad do it all night long, from the minute her dad gets in to the minute they fall asleep. Sometimes they do it right round till morning. Sarah has heard them. She finds it quite upsetting and that is why she never does it herself. She just laughs if people try to quarrel with her.

I don't quarrel, because of not having any bottle. If I'd got bottle I'd have said something to Elinor Hodges for calling my mum immoral. That is a hateful thing to say about someone's mum. I bet Sarah would have said something. She wouldn't have quarrelled, but she would have said something. I wish that I had!

I like going to Oakfield. I even like wearing the

uniform, which some people think is naff.

It is bright red, and I think that is far more interesting than brown or navy, which is what most schools have. I like the little waistcoats, as well; I think they are cute. I even like the Latin motto on our blazer pockets.

It means, through hard work to the stars. The stars are what I am aiming for! But it is true that you have to work hard to reach them.

Doing ballet is *very* hard work. I can't wait to get back to it! Every day that I'm not taking class is a day lost from my life. Miss Runcie says, "Don't worry, you're still young and flexible. You'll catch up." But soon I will be twelve, and twelve is not young! Not for ballet.

I can't afford to waste any more time. I must go back to class *immediately*.

It is no use thinking about ballet just at the moment. I am thinking about Oakfield now. I am thinking about what a good school it is and how lucky I am to go there. That is what I am thinking about.

We do lots of interesting things at Oakfield. School plays, for instance. And carol concerts, where we raise money for charity. We all get to vote which charity we're going to do it for. Sometimes it's children, sometimes it's animals, sometimes it's for people that are starving. There was a picture in the school magazine last Christmas of Elinor Hodges presenting the cheque. She only got chosen because she had less order marks than anyone else. In fact she didn't have any at all, which is because she never does anything wrong. Sarah says it's sickening, but I suppose she can't help it. It's just the way she is.

Sarah gets order marks for being cheeky and answering back. (A bit like Mum!) I get order marks for being what Sarah calls "daffy". By this she means that I sometimes daydream instead of paying attention so that when I am asked questions I haven't any idea what the teacher has been asking me, and as a result I give these really silly dumb replies. And then I get given order marks!

What I daydream about, mostly, is being on stage with Darcey. She might be dancing Princess Aurora, for example, and I will be dancing the Lilac Fairy.

Or she will be Swanhilda and I will be one of her Friends.

Or maybe we will be in *Sylphides* together.

Those are the sort of things I dream about.

Per ardua ad astra! Nothing that is worth getting is got easily. That is what Uncle Eddy says.

11. I Meet a Famous Author (and Write a Book)

Something quite exciting happened to you at Oakfield.
Yes! We had a Book Week and I met this
famous author.

Last year, it was. We had this Book Week. A person came from a publisher's to tell us all about how books were made and an author came to tell us how she writes her stories, and at the end of the week we all dressed up as Characters from Literature and did a quiz. I got two prizes! One was for dressing up as Pocahontas (I would really like to have dressed up as Posy, from *Ballet Shoes*, but I didn't think anyone would recognise me) and the other was for coming second in the quiz. I was given two book tokens and I spent them on a book about Darcey!!!

When I got the prize for being Pocahontas I

heard Greta Lundquist whisper to Susie Smith, "You know why they gave it to *her*?" and I saw Susie nod. They weren't being nasty, or anything. I mean, they didn't know that I could hear. But I wondered if that was what everyone else was thinking and if I really had only been given the prize because of people feeling sorry for me.

I don't want people to feel sorry for me! It is horrid when you think that they are looking at you and thinking things.

I would like to ask Sarah if she thinks things, but I am too much of a coward. Zoë is the only person I can talk to about it. She is the only one who understands. And Zoë agrees with me. *We do not want people to feel sorry for us.*

Except ourselves, because sometimes you can't help it, though I try hard not to. I think that self-pity is a negative emotion. It doesn't lead to anything positive but just to tears, which makes you feel worse.

The author who came to our Book Week was a lady called Jane Rue. There are some of her books in the library but I had never read any before she came. Then we did one in class and it was quite funny so that I was looking forward to the visit, though some people groaned and said that it would be a dead bore.

Susie said, "An *author*. Yuck!" and screwed up her nose.

Someone else said, "I'd rather do maths!" Other people got fussed in case she wanted us to write things, but Mrs Rowe said all she was going to do was talk to us and tell us about her books, and then we would be expected to ask questions. So Elinor Hodges immediately went away and prepared a huge long list that would have taken about ten days if she'd asked all of them.

Before Jane Rue came, we speculated what she would look like. Sarah said she would be old, because authors were always old. Andrea Francis thought she would be rich and arrive in a Rolls-Royce. I didn't know what to expect, never having seen an author before, but I thought she would probably be very smart with high heels and a handbag and maybe wearing a fur coat, though hopefully not a real one.

I was so amazed when she came walking into the hall behind Mrs Rowe and Mrs Rowe introduced her! I couldn't believe that she was an author! She just looked completely ordinary, like a person that you might meet anywhere. She was older than Mum but not old, like Gran was old. She didn't have grey hair. And she wasn't dressed in the least bit smartly, just in jeans and a sweater, without a fur of any kind. She didn't have a handbag, either – or high heels! All she had was a huge big shoulder bag containing lots of books.

She dumped all the books on a table, and out of the corner of my eye I could see Susie pulling faces. Susie doesn't go for books. She reckons they're dinosaur material. But I quite like reading, and so I was interested. Had this author really written so many?

She had! She had written *dozens*. I couldn't imagine where she would get all her ideas from, but she said that that was what she was going to tell us.

She said that she started writing when she was little because she was very shy and couldn't make any friends. So that was why she started writing. She made up her own friends and put them into books.

She said that the very first book she ever had published was a book about a girl who becomes a dancer. That made me sit up! She said that she always desperately wanted to be a dancer herself but that her mum and dad couldn't afford for her to have lessons and so she became very unhappy and frustrated. So then one day when she was about fifteen she thought she would write a book about a girl who wanted to learn ballet, and so she wrote this book called

Castanets & Ballet Shoes, in which the girl becomes hugely successful, and guess what? She ends up dancing Odette!

I was *really* interested in that. Everyone turned round to look at me and I could feel myself growing bright scarlet. Mrs Rowe said, "We have our own little ballerina here," which truly embarrassed me. I could have fallen through the floor! Fancy calling me a ballerina! When I'm not yet even a member of the corps de ballet! But people that aren't dancers don't understand.

The more this author talked to us, the more I realised that she wasn't as ordinary as she looked. She was a very amusing and witty person. She told us, for example, how she and her husband had all these animals that they had rescued. Pigs and goats and chickens. And two Shetland ponies and some sheep. Not to mention fifteen cats and six dogs!!!

She showed us pictures of the cats and dogs and told us how they spoke, using different voices. Susie, thinking she was being very clever, put up her hand and said, "Excuse me, but animals can't talk," and the author said, "Excuse me, but mine can!"

She told us how, if you listened very carefully and took the trouble to get to know them and to really understand them, then you would hear them talking. It is true! Bella and Bimbo talk all the time. They are very superior and have upper-class voices like the Queen.

Caviare! bring me some Caviare!

I don't think Kitty would have had an upper-class voice. I think she would speak what Mum calls "common". But I still love her best!

Another thing the author told us was that all the dogs slept in the bedroom with her and her husband, and that four of them actually slept in the bed so that they had to have this really huge great bed taking up most of the room. I could hardly believe what I was hearing. Four dogs sleeping in bed with you!

We were all giggling like crazy because some of the stuff this author was telling us was really funny, like about this one dog, Benny, that is a deaf dog and looks like a walking hearth rug and sleeps in the middle of the bed with his head on the pillow. She said he has this habit of suddenly standing up underneath the duvet so that all the cold air comes billowing in. And then he starts shaking his head so that his ears go flap

flap flap and the cold air whirls all about. And then when he has done that he starts turning in circles and trampling up and down as he makes a nest for himself. And the duvet goes in circles with him so that in the end he is all wrapped up in it like a big walnut whip and she and her husband are left without any.

Everyone laughed at this except for Elinor Hodges. Even Susie laughed. You could tell that Elinor was being all disapproving and thinking that it was not hygienic to let dogs sleep in the bed and that dogs should be kept outside in kennels. Which is what I personally do not agree with, and neither would the author have done because she was a real animal person.

She told us that some people thought she was mad, but that she didn't care. She said, "Some of you probably think I'm mad," and she looked at Susie as she said it. And Susie turned pink and couldn't think what to say, which is the first time I have ever known her to be at a loss for words!

At the end we were told we could ask questions, so Elinor Hodges at once stood up with her great long list and started asking these really dreary, boring sort of questions such as "How long does it take you to write a book?" and "Do you have a word processor?"

The author said she didn't use a word processor, she always wrote her first draft by hand and then typed it out on an ordinary typewriter. She said, "I'm afraid I'm a bit of a technological dinosaur."

Susie turned round at this and made an "I-told-you-so" face at me and Sarah. But then the next minute she was waving her hand in the air to ask a question and the question was, "How much do you earn?"

Mrs Rowe was absolutely furious! She told Susie off for being impertinent and vulgar, though the author didn't seem to mind. She explained to us that she didn't earn a fortune and that hardly any authors did. She said, "You don't write books for the money, you write them because you feel you have to," and Susie raised her eyebrows right up into her hair as if the author was a bit simple, or something. Susie is really into making money. She understands all about stocks and shares and compound interest, which to me is just boring.

When I got home I told Mum all about the visit and about the author having all these animals and four dogs sleeping in the bed, and Mum said that she was obviously mad.

I told Mum that lots of people thought she was mad but that the author didn't care, and I said that I personally thought it would be lovely to have four dogs sleeping in bed with you. You could cuddle them and never get cold, and if you woke up and felt a bit lonely or frightened there would always be someone to lick you or snuggle up to.

Mum cried, "Oh, darling!" and held out her arms. She said that if I ever woke up and felt lonely I could go into her room and sleep in bed with her. She said, "You can snuggle up to me any time you like. You know that."

I do know it, but it seems childish at my age to sleep with your mum.

After the author had been to visit us I wrote to her telling her how totally brilliant her talk had been and how interested I was in her having wanted to be a dancer because I hoped to be a dancer myself one day. She wrote this long letter back, which I still have. I will never get rid of it! It is a precious object. Right at the end she wished me luck and said that she would watch out for my name on the posters.

So that is two famous people who are going to watch out for me! Jane Rue and Darcey.

When I am on *This is Your Life* I very much hope

that Ms Rue will be a guest because then I can tell her how her visit inspired me.

One of the other things she said in her letter was that I used words very well and that maybe one day I would write a story myself. "A ballet story, perhaps." She said, "It was a great comfort to me when I wrote *Castanets & Ballet Shoes*. It didn't stop me yearning to be a dancer, but it took away some of my frustration." She said that writing is a very good way of exploring your emotions and can be a great solace.

I thought about what she said and last term I wrote this book about a girl called Bryony who wants to be a dancer only she gets ill with AML and has to go into hospital and have drugs and everyone thinks she is going to die, but she doesn't. Instead she goes into remission and starts at the Royal Ballet School when she is twelve years old and when she is seventeen she is taken into the Company and dances in *Swan Lake*. She dances Odette and everyone applauds and she is given a big bouquet of flowers and that is how it ends.

The book is thirty-five pages long. I typed it out on the word processor with wide margins and double-spacing, like Jane Rue said you had to. She said that publishers cannot read handwriting, they can only read typing. I don't know why this is. Perhaps their eyesight is poor because of all the books they have to look at.

I had to use the word processor when Mum was out as the book is *A Secret*! There is only one person I have shown it to, and that is Uncle Eddy. He thinks it is good enough to be published, maybe, but I am not sure about this. For one thing I don't think the spelling is quite right, though Uncle Eddy says that doesn't matter. He says the publishers would see to it. He says the only thing that I would have to do is to explain about AML, as not everyone will know what it is.

I would have to explain that it is *acute myeloid leukaemia* and that acute means it is not something that goes on for years and years just the same but is something that happens quite quickly, like for instance a pimple that comes to a head and bursts, and that myeloid is to do with bone marrow, and that leukaemia is a sort of cancer that attacks the blood.

When you go into remission it means that the drugs have worked and you don't have it any more, but sometimes the remission doesn't last and then you have to go and have more drugs.

People that know about it, like doctors, or people that have got it, quite often just call it AML. There are lots of other sorts, but AML is what Bryony has got. It is not as common as the other sorts except in older people, so that Bryony is a bit unusual. Most children that have leukaemia have the other sorts.

I called my heroine Bryony because I think it is a nice-sounding name and good for a ballet dancer. It is a kind of flower, as a matter of fact, which grows in hedges.

Mum showed it to me once when we were out for a walk and I thought that it was pretty. I didn't know then that I would be writing a book about it!

Born to Dance by Becky Banaras

Born to Dance

This is the story of Bryony in the book that I wrote.

One day when Bryony wakes up she has a pain in her leg. She tells her mum and her mum says she has probably strained it. "Doing all those ballet exercises." Bryony thinks that maybe it was when she was doing *grands battements*.

But she thinks she will be able to work her way through it, because quite often that is what dancers do when they have aches and pains. So that afternoon when she goes to class she tries to pretend that everything is the same as usual and to forget about her leg and how it is hurting.

But next day it is worse and when she goes for class her teacher notices and says to her that she must rest for a while and not come to class until it is better. She says that she has probably pulled a muscle and it is best to rest it.

Bryony really hates to miss class but her leg is so bad she can hardly bear to walk on it. Also she is feeling quite tired and people start to say how pale she is.

At first her mum doesn't worry because she has always been pale. Once at school some unkind girls made a nickname for her and the nickname was "Pasty". But then one morning Bryony wakes up and she has a pain in her other leg as well, and now her mum starts to get a bit anxious and tells the au pair to take her to the doctor. Bryony's mum cannot go to the doctor with her as she has to be at work. She is a big television star and they are doing some important filming, but the au pair, who is called Rosa-Maria, is quite nice. Bryony doesn't mind going to the doctor with her.

The doctor is also quite nice. He has been to see Bryony before, when she has had mumps and chickenpox. He says to

Rosa-Maria that she must take Bryony immediately to the hospital to have a blood test so that they can find out what is wrong.

The blood test means having a needle stuck in her arm and a tube of blood sucked out, which is not very pleasant, but Bryony is eleven and so she is brave about it.

When her mum comes home that day she cannot understand why Bryony has had to go to the hospital to have the blood sucked out. She says, "Why does she need to have blood sucked out for a pulled muscle?" Rosa-Maria says that the doctor thinks maybe Bryony might be anaemic. (Which is something else Uncle Eddy said I would have to explain.)

Anaemic means not having enough red blood cells which carry the oxygen round your body and give you energy. If people don't have enough red cells, then they get tired.

At six o'clock that night the doctor rings up and speaks to Bryony's mum. He says he has had the result of the blood test and would like to come round to discuss it.

Bryony's mum turns pale. She says, "I hope it isn't anything serious?" But the doctor won't tell her until he comes.

When the doctor arrives, Bryony is told to go and watch television with Rosa-Maria and her little brother Joseph. She doesn't hear what the doctor says, but afterwards, when he has gone, she sees that her mum has been crying. Her mum tells her that she is anaemic and that is why she has felt tired. She says that she has to go back to the hospital so that the doctors can find out what is causing it.

When they go to the hospital a second time it is a different hospital, it is a hospital that deals only with children, and Bryony's mum goes with her. Bryony is glad that it is her mum and not Rosa-Maria. She likes Rosa-Maria but it is not the same as being with her mum.

At the hospital they are taken to a room with four beds in it. Two of the beds are empty but in one bed there is a girl of about Bryony's age. She is sitting up against the pillows and listening to music through headphones. She is very pretty with blonde hair and a red nightdress with white dots. She smiles at Bryony but Bryony is too frightened to smile back. What has frightened her is that this girl has plastic tubes coming out of her nightdress. The tubes are stuck to the side of the bed and are attached to plastic bags that hang off a metal stand.

You can see inside the plastic bags. One of them has something that looks like blood in it. Bryony feels sick and scared. Is this what is going to happen to her?

The girl takes off her headphones and says, "Hi! I'm Chloë. Are you a new patient?"

Bryony is too scared to say anything at all so her mum has to say it for her. Bryony is a bit of a coward. She hasn't any bottle. She is even scared of being X-rayed! This is silly, because X-rays don't hurt. But then she has to have an injection so that the doctor can take a sample of her bone marrow. He has to punch a needle into her hip, and that is nasty. That is *really* nasty. Her mum tells her to be brave and Bryony tries hard but she is scared and trembling all the time even though her mum is with her.

After that she is taken back to the room with the four beds and she has to get into one of the beds and have blood dripped into her from a plastic bag hanging from a metal stand, just like the girl called Chloë, except that Bryony only has one plastic bag. While Bryony's mum is outside talking to the doctor, Chloë tells Bryony that she'll probably have lots once they start treatment.

Bryony is horrified to discover that she is going to have to stay in the hospital. She had thought she was going home! She says to her mum, "But what about my dancing classes?" and her mum has to explain to her that she can't have dancing classes for the moment. She says, "You have to wait until you're better."

Bryony asks how long that will be and her mum looks grave and says, "It could be a month or two."

That is the *worst* news.

It is only later that her mum tells her what is wrong with her. She tells her that she has AML and that the doctors are going to give her drugs that will cure it.

After Bryony's mum has gone and Bryony and Chloë are alone, Chloë tells Bryony that she has leukaemia as well, only hers is a different sort. Hers is called ALL. ALL stands for *acute lymphoblastic leukaemia*. She says that to begin with she couldn't ever remember the word *lymphoblastic* but that now she can. But she doesn't know what it means! Not properly. The doctor has told her, but she can't make sense of it. It is too complicated.

Chloë says that ALL is what most children have. Not so many have what Bryony has got. Bryony doesn't know whether this is a good thing or a bad thing, but Chloë tells her not to worry. She says, "They can almost always cure it nowadays. They just give you chemo and then you go into remission."

Bryony is so ignorant she doesn't know what chemo is or what remission means! Chloë tells her that chemo is chemotherapy and means drugs. She says, "They make you feel sick but it's worth it if it puts you into remission." She says that remission is when the leukaemia goes away and you don't feel tired any more or get bruises.

Bryony says that she never got bruises, she just got pains in her legs. Chloë says that what she got was headaches and a high temperature. But she says that it's different for everyone. Chloë has been in the hospital for a few days and already seems to know everything.

It helps Bryony, having Chloë there to talk to. They become best friends. Best *hospital* friends. When one of them is sad the other cheers her up, or if one of them is frightened the other makes her brave. Chloë has lots more bottle than Bryony but even Chloë gets frightened sometimes.

After a few weeks Bryony is allowed to go home because she is in remission, which means there are no more cancer cells in her blood. Everyone is happy and Bryony's mum takes her to have a special tea at a smart hotel to celebrate. The hotel is in the West End. It is full of palm trees and beautiful blue carpet and Bryony eats cream cakes, as many as she likes.

She is not worried about being too fat for ballet because she has lost lots of weight and the doctor says she must try to put it on again.

She is told that she can go back to her ballet classes but not as many as before.

Only one a week to begin with. But one a week is not enough! Her mum says, "Give it a while and we'll see."

She still has to have chemo and all her hair is falling out. This is because of the drugs. Chloë's hair has fallen out, too. It happens to most people, but Bryony knows that it will grow again. The doctor has told her so.

One day when Bryony goes to the hospital for her blood test they tell her that she is no longer in remission. The leukaemia has come back and she must go into hospital again. She is very ill and her mum cries and so does Rosa-Maria because they think she is going to die. Everyone thinks she is going to die. Even the doctors and nurses. They think they are hiding it from her but she knows what they are thinking. When her Uncle Ted comes to visit her, she tells him that this is what they think and he says to her, "What do you think?"

Bryony says, "I'm not going to die! I'm going to get better and become a famous dancer!"

And Uncle Ted says, "If that's what you believe, then that's what will happen."

And it does, and everyone is amazed because they didn't think it was possible.

She dances Odette and is famous and that is the end.

THE END
A book by Rebecca Banaras

Uncle Eddy says the best bit is where Bryony says she's not going to die and she doesn't. He says that most of the book is sad and makes you weep, but that the ending is "brave and beautiful". He says that it ought to be published because it would give hope to other children that have got leukaemia.

He means children like me.

13. The Bad Times

*When you were ten years old, something happened
and you had to go into hospital.*

The same as Bryony. I have got what Bryony's got. I suppose, really, that's what made me write the book.

Uncle Eddy is the only person who has read it. I can't show it to Mum because she would start crying. Mum cries very easily. And Sarah wouldn't like it because she doesn't like anything to do with illness. She likes to pretend it isn't happening.

I can't even show it to Zoë. Zoë is the same as Chloë in my book. Chloë is her.

Zoë was the one who told me right at the beginning that you have to stay in remission for five years before you are properly cured. If you come out of remission before that time, then you probably won't ever be cured.

The sooner you come out of remission, the worse the prognosis is. That is what Zoë told me.

Prognosis is just a word which means outlook. Like, the outlook is good. Or the outlook is bleak.

If you come out of remission in the first year, then the outlook is very bleak.

That is what Zoë told me. Right at the beginning, when I didn't even know what chemo was.

I don't know how she found out about all these things. Asked the doctors, I expect. Zoë always wants to find out about everything. She's ever so much braver than me.

She'll come on my programme for sure!

Zoë is like a lion! The only thing that really upsets her is not seeing her dad.

The first time Uncle Eddy came to visit me, Zoë went and buried herself under the bedclothes and wouldn't come out. When he'd gone I heard her crying. I'd never heard her cry before. Not even when they stuck a tube in her chest so that the drugs could be dripped straight in without having to be injected. She really didn't want them to do that but she still didn't cry. But she cried that day when Uncle Eddy came.

When I asked her what the matter was she said, "It's all right for you, you've got a dad!" She thought Uncle Eddy was my dad! I didn't know then that Zoë's dad never came to see her. Her mum came as often as she could but even her mum couldn't come every day because she lives out in Essex and she couldn't always afford it. So that was when I decided to share Uncle Eddy with her. I think it cheered her up a bit to know that I hadn't got a dad, either.

We were in hospital for ages together, me and Zoë. They couldn't get us into remission. With some people it happens almost at once, but with me and Zoë it took weeks. And then Zoë went and got sick with this infection, which was the only time her dad ever came to visit her.

It was horrid when she had the infection because they separated us and I wasn't allowed to see her in case I caught whatever it was. I missed her so much! We always told each other everything, Zoë and me. We used to compare notes about what the doctor had said and what the results of our blood tests were and how we were both doing. And now I was on my own!

They put another girl in Zoë's bed. She was only little, only about seven years old; she didn't know what was happening. She kept screaming whenever the nurses came to take blood samples.

I felt sorry for her, but she was too young to talk to the way I could talk to Zoë. I was terrified in case Zoë didn't come back. Or in case she died and they didn't tell me.

I knew that people died. There was this little boy called Kris that was only a baby. He was only about Danny's age. He died. A girl that was there, a big girl called Amanda, she tried to tell us that he had gone home. I believed her. It was Zoë found out what had really happened. She found out that he had died. Zoë always finds things out. She's like a magpie. Inquisitive. But she says it's better to know than not.

I suppose she is right.

My favourite nurse is Carol. I'd want her to be on the programme!

She used to be on nights, but now she's on days so I see more of her.

When Zoë had her infection, Carol knew that I was frightened. She told me not to worry, that Zoë was going to be all right. And she promised to make sure she was put back in the same bed.

I wanted to believe her! But Zoë had already warned me about them not always telling the truth. She said that when she first came, there had been someone else in my bed. There had been a girl called Trudi. One day she had disappeared and not come back and Ellen, who is another nurse, told Zoë that she had gone into remission. It was only later Zoë discovered she had died. So I still went on worrying, until one afternoon I woke up and there was Zoë, grinning at me from the next bed. She said, "I'm back!" and Carol said, "I told you so," and I felt mean for not trusting her.

Zoë said, "Why feel mean?" She said, "They lie all the time. I can't stand being lied to!"

I don't think they lie, exactly. I think they just want to protect us. They don't want to tell us bad things unless they absolutely have to. They think we will find it upsetting, knowing that people the same age as us are dying. But as Zoë says, we're not babies. When you're eleven, you know what's going on.

I think personally it would be a comfort if you knew you could always rely on them, the doctors and the nurses. And parents, as well. If you knew that they would tell you the truth. That way it would mean you wouldn't get to worry quite so much.

This is why Zoë and me made a pact that we would always tell each other what was happening and not smile brightly and say everything was all right if it wasn't. Like if we'd just had a bad result from a blood test, we would tell each other. Which we always did.

When we had been having chemo for a few weeks, our hair started falling out. Zoë's started first, because she'd been having chemo longer than me. She said, "It doesn't happen to everybody. Maybe you'll be lucky." But then I woke up one morning and found bits of hair all scattered about the pillow and I knew that it was happening.

I kept trying to pretend to myself that it wasn't but every time I brushed my hair the brush would be all full of it, and I kept looking at Zoë and seeing these bald patches and I just couldn't bear it, the thought that I was going to end up looking like that.

Zoë did her best to make me brave. She said things like, "It's only temporary," and "It's only hair," and "What does it matter so long as we're going to get better?" She said that lots of children with leukaemia get completely cured. "But they have to lose their hair first."

I wailed, "But I grew mine long, specially! Specially for ballet! It took me ages!"

Zoë said, "It'll all come back again. Mine did."

At first I didn't realise what she was saying, but then I said, "What do you mean, yours did?" And then she told me, she'd had chemo before. She'd had it when she was seven years old. She said, "I've been in remission all this time. Almost five years! If you're in remission for five years, they reckon you're cured."

Another few months, and Zoë would have been cured. But she said she wasn't worried. She said, "The longer you stay in remission, the better your chances are." She said if she'd only been in remission for a month or so, then she would know that she was probably going to die. But as it was, she was going to go back into remission and this time she was going to stay in remission and when she grew up she was going to be a nurse and come and look after other children that had leukaemia.

"Because then I'll be able to tell them that I've been through it."

We talked a lot about what we are going to do when

we're grown up. Zoë said that when I was a famous dancer I would have to come and visit her in her hospital ward and talk to all the children with leukaemia and tell them that I'd been through it, as well. I promised that I would. We agreed that it would be nice if some well-known person that had had leukaemia and their hair had fallen out would come back and talk to us. It would cheer you up.

There must be *some* well-known people that have had it.

Mum told me that there is a famous singer called something I can't remember, something Spanish, and that he has had it, but it is not the same because he had it when he was grown up, not when he was a child. And I don't know whether his hair fell out or not. Maybe it doesn't if you are grown up. Or maybe it had fallen out anyway, like Mr Tucker's at school, simply because he is old. It wouldn't be so bad if you were old. It is horrid when you are still young.

It's not only hair falling out, it's other things, too. Like your mouth getting sore and your gums bleeding so you can't clean your teeth properly. And people sticking needles into you all the time to take samples or give you drugs. Some of the drugs are foul, they make you feel really ill, and some of them make your skin burn. Zoë said she didn't have to have these ones when she was only seven but they were giving them to her now because of her having relapsed, which is what it is called when you come out of remission.

These are the ones that made me cry. I told Uncle Eddy I didn't want them any more and he held me and let me weep over him and said that I was his brave girl. But I'm not! I'm not in the least bit brave! I haven't any bottle at all. I hate it!

Even Zoë hated it when her skin got burnt. It's really painful. But Zoë never cries. She just gets cross and swears. I wish I was more like Zoë.

Something that happened to me and not to her was nosebleeds. I've had dozens of them. I've had so many I've sometimes thought they're never going to stop. Once I bled all over a picture of Darcey, in a book that Mum gave me for Christmas. That made me cry again, when that happened. It seemed so terrible, to nosebleed over Darcey. Zoë tried to rub her clean for me but there were still all these horrible browny smears.

When mum came to visit me she couldn't understand why I was so weepy, and when I showed her the picture she said, "Oh, darling! Don't worry about that. I'll buy you another copy." But I still felt awful. I hate my body doing all these horrible, disgusting things and me not having any control over it.

I've tried explaining this to Mum but all she says is, "That's the problem with being a dancer. You expect too much of yourself. You ask the impossible."

She says there are times when you can't expect to have control. She said, "Like, for instance, when I was pregnant with you... there you were, growing away inside me, and me getting fatter and fatter, and not a thing I could do about it except just wait for you to get big enough to come popping out."

That is true, but Mum *wanted* to have me. I didn't want to have AML. I didn't want to get sick and bald and bleed all over Darcey! Mum had a baby to look forward to, but what have I got?

Mum says that I've got the future. She says, "That's what you must hold on to. You're putting up with all this now, so that in the future you can be well and strong. Whenever you feel low, you just keep reminding yourself."

I do try, but sometimes it's not easy. Sometimes it seems as if I'm just saying it to myself and it doesn't really mean anything. Sometimes I think I'll never be well and strong.

It was better when Zoë was here. I felt braver when I had her to talk to.

Zoë got out of hospital before me. She went back into remission and they let her go home. She promised she'd come and visit me, and she did for a little while, because she still had to come back to the hospital once a week for tests, but then I went into remission as well and we didn't see each other very much after that. Only just now and again when we had an appointment on the same day, except once when Uncle Eddy had to drive down to Essex and he took me with him and left me at Zoë's and we spent the day together.

We went up to her bedroom and looked at ourselves in the mirror and giggled because Zoë said, "We're like a pair of boiled eggs!"

Usually I didn't look like an egg because I wore my wig that Mum bought for me. It's a special one made out of real hair the same colour as mine, so that nobody at school ever knew that really I was bald. But Zoë's mum couldn't afford a wig, so when I went to her place I didn't wear mine. I took it off and left it in the car so as not to upset her.

Lots of children, when their hair has fallen out, they wear scarves, but Zoë is too proud. She just went walking round bald and didn't care who saw her. "It's trendy," she said. "It's the new fashion." I think that is *really* brave.

I am too vain, I suppose.

14. Jokes!

At last, you went into remission.

We had celebrations when I came out of hospital. Uncle Eddy came and we all went for a meal, me and Mum and Uncle Eddy. We left Danny at home with Ana-Maria, who's our au pair, because he is too young. He is just a silly nuisance in a restaurant.

Mum bought pink champagne, and we all got to drink it. Even I was allowed a glass!

Mum and Uncle Eddy toasted to me. They clinked glasses and said, "To Becky!" Then Uncle Eddy winked and said, "Here's looking at you, kid!"

As a matter of fact, everyone in the restaurant was looking at Mum. They always do. She can't go anywhere without being looked at. But that evening she didn't mind. She was really happy! She hugged me and said, "Darling, I know the drugs are perfectly horrid, but you see, it has been worth it, hasn't it? Now you can concentrate on getting strong again!"

All I wanted to do was start back on my ballet

classes. Dr Stanhope, who is my doctor that looks after me at the hospital, said that I could do one class a week but that I was to stop if I got tired. Mum was scared it would be too much for me, but Dr Stanhope talked to me about it and I told him how I was going to be a dancer when I grew up and how important it was to me to have classes, and he spoke to Mum and then it was all right.

I really like Dr Stanhope! He is another person I will have on my programme.

He is a person who understands. He told Mum that if ballet meant so much to me, then I must be allowed to do it.

Uncle Eddy agreed with him. I heard him talking to Mum when they didn't know I was there. He said, "I know it's difficult for you, kid." He calls Mum kid just like he calls me, even though she's older than he is. He said, "I know the temptation to wrap her in cotton wool, but she's got to be allowed to live her life."

Uncle Eddy understands as well! I don't think Mum always does, or maybe it's just that she worries more. Every week when I had to come back to the hospital for tests she would ring up from the studios to check if everything was all right. She said she couldn't concentrate properly until she knew.

Ana-Maria used to bring me to the hospital. I would have rather it was Mum, but on the other hand at least Ana-Maria never got nervous, like Mum did when she came. When Mum came she gave me the jitters. I didn't have the jitters as a rule because I was used to it. Also, I knew everybody. People used to say hello to me. The nurses and the doctors and the men with the trolleys.

And sometimes Zoë would be here and then we would have fun, giggling together.

me↓Zoe

I always giggle with Zoë. When I am a dancer and she is a nurse and I go back to visit her to talk to her patients, we will probably still giggle. She is the sort of person you can't help giggling with.

I haven't got anyone to giggle with now. Now that I'm back in the hospital. I just lie here and think. What I think about mostly is dancing *Swan Lake*. I dance it in my head and imagine that I am on stage. So long as I can imagine that, I am all right.

It is just sometimes, when it stops being real and I know that I am only dreaming it, that I get frightened. Time is rushing past and I am missing all my classes. I should be having at least three a week! I haven't had any for at least two months. How am I going to be a dancer if I can't have classes? And my hair was growing back and now it's all starting to fall out again and I hate these horrible drugs that make me feel sick, I feel sick, sick, sick all of the time and my mouth hurts and I'm having nosebleeds again and sometimes I think that I am going to die.

Sometimes I think that I wouldn't mind dying if it meant no more of the horrible drugs.

But I am not going to! I am going to live to be a hundred!

I am going to be like Bryony and dance in *Swan Lake*. And then they will say *Leukaemia girl beats illness to become ballerina*. That is the sort of thing that they say. And there will be interviews on radio and television and in the magazines. People will come to the theatre, to my dressing room, to talk to me and write articles, like they do with Mum. But unlike Mum I will not be recognised all over the place in supermarkets or when I am walking down the street as not so many people recognise ballet dancers. Lots of girls at school didn't even recognise Darcey until I told them who she was!

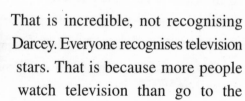

That is incredible, not recognising Darcey. Everyone recognises television stars. That is because more people watch television than go to the ballet. But that is all right. I don't specially want to be recognised. I just want to dance!

I have got to get better *quickly* or it will be too late.

I am trying to think of some jokes.

What did one magnet say to the other magnet?

"I find you attractive."

Ha ha. That is not very funny.

Where did the Vikings drink?

At a Norse trough.

Neither is that. They are the sort of jokes you find in Christmas crackers.

I have just remembered one that someone told me yesterday.

This is the joke. There's this boy who's just started at a new school. The teacher asks him if he can read and write. He says, "I can write, but I can't read." So the teacher says, "All right. Here's a piece of paper. Show me how you write your name." So the boy writes something on the paper and the teacher picks it up and looks at it and it is just scribble. "What's this?" she says. And the boy says, "How should I know? I told you, I can't read."

Ho ho! That is a really stupid one.

I'm not very good with jokes as I can never remember the end of them. Well, hardly ever. I only remembered this one because it's so stupid. Zoë used to tell me lots, only hers were really funny.

I wish she was here now and then I could ask her to tell them to me again. This time I might be able to remember the endings and then I could tell them to someone else.

There is a girl in the bed opposite who would probably like to hear some jokes. This is the first time she has been in hospital and she keeps crying for her mum. Her auntie is with her but her mum is in hospital as well. I think that is so sad. I would like to be able to cheer her up.

Maybe when Uncle Eddy comes I will ask him to go over and tell her some jokes. He is good at making people laugh. But I don't know when he is going to be able to come. He is in Africa.

He sent me a card with lions on it.

On the back he wrote, "Here's looking at you, kid!" He is always saying that, I don't know why. But I like it when he says it.

I hope he comes back soon! I want him to be here! I only feel safe when Uncle Eddy is here.

He's going to be in Africa for another whole fortnight. But I know that he is thinking of me. He told me before he went. He said, "Sweetheart, when I'm away from you never a day goes by but you're in my thoughts."

I am going to concentrate on being in Uncle Eddy's thoughts. That way it will keep me safe.

Here is another joke I have thought of.

What did the dentist say in court?

I swear to tell the tooth, the whole tooth, and nothing but the tooth.

I suppose that is quite funny.

Sort of.

I can't think of any more.

It is no use asking Mum. She is like me, she can never remember the ending.

The ending of a joke is called "the punch line". It is a catastrophe if you cannot remember your punch line.

You would think that Mum would be able to, being an actress. But she has always had trouble with her lines. I have always had to help her.

I don't know who would help her if I was not here. She would have to manage on her own.

Danny is too young. He wouldn't be any good.

So nothing must happen to me or Mum won't ever be able to learn her lines!

Sarah told me a joke once. Something about seaweed.

Why is the sea wet? – Because the seaweed.

I think that was how it went. I can't really remember.

It was something like that.

Perhaps I am not a very jokey kind of person. Just a weedy wimpy sort of person who isn't very brave.

15. Wonderland

You'd only been out of hospital for a few months when you were told that you had to go back in again.

Mum cried when Dr Stanhope said I had come out of remission. She tried not to show it, but I knew she'd been crying because her eyes were all red and swimmy. So I knew that he had told her something bad.

Mum said that I was a little bit anaemic, "Just a little bit", and that Dr Stanhope wanted me to go back into hospital for some more treatment. I said, "Why do I have to go back into hospital for it?" Mum said, "Well, it's easier for them to keep an eye on you if you are in hospital. But I'm sure it won't be for very long."

I knew she wasn't telling me the truth. I knew that I had stopped being in remission. I do think it would be better if they didn't try to protect you. We can always tell.

When Dr Stanhope came to see me, I said, "Will you have to give me more chemo?" and he said, "I'm sorry, Becky, but I'm afraid we will." I said, "Is that because I'm not in remission any more?" and he said, "Yes, but let's hope it's just a hiccup."

When he said that I hiccuped, because that is the sort of thing they like you to do. They like you to be bright and sparky and have a sense of humour.

Dr Stanhope was pleased when I hiccuped. He laughed and said, "That's the spirit!"

Another time I said to him that someone had told me if you came out of remission before five years, it meant you probably wouldn't ever be cured. I didn't say it meant you would probably die, because I am not brave enough.

Dr Stanhope said, "It doesn't necessarily mean that at all. But it does mean it's more difficult. It does mean that you have to be extra specially brave and put up with another lot of treatment."

Zoë had to put up with another lot of treatment. So did Bryony, in my story that I wrote. And she grew up and danced in *Swan Lake*!

I know that Mum doesn't expect me to grow up. Nobody expects me to. Not even Dr Stanhope.

I suppose I don't, really. Deep inside myself. I know that what Zoë told me is true because Zoë is the one person who always tells the truth.

If Zoë were here I could talk about it with her. I

can't talk about it with Mum, it upsets her too much. She tells me not to be morbid. She says, "Oh, Becky, darling! Don't be so morbid!"

I don't think it's being morbid. And I don't think it's being negative, either, which is another thing Mum accuses me of. She says, "You must think positively, sweetheart! Otherwise you're not giving yourself a chance."

I don't see that it's being negative to wonder what is in store for you. I think it is simply facing up to things.

I've been thinking just lately about what Gran said. Gran said that when you die you meet all the people that have gone before. But wouldn't this make it terribly crowded? In heaven, or wherever it is that you go?

I tried asking Uncle Eddy about it. He is the only person I can really talk to, now that Zoë is not here. I said, "If everyone that's died is going to be up there, won't it be a bit like Oxford Street at Christmastime?"

I went to Oxford Street last Christmas with Ana-Maria to see the lights.

There were so many people you could hardly move.

Uncle Eddy said, "It will only be like Oxford Street if that is how you would like it to be. Is that how you would like it to be?" I said, "No, it isn't! I'd hate it!

Everyone pushing and shoving."

So then Uncle Eddy said, "In that case, think how you would like it to be, and that is how it will be."

I have been thinking and thinking. All I can think of is that I want Gran and Kitty to be there.

And maybe some of the really great dancers that I have seen pictures of. Margot Fonteyn and Rudolf Nureyev and Anna Pavlova.

It would be brilliant if I could get to meet them! But mostly I just want Gran and Kitty.

I knew when Uncle Eddy came back from Africa specially to be with me that I was more ill than Mum let on. Poor Mum! She can't face up to it.

I can! I think.

Sometimes I can. Other times it just doesn't seem real, the thought of life going on without me.

Well, but it is not going to! Not yet. I am not ready to leave yet. I am going to go on *fighting*.

I was ever so pleased when Uncle Eddy came back. It was a truly golden moment when I saw him walking into the ward. I love him so much! And we have been able to have long, long talks like I can't do with Mum.

me and Uncle Eddy, talking

We chat for ages together! About all sorts of things. There's nothing I can't talk to Uncle Eddy about. Like for instance one time I asked him whether he really thinks there are lots and lots of people waiting for us when we die. If I'd tried asking Mum she'd have said, "Oh, darling! Don't be morbid. What's all this talk of dying?"

Uncle Eddy never tells me that I'm morbid. He understands that there are things I need to know. He said, "For sure! Lots and lots. No one will ever have to be lonely."

I said, "But do people wait? Do they wait for people?"

Like Granddad, for example. Granddad has been dead for a really long time. Longer than I have been alive. Suppose he got tired of waiting for Gran and found someone else?

Uncle Eddy said that he wouldn't have got tired. He said, "Time is different there. There is no time. Time stands still... for ever and ever. To Granddad it will have seemed like no more than a few seconds have passed."

So then I asked him something else that had been bothering me. Granddad was only fifty when he died, but Gran was quite old. How would Granddad have felt about his wife being an old person? How would Gran have felt about it? Would she mind him seeing her with grey hair and wrinkles while he was still young? Wouldn't it have upset them both?

Uncle Eddy said, "No way!" He said that things like age simply wouldn't matter any more. He said, "If it was Gran's dream to be young again, and to meet Granddad when he was young, then that is what she will have done."

He said, "We will all find whatever we want to find, and be just as we want to be. I promise you."

I said, "Are you absolutely sure?" Uncle Eddy said, "I'm absolutely positive."

So then I said, "But how can you *know*? How can anybody *know*?" and he said, "Trust me! I know."

I do trust Uncle Eddy. But I still can't help being anxious. I don't want to go there if I can't be with Gran and Kitty!

Another thing Gran said was that dying was worse for the people that are left behind than for the people it happens to. I suppose this is because of time in heaven standing still while time on earth just creeps. Like for Granddad it would only have seemed a few seconds while for Gran it was years and years.

Perhaps it is a sort of comfort to think that people who have died are not being lonely and missing you. If I die it will only be seconds before I see Mum and Danny and Uncle Eddy again.

But I am not going to die! I don't want to! I want to dance Odette and go to Wonderland!

It's Danny I feel sorriest for. He is the one I worry about. I know that Mum will be sad and cry but she is always so busy with her television work and Uncle Eddy has his filming but Danny is only just a little boy. He won't understand! He won't know about time seeming like seconds. He won't know that there are people up there waiting for you.

Danny is going to miss me more than anyone. He'll be all on his own with Ana-Maria. And if she goes back to Spain he will have to get used to someone else and he is so shy, he hates having to meet new people.

I think Mum ought to have another baby to keep him company. I wouldn't mind her having another one. But first she will have to get married again and I don't know who she could marry. She hasn't even got a man friend at the moment. But it isn't fair to leave Danny on his own! He needs someone to look after him.

I wish I'd been nicer to him when he was a tiny baby. I wish I hadn't been jealous, because of him having a dad and me not. It wasn't his fault. He didn't ask to be born. Nobody asks to be born. I wish I'd cuddled and kissed him more. I love him ever so much!

When we go to Wonderland, Danny is going to come with us. I'm not going to go if Danny can't come! We oughtn't to have left him behind that night when we went to celebrate. The night Mum bought champagne. He can't help it if he's a silly babyish nuisance and bangs on the table and tips his chair back and does all those things that make Mum mad.

"He'd only ruin it for you." That's what Mum said. But I wouldn't have minded!

When we go to Wonderland, we will go on Concorde.

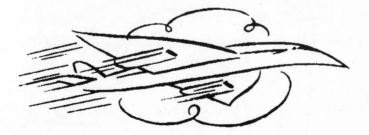

Mum has said that we can! She says it will be a special treat, for being twelve.

I shall be twelve in… a few months.

Three months!

Less than three months.

Soon.

Then we'll pack up our cases and Mum will say, "Have you put your toothbrush  in?" And Danny will want to take his teddy bear and Mum will groan and say, "Can't we go *anywhere* without that wretched bear?" But it's the only way that Danny will sleep.

He has nightmares if he's parted from Teddy.

Danny will take Teddy and I will take my signed photograph of Darcey. I don't go anywhere without my signed photograph. I've had it on my locker all the time I've been in hospital. The nurses call me their little dancer. They all know I'm going to dance in *Swan Lake*. Once when it was Carol's birthday they had a party for her on the ward and I did a snowflake dance that I made up myself, specially for her.

I danced it in my nightie! It was the nearest I could get to a proper ballet dress.

I made it about snowflakes because outside it was cold and snowy and people's mums and dads kept saying things like, "My goodness, you're in the best place in here!" It made Zoë ever so mad. She said, "How would they like it if they had to be in here?"

Zoë's at home now. She's doing really well. She sent me a card the other day.

I have good feelings about Zoë: she is going to be all right.

POST CARD

Hi Becky.
I'm well, why aren't you?
What are you doing in
hospital??? Get back
into remission!!! Quickly!!!
That is an order.
I MEAN IT.
ZOE × × × × × × × × ×
× × × × Your friend × × ×
× × × × × × × × × ×
× × × ×
P.S. Do it soon. OR ELSE!

Beck
Bar
Tu
In

I still wish she could come to Wonderland with us! It is going to be the very best birthday present I have ever had. Uncle Eddy will come and pick us up in his car

and we will all drive to the airport together.

Then we will get on the plane

and do up our seat belts

and fly high up into the air

all across the seas and the oceans and the mountains

high amongst the clouds

and all through the stars

until we come to Wonderland!

All our favourite characters will be there.

There will be Jo, and Alice, and Peter Pan, and Lassie, and the Little Princess, and Dorothy – and Toto!

And my gran! My gran will be there! She'll be there, waiting for me!

I can't wait to be twelve and go to Wonderland!

That is the end of Becky's story.

She would have been so proud if she could see her name in print!

Who knows? Maybe she can…

In memory of our brave
little Becky Bananas
aged 11 years and
10 months
Be happy sweetheart
We love you
Mum, DANNY
and Uncle Eddy
'She had lots of bottle'

JEAN URE

Illustrated by Mick Brownfield

For my very own Fruit & Nut Case...
and for Sydenham High School who gave me
such a warm welcome

Chapter One

My dad's an Elvis Presley look-alike. He's got a white suit just like Elvis had, and a guitar, and he sings all the songs that Elvis sang. *Blue Suede Shoes*, *Hound Dog*, *Love me Tender, Love me True*. He knows them all!

I've drawn a picture of my dad being Elvis on my bedroom wall. I'll draw it again, now.

I'm always drawing on my bedroom wall. When I've filled up all the space I'm going to start on the ceiling. I'll be taller by then. I'll stand on a stepladder and I'll be able to reach.

This is how one bit of my bedroom wall looks.

It's instead of having a garden. As a matter of fact there is a garden at the back of this house, but it belongs to old Misery Guts that lives downstairs and she won't let me play in it. It's only a bit of moth-eaten grass and dustbins, anyhow. If I had a garden I would grow all flowers in it.

My *garden* wall is right opposite my bed where I can see it when I wake up in the morning. My *people* wall is by the windows.

Unfortunately, that is all the wall there is as the room is not very big and there is a huge great enormous old-fashioned wardrobe just inside the door, taking up loads of valuable space.

The wardrobe used to belong to my nan. I hate it! When I was little, like four or five, I used to think fierce monsters lived in it. I don't now, of course; now that I'm older. But I still hate it because it is *ugly*. I hate things that are ugly!

Dad is always promising that he will chop it up and make me a shelf out of it, but so far he hasn't. He's better at being Elvis than at D.I.Y.

Sometimes, like if we're having a bit of a party, Dad will put on his Elvis suit and sing *Love me Tender* specially for Mum. *Love me Tender* is her favourite. She goes really gooey over that one!

In case there is anybody who has just dropped by from another planet and is thinking "Who is this Elvis person?" I maybe ought to explain that Elvis Presley was a very famous singer way back in my nan's time. Mum says he was called Elvis-the-Pelvis because he used to wiggle his hips around as he sang, but Dad says he was the King of Rock, and that is what some people still call him, "the King".

My dad is a dead ringer for the King! He looks really great when he brushes his hair back and puts gel on it so that it puffs up in front, the way the King's did. And he wears his white suit and his high-heeled boots and he sings all these old songs. OK, and Mum loves it.

They get all moony and swoony the pair of them. It's like they're teenagers again, before I was born.

Once upon a time, Dad used to do Elvis gigs in the local clubs but he hasn't done one for a while now. Last time he did one he had a bit of an accident. He tripped over his guitar lead and fell off the stage and busted his ankle.

🐱 astrophe!

Dad's always doing things to himself.

He's a real disaster area!

My mum's not much better. She does the daftest things!

Honestly, my parents! They're going to turn me into a right fruit and nut case, I know they are.

I try to look after them, but I can't have my eye on them all of the time.

Dad gets ever so impatient when Mum messes up the dinner or burns his shirts. But she can't help it! It's just the way she is.

Like Dad flying off the handle. He can't help it, either; he's just a live wire. He doesn't mean anything by it. But it gets Mum all flustered and nervous and I have to go jumping in really fast and make them laugh. I can always make them laugh! Usually.

When we're having fun together, like when Dad's being Elvis singing his songs, and Mum's dancing along to them, life's absolutely brilliant. I think they're the best mum and dad in the world and I don't care a row of pins that we haven't any money and have to live in the upstairs part of a rotten crumbly old house with Misery Guts lurking like some horrible evil spider waiting to catch us in her web. It just doesn't bother me in the slightest little bit. It doesn't bother me *where* I live so long as I'm with my mum and dad.

It's when Mum does something daft and Dad flies off the handle and makes her cry that I get a bit fussed. What scares me is in case they stop loving each other and Dad goes off to live somewhere else, so that we're not a family any more. That is the ONLY THING in the universe that I am scared of. I'm not scared of climbing trees right to the very top, I'm not scared of big fierce dogs that run barking at you, I'm not scared of Tracey Bigg and her gang of stupid bullies, no way! I could bash Tracey Bigg to a pulp any time I want. But I don't think I could bear it if my mum and dad split up.

Every night before I go to sleep I say this special prayer. I haven't ever let on to anyone about my prayer before, not a single living soul, but Cat told me I'd got to be honest.

Cat's the one who said I ought to write a book. She said, "I just know that you can do it, Mandy!" I said, "You mean, like... a book about *me*?" and Cat said, "Well, and why not?" So then I didn't know what I would have to write about, or what sort of things she'd want me to put, and she said, "It'll be a true story, right? *Your* story. So just tell it like it really is."

All this stuff about myself. I dunno! It seems weird. But if it's what Cat wants.

So, all right! I'm being honest. I AM BEING HONEST! Watch my lips.

i am being honest!

I don't know – *honestly* – whether I really believe in God, but that doesn't stop me saying my prayer. This is what I pray:

Please God don't let Mum and Dad get divorced

Actually, I don't do that. Kneel, I mean. I sort of put my hands together, but I do it under the duvet when I'm lying in bed. I've been doing it for almost two years, now.

Two years is a long time to keep on saying the same prayer. But it's worked, so far! Even if Dad does sometimes fly off the handle. Even if Mum does do the daftest things. We're still all together! I wouldn't ever dream of going to sleep without saying my prayer.

"Please, God, don't let Mum and Dad get divorced. Please, God! Let them be together for ever and ever, and ever and ever, and ever and ever, and ever and ever, and ever and ever, amen."

I have to say it ten times, to match my age. The older I get, the more difficult it will be to keep count of all the for evers! But I will still do it. I will always do it.

My life is quite uneventful, really, and I cannot think there is going to be very much to record, but Cat says, "Go for it! Just put whatever occurs to you. Whatever's important."

But now that I've said about my prayer, and about Mum and Dad, I can't think of anything else! Just being together as a family is all that is important.

Maybe I should describe "A Day in the Life of Mandy Small". It is not what I would call very interesting, but I expect Cat would like it.

OK. Well. I always set my special Mickey Mouse alarm clock so's to be sure of waking up on time in the morning. As soon as it rings I leap madly out of bed and hurriedly rush into my clothes.

If it's summer I do it more slowly, but in the winter I have to rush or I would freeze to an icicle before I got through dressing. This is because we don't have any central heating in this crumbly old house. Sometimes it is so cold that when I wake up there are frost patterns on my window, all swirly and beautiful.

Once I am into my clothes I go racing to Mum's room to make sure that she is awake. Dad has to leave home at six o'clock to go and clean windows with his friend Garry, and sometimes after he's gone Mum falls asleep again. If I don't wake her she would be late for work and then she would be threatened with the sack, which is what happened once before.

My nan says, "Oh, really, Sandra!" (Sandra is my mum's name.) "Fancy having to rely on a child to get you up! Why on earth don't you set your alarm?"

But the one time Mum set the alarm for seven, after Dad had gone off, she forgot to put it back again to 5.30 and Dad didn't wake up next morning, so then *he* was late and that made him fly off the handle, and that is why I have taken charge. It is easier for me to do it. I don't mind waking up.

After I have shaken Mum, I go into the kitchen and make some tea and toast. I then go back to Mum's room to check that she is still awake. Sometimes she is, but more often she has gone and nodded off again. It isn't Mum's fault that she can't wake up in the mornings. She's just not very good at it. Some people are and some people aren't, and Mum is one of the ones that aren't. But it's all right, because she's got me. She says, "What I'd do without my Mand, I don't know."

Mum is Sand and I am Mand. I think that's really neat!

Dad is Barry. It occurs to me that if they had another baby and it was a boy, they could call it Harry and then we would have Barry and Harry, and that would be neat, as well. I'd quite like a baby brother, but Nan says, "Heaven forbid! They can't even cope with one of you." So I don't think, alas, that they will have another baby. Apart from anything else, where would it sleep?

All we have in this upstairs part of the house is one bedroom for Mum and Dad, one (*tiny* little) bedroom for me, one room for sitting in, one which is a kitchen, and one which is the bathroom, though that is just a measly bit of room shaped like a wedge of cheese, half-way down the stairs, that we have to share with old Misery Guts, who moans like crazy about tide marks round the bath and hairs in the wash basin. She also used to moan about us using her loo paper, so now she carries her own roll with her whenever she goes there.

Now I've forgotten where I was.

I know! Telling about my day.

So. Right. As soon as I've eaten a bit of toast, and Mum's had her cup of tea, we go down the stairs, on tiptoe because of Misery Guts, and close the front door behind us *really quietly*, and run up the road together, laughing, as it is always a relief to know that a) Mum is not late and won't be threatened with the sack and b) we have not disturbed old Misery Guts and been yelled at.

Poor Mum! She hates being yelled at. She's quite a timid person, really. I am more like Dad. I am FIERCE. What my nan calls "aggressive and up-front". But she can talk! We both take after her. Dad's dad, my grandy, is well under her thumb. That's what Mum says, anyway.

Mum hasn't got a mum and dad. She was dumped when she was just a little kid. I think it must be so terrible to feel that you're not wanted. That is something I have *never* felt. I know I was a mistake, because Nan has often told me so. She says that Mum and Dad were "no more than children themselves" and "far too young to go having babies". But once they'd got over their surprise they were really pleased. Mum says I'm the cleverest thing she's ever done. She says, "Your dad was so excited! He even came to the hospital to see you arrive!"

So I know that I am loved and wanted. I just wish I could be certain that Mum and Dad love and want each other. I think they do, 'cos they always kiss and make up and Dad is always buying Mum little presents to show how much she means to him. But it just would be nice to be certain *sure*.

Now I've gone and lost track again. Miss Foster – she's our teacher at school – she'd say I'm not concentrating. She's always accusing me of not concentrating.

OK. So now I am! This is what happens after me and Mum have left the house.

We walk as far as the tube station together, then Mum kisses me goodbye and I go on to school. I always turn at the corner and wave, and

Mum waves back. For the rest of the day, I can't wait for school to end so that I can go back home again.

I can't stand school. There's this girl in my class called Tracey Bigg who really bugs me. She's really got it in for me. This is because one time when Oliver Pratt was blubbing and Tracey Bigg and her mates were making fun of him, I went to his rescue. Like Tracey was jeering at him and calling him a crybaby so I told her to stop it and she said, "Who do you think you are?" and I said I knew who I was and if she didn't shut her mouth I'd shut it for her and she goes, "Oh, yeah?" and I go, "Yeah," and we have this huge big fight and Oliver just stands there with his finger in his mouth, gorming. I mean, he is a total nerd but he can't help it. I don't expect he can. It isn't any reason to be horrid to him. But lots of people are, like Billy Murdo and his gang. *Bully* Murdo, I call him.

See, if you're not the same as all the rest, you get picked on. Oliver's not the same 'cos he's a bit, well, sort of slow; and I'm not the same 'cos – I don't really know why I'm not the same. But Miss Foster's always getting at me and making me feel like I'm useless. I wish I could go to an acting school! One of those places where sometimes the kids get picked to be on telly. I bet I'd be good at that! But probably, I expect, you need lots of money, like you do for most things. So until some big pot film person catches sight of me and goes "Hey! Wow!" and instantly offers me a Lead Part in his next production, it looks like I am *stuck*. Worse luck.

The minute school is over I go scooting off just as fast as I can to collect Mum from her baker's shop, where she works, and we go round the supermarket together and buy stuff for tea and carry it home and hope old Misery isn't waiting to pounce on us the minute the front door opens, which all too often she is.

After we've listened politely to old Misery and meekly promised to mend our ways, we go upstairs and have a cup of something and a giggle before getting the tea ready for Dad. Me and Mum do a lot of giggling. We're like sisters, sometimes, the two of us.

Dad comes in at five o'clock and I always go rushing to meet him. Sometimes, if old Misery's caught him, he'll be in a right grumpy mood. And when Dad's in a grumpy mood, BEWARE! Mum gets flustered, and that's when things start to go wrong – specially if she's done something daft and ruined his tea.

But if he's in a good mood, then whoopee! We have fun. Maybe he'll sing some Elvis, or we'll play a game of cards, or just settle down to watch the telly like any other family. If it's summer I might perhaps go into my room to do some more wall-painting. I aim to get the walls filled up by the time I'm eleven! Then it's the ceiling. After that, who knows? The floor???

Nan thinks it's terrible I'm allowed to paint on the walls, but Dad says it's my room, so why shouldn't I? He says, "Other kids get to play with their computers: Mandy gets to paint her bedroom."

That is one of the very *best* things about my dad. He always, always sticks up for me!

I'm not really actually writing this. I am saying it into a tape machine!

It was Cat's idea. Cat is the person who comes into school every week to help people like me and Oliver with our reading. She is my friend. And it's all right for me to call her Cat and not Miss Daley; she said that I could. She didn't say that Oliver could. Just me. Because we're friends.

Cat knows I'm not very good at writing. But I'm ace at talking! Usually. It all depends who I'm with; I don't just talk to anyone. My nan complains I never stop but that's not true. Sometimes I don't say a word for minutes on end. And when I'm at school I don't hardly talk at all, except just sometimes to Oliver, 'cos of feeling sorry for him. If I didn't talk to him, nobody would. So we talk about a few things, but nothing important.

Cat is the only person I *really* talk to. I can talk about anything to Cat! What I usually do, I tell her the latest joke I've heard or something funny about old Misery Guts and we have a bit of a laugh. I don't tell her about hating school or Miss Foster having a go at me or anything like that. That would be whingeing and I hate people that whinge. But I *could* tell her. If I wanted. And I know that she'd listen 'cos she's that sort of person. She's not just my friend, she's my *special* friend; and that's why I'm doing this book. Because she asked me.

When I've filled up the tape, or done as much as I can, Cat's mum is going to type it out on her word processor and then Cat is going to get it printed. It will all be spelt right, with lots of commas and full stops and little squiggly bits like : and ; and ! so that it looks like a real book.

I am going to do the drawings! Lots of them. I like books with drawings. Sometimes I think it would be better if books didn't have anything *but* drawings. No words. Cat doesn't agree; she says you need both. I don't see why but, anyway I am going to do drawings instead of draggy descriptions that go on for ever and make you lose interest.

Like, for instance, I *could* say that Cat is...

Very tall and thin with lots of bony bits
and that she has:

a round jolly face

a wide mouth

sticky-out teeth

a blobby nose –
and that she wears:

eee-normous glasses

tight sweaters

short skirts

black tights

and long boots.

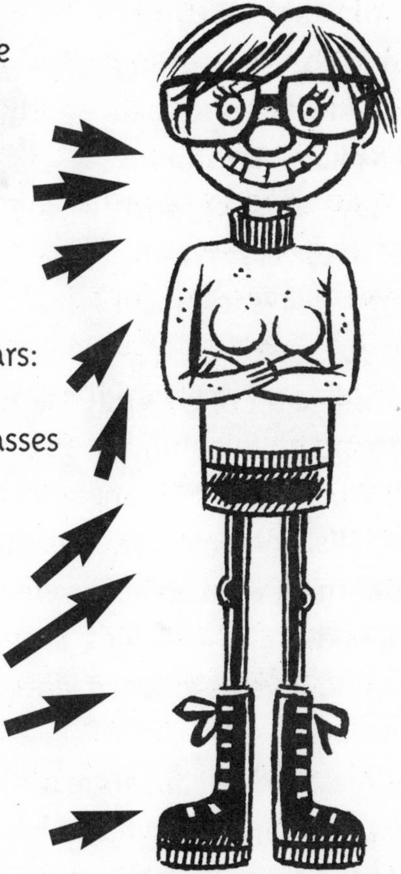

This is Cat

But I think that would make people go "Yawn!"
and not read any more. It's ever so much more fun
to draw!

I hope she doesn't mind me drawing her! I

can only do funny drawings. Even when I draw me I make me look funny. This is me:

All the drawings that I do, I'm putting with the tape so that Cat's mum knows where to leave a space when she does the typing. Then I will stick them on!

I still can't really understand why Cat wants me to record all this stuff. All about me and my boring life. When I asked her she said, "Well, look at it this way. It's not everyone can say they've written a book. Think what an achievement it would be!"

I said, "But nothing's ever happened to me." Meaning, I've never been kidnapped,

or lost at sea

or rescued anyone from drowning

or been in a plane that's been hijacked.

I have never been on a plane full stop. A BIG full stop.

I've never been abroad, I've never been on a boat, I've only been to the seaside once and that was two years ago

when Nan gave us the money to go to Clacton and stay in a bed-and-breakfast. Even then it rained all the time. And Mum put some clothes to dry on the heater and the clothes caught fire while we were out and set light to the curtains and Dad got in a hump and spent all our money playing the fruit machines down the pub which meant we had to come home three days early and the bed-and-breakfast lady kept sending threatening letters about her curtains!

Nan and Grandy had to pay her in the end, to buy some new ones. Nan was ever so horrid about it. She said that Mum was like a child and that Dad was irresponsible and we didn't deserve to have holidays. So we've never had one since and now I don't suppose we'll ever have one again. See if I care!

That Tracey Bigg, she goes off all over the place. Places like Florida and Gran Canaria (wherever that is). She's always boasting about it. I haven't got anything to boast about. I just don't see what Cat wants me to say into this tape machine she's given me.

I said this to Cat and she chirruped, "Oh, Mandy, you've got all sorts of things!" Cat's always chirruping and chirping. She's ever such a cheerful person. So am I, I suppose, really. On the whole. Maybe that's why we're friends. She told me that things didn't have to be big and dramatic to be put into books.

"Just ordinary everyday happenings. That's what interests people."

Does she mean that other people are going to read about me???

I could be famous! I could be rich! They could make a film about me!

Yes, and if they do I know one person that's not going to be in it, and that's Tracey Bigg. If anyone gets to play her it'll be some ugly, cross-eyed, po-faced *tub*.

Serve her right! I can't stand that girl.

Chapter Two

This is her.

Tracey Bigg. She's always picking on me, just because she's Bigg and I'm Small. Which we really are. *Unfortunately*.

She's horrible! I hate her. She says these really mean and spiteful things just to try and hurt people. Like at the beginning of term when Miss Foster said we'd all got to read as many books as we could and get people to sponsor us, and the money we raised was going to go to charity, and Tracey Bigg sniggered and said, "What happens if we can't read, Miss?" and everyone knew she was talking about me.

Me and Oliver Pratt. Not that I cared, I don't care what anyone says, but Oliver went red as radishes and I felt really sorry for him. I mean, for all Tracey Bigg knows we've got that thing where you muddle your letters,* which is a sort of illness and nothing to do with being lazy or stupid. It's like being handicapped and people mocking at you.

Tracey Bigg is the sort of person that would mock at anyone that was handicapped. She'd kick a blind man's stick away from him just for fun, she would.

Tracey Bigg is garbage.

Miss Foster said that anyone that found reading difficult could choose books with pictures, but it didn't make any difference, I couldn't have found anyone to sponsor me anyway. I knew I couldn't ask Mum and Dad 'cos they were already worried about money, where is the next penny going to come from? and how are we going to pay all the bills? And I couldn't ask the neighbours 'cos Mum doesn't like me to do that. She says if I ask them, their kids will ask her, and then she'll feel embarrassed when she has to say no. And I could just imagine what would happen if I tried asking old Misery Guts!

"Go away, you repulsive child! I would not give you the droppings from my nose"

When it was time to give the forms back I had to pretend I'd lost mine. Miss Foster got really ratty with me. She said, "Mandy Small, what is the matter with you? You are the most careless, thoughtless child I have ever met!" And Tracey Bigg was there and she didn't half sneer. 'Cos she'd read more books than anyone, hadn't she? *And* made a load more money.

When we went into the playground at break she kept going on with this rhyme she'd made up.

> *"Mirror, mirror on the wall,*
> *who's the dumbest girl of all?*
> *Mandee! Mandy Small!"*

She taught it to Aimee Wilcox and Leanne Trimble that are her best friends and they went round chanting it all through break and doing this stupid dance that made everyone laugh.

I just took no notice. I mean, my skin is really tough. It's like I'm wearing body armour. You could shoot arrows at it and they'd just bounce off. You could shoot bullets. You could hurl dead elephants.

Tracey Bigg can't hurt *me*. But all the same, it does get on my nerves. You get to feeling like you're on the point of exploding. Like a bottle of fizzy pop that's been all shaken up and the cork is just about to b...*low*!

That's what happened back at half term. My cork just blew,

and I bopped her one.

Actually, I bashed her. Right on the conk.

She bled gallons! She bled everywhere. All down her chin, drip-drip-drip. All down the front of her dress, drip-drop, drip-drop, *splodge*. What a mess! But it was her own fault. She asked for it. See, what happened, Miss Foster gave us these forms to take home. *More* forms. She's always giving us forms. Usually I just chuck mine away. I mean, I can't keep bothering Mum all the time. She'd only get fussed.

This lot was forms for going to summer camp. Down in Devon, on a farm.

"I don't expect most of you have ever been on a farm, have you?"

Tracey Bigg had. *Of course*. She's been everywhere. She's been to America. She's been to Australia. She's been to Switzerland and gone skiing in the mountains. She would!

I haven't ever been anywhere except to Clacton where it rained and Dad spent all our money. Oh, and to my nan's, but that's only a tube ride away. I would quite like to have seen a farm but I didn't think I could leave Mum and Dad for a whole fortnight even if Nan and Grandy offered to pay, which they might have done as on the whole they are quite generous. But I am always frightened that if I'm not there something disastrous will happen. Like I'll get back and find that Mum has burnt the house down or Dad's gone through the roof. Or even worse, that one of them has run away.

So I told Miss Foster I couldn't go and she seemed disappointed and said, "Oh, Mandy, that's a pity! I feel a change of scene would do you good."

I don't know what she meant by that. I don't need any change of scene! I'm quite happy where I am.

Anyway, out in the playground afterwards Tracey Bigg made up another of her stupid rhymes.

That was when I bashed her. And she yelled, and grabbed my hair, and tried to scratch my eyes out so I kicked her, really hard, on the ankle

and she tore at my sleeve and that was when Miss Foster and another teacher came running across and separated us.

'Course, I got into dead trouble for that.

Dead trouble. Tracey said it was all my fault, and so did Aimee and Leanne. They said, "She attacked her, Miss."

Nobody ever asked me *why* I'd attacked her, and I wouldn't have told them even if they had. Not any of their business. But they didn't ever ask.

It's like I've got this reputation for being aggressive and Tracey's got this reputation for being *good* and that's all anyone cares.

But sometimes I think you have to be a bit aggressive or people just stamp all over you. Like with Oliver, and Billy Murdo's gang.

They bully him something rotten and no one ever does a thing about it. That's because they do it where the teachers can't see. And Oliver, he's such a sad, weedy little guy, he never sticks up for himself.

I bet if he did, Miss Foster would say it was all his fault, even though Billy Murdo's about ten times bigger.

Sometimes you just can't win. But on the other hand, you can't just sit back and do nothing. I don't think you can.

Half-past three is when school ends. I can't wait to get out! I never stay behind for anything; not if I can help it. I run like a whirlwind to Bunjy's to pick Mum up and go shopping with her.

Bunjy's is the name of the baker's where Mum works. But the lady who owns it, the one who keeps threatening to give her the sack, isn't called Mrs Bunjy but Mrs Sowerbutts. Mum calls her old Sourpuss. She's not quite as bad as Misery Guts, but they both give Mum a lot of hassle.

Sometimes when I get there I'm a few minutes early. If old Sourpuss is around Mum pulls this face at me through the window and I know that I will have to wait.

Old Sourpuss wasn't there that day, the day I bashed Tracey Bigg and made her nose bleed. Mum came waltzing out looking all happy and giggly 'cos she'd left a few minutes before she ought!

I love it when Mum behaves like that. It means we're going to have *fun*!

Before we went home we called at the supermarket to buy some food for Dad's tea. Mum wanted to do him something different, something a bit posh. She started talking about making pastry and putting things inside it, but I managed to talk her out of *that* idea. Last time Mum tried making pastry it was an absolute disaster. It came out all hard, like a layer of cement. Dad said, "Blimey O'Reilly, you'd need

405

a hammer and chisel to make any headway with this!"

I don't know why Dad says Blimey O'Reilly, but he only does it when he thinks something is funny. Sometimes he just doubles up laughing at Mum and her cooking. Once she put the sugar in the oven to dry and it melted all over the place, and Dad said she was daft as a brush. He said, "Oh, what a yum yum!" And we all fell about, including Mum.

But other times, like if he's had a bad day or old Misery's had a go at him, he doesn't say Blimey O'Reilly he says things that are cross and unkind and Mum gets all upset. So it seemed to me it was silly to take chances. I reckoned Mum ought to get him something he liked. Food is terribly important to men. They get really upset if they come home and their dinner isn't ready or it's not what they want. Women don't care quite so much. Well, that's how it seems to me.

So in the end we bought his favourite pie, which I reckoned even Mum couldn't ruin as all you have to do is just put it in the oven. Mum said, "We'll have toast fingers and a bit of paté to start with," 'cos she still wanted to be posh.

Well, we got in and first thing we know is old Misery Guts is there waiting for us, hiding behind the door. All in one breath she says, "Mrs-Small-I-really-must-complain-about-the-state-of-the-bathroom-it-looks-as-if-a-bomb-has-hit-it." To which Mum chirps, "We should be so lucky!" and goes racing up the stairs two at a time with me giggling behind her.

The reason the bathroom looked as if a bomb had hit it was that the hot water thingie had blown up when Dad was running his bath. The hot water thingie looks like an ancient monument.

Before you can get any hot water out of it you have to move lots of little levers and turn on lots of taps and then light a match. I'm not allowed to touch it in case I blow myself up. Half the wall is down, now.

"That Misery Guts," panted Mum, as we pounded up the stairs to our own floor. "A pity it couldn't have blown up when she was in there!"

"In the bath," I said. "All naked."

Sometimes old Misery Guts makes Mum's life a real pain, but we just laughed about her that day. Mum was in a really giggly sort of mood. She turned the oven on, to heat it up for Dad's pie, and we had a cup of tea and watched a bit of telly, and then Mum put the pie in and I laid the table and we got the bread out for toasting.

"Let's do some thing special," said Mum. "Let's cut the toast into funny shapes. We'll cut one into a Misery Guts shape and see if your dad can guess who it is!"

So that was what we did. We made a Misery Guts shape and an old Sourpuss shape, and Mum made Nan and Grandy shapes, and I made Tracey Bigg and Miss Foster shapes, and then we just went mad and made any old shapes that took our fancy. Shapes with big heads, and shapes with big feet, and shapes with big bums. Fat shapes, skinny shapes. Tall shapes, short shapes. Shapes of all kinds!

We ended up with way too much toast!

"We've used up the whole loaf!" said Mum.

But we just giggled about it, 'cos that was the sort of mood we were in.

Dad got in at five o'clock. He swung me up in his arms and said, "And how's our Mand?"

"We've been making toasted teachers," I said.

"That sounds a bit dodgy," said Dad. "I hope they're not for my tea?"

"Only for starters," said Mum, proudly. She

was really chuffed with her posh starters. Paté and toast! That's what the nobs have.

"So what's for enders?" said Dad.

"Enders is trifle," I said. We'd bought some little pots of it at the supermarket.

"And middles?"

"Middles—"

"*Oh!*" Mum clapped her hand to her mouth. I ran for the oven. Too late! Dad's beautiful pie was ruined. We'd been so busy making toast shapes that Mum had forgotten to turn the oven down. The pie had burnt to a cinder!

I looked anxiously at Dad.

Dad said, "What's this supposed to be, then? My tea?"

Mum, all tearful, said, "There's always baked beans."

"*Baked beans*?" roared Dad. "I don't want baked beans!" He banged with his fist on the table. "I want a man's meal, darling!"

Please dont let Dad get cross with Mum. Please dont let him make her cry!

I could see that any minute Mum was going to burst into tears, and I knew if she did that it would

410

only get Dad even madder. So I rushed to put all the toast shapes on the table and said, "We could have baked beans on toasted teacher! Look, this one's Mr Phillpots, with his big bum! And this fat one is Mrs Duckworth. Or you could have beans on Misery Guts. This one's Misery Guts. See? Mum made her. 'Cos she moaned about the bathroom, so I reckon she deserves to get eaten. I think you should eat her and Mum should eat old Sourpuss. You could start with the head and work down. Or start at the feet and work up. Yum yum! Lovely bum!"

I'd picked out old Misery Guts and was pushing her at Dad and by this time he was laughing, and Mum was smiling a little tearful smile, so I knew that I could relax. Everything was going to be all right.

"Honest to God," said Dad, wiping his eyes, "I don't know where we'd be without you, Mand!"

My mum and dad really do *need* me.

I'm really enjoying telling my life story! I didn't think I would, I thought it would be a real drag. The only bit I was looking forward to was the drawings. But now I have discovered that I can put on different voices. Like for instance when I'm being Dad I put on this voice that is very grrrrrruff and

And when I'm being Mum I speak very high and light like soap bubbles.

Old Misery Guts, she's got a voice like a rusty tin full of nails. And when she speaks, her mouth goes like a prune.

So that's what I make my mouth go like when I'm being her.

Cat has a really **nice** voice. All warm and round and bubbly, like honey glugging out of a jar.

And she has this north country accent, which is fun.

If I'd have known I could do all these voices and act out being different people I could have been in our Christmas play. I could have played the lead instead of — guess who?

You've got it! Tracey Bigg. Aimee Wilcox said she was picked because she speaks nice. But I can speak nice! If I want to. I don't always want to. Anyway, I bet it wasn't 'cos she speaks nice, I bet it was 'cos she speaks

LOUD.

I can speak loud.

Not that Miss Foster would pick me. She wouldn't ever. She reckons I'm useless and that my mum and dad are useless and that we're all a bunch of no-hopers. She won't half be surprised when my book's published!

Dad said the other day, "So! We're going to have a famous writer in the family, are we?"

I have thought about this, but while I would quite like to become famous (just to show Tracey Bigg and Miss Foster, and also, of course, to earn a lot of money) I don't think that I shall become famous by writing books. For one thing, I don't expect that Cat's mum would want to keep on typing them out for me. And for another, what would I write about??? Once I have told my life story, what is there left?

Maybe I will become a famous actress! Or a funny person on the telly, pretending to be well-known people. Taking them off. I bet I could do that! It would be a bit like Dad being Elvis. I could be... Madonna!

I could be a Spice girl!

I could be the Queen!

I could be anyone!

Dad has heard me doing my voices. He'd really love to know what I'm talking about! He said, "You're not talking about us, are you, Mandy? Me and your mum? You're not giving our secrets away?"

Mum told him to let me alone. She said that I was doing it for Cat (only she calls her Miss Daley) and if Cat thought it was a good thing, "We oughtn't to interfere."

Dad said, "I'm not interfering, I just want to know what she's telling her."

He's tried wheedling and coaxing me, he's even tried bribing. He said, "Give you half a dollar if you'll let me have a listen!"

But I don't know what half a dollar is, and in any case what I'm talking about is strictly private.

strictly private

Well, almost strictly private. Just between me and Cat. And Cat's mum, of course, but I don't count her. She's only typing it out. It's not as if she knows us. She doesn't even live near us. She lives in Northwood, which is a dead posh area. We're nowhere near her. So I don't mind if she gets to hear what I'm saying, but no way do I want Dad to!

I was hoping, when I'd filled one tape, that Cat would say I could stop now, but she said, "Oh, no! You don't get let off that easily. I want a whole book out of you, young woman."

I said, "A whole *book*?" thinking that I would still be filling up tapes when I am old and ancient.

Cat said, "Well, several chapters at any rate."

I said, "How many is several?" and she said, "Mm... seven or eight?"

Seven or eight! I said, "I haven't lived long

enough to do seven or eight!" But Cat only laughed and said, "Get on with it, you're doing fine," and handed me another tape.

I suppose I don't mind, really.

Just so long as Dad doesn't get to eavesdrop!!!!

But I don't think he would.

Chapter Three

Here I am, starting over again. Testing, testing. One, two, three. This is Mandy Small telling her life story.

Now I'm going to play it back and see if it's come out OK.

Hearing your own voice is really strange! I don't sound a bit like what I thought I did. I thought I'd sound like someone on the television, maybe.

Talking posh.

Like Tracey Bigg.

Cat asked me once how I felt about Tracey Bigg. She said, "I get the feeling she upsets you."

She doesn't upset me! I'd just like to jump up and down on her a few times and squash her *flat*.

hi! this is menday Small, tellin her laif story.

Then when I'd done it, I'd roll her up like an old carpet and stuff her in the bin.

I'm not supposed to be talking about Tracey Bigg. This book isn't about Tracey Bigg, it's about me! I don't know how she got into it again. She keeps getting into things. From now on I am going to *keep her out*.

That'll settle her.

Now I'm back to telling my life story, only I don't quite know what to tell. When I asked

Cat, she said, "Just tell it like it is! Why not pick up where you left off?"

Where I left off was the night Mum burnt Dad's tea and we all ate toasted teacher and baked beans.

The next day was Saturday. I like Saturdays! They're one of my favourite days. *No school*, for one thing. For another, Mum doesn't have to work and neither does Dad.

Dad and I always go down the shops of a Saturday morning. Mum stops behind to catch up on stuff like the washing and the ironing. She has her treat on Sunday when she stays in bed. Sometimes she stays there until twelve o'clock! Sunday is Mum's day. But Saturday is mine and Dad's.

Dad was in a really good mood that particular Saturday. He fooled around doing his Elvis act as we walked down the road and Mrs Stern that lives at No. 4 called out to him.

"Hi, Barry! When we gonna see you down the *Hand & Flower* again?"

Mrs Stern is a huge fan of Dad's. She also does *a lot of drinking* in the *Hand & Flower*.

The *Hand & Flower* is where Dad fell off the stage in the middle of his Elvis gig. But Dad had not been drinking. He is just accident prone.

When we got to the shops Dad said, "Let's give your mum a surprise... let's go and buy some stuff to fix that kitchen cabinet she's always on about."

Mum had been on about the kitchen cabinet for weeks. *Months*. It's this little cupboardy thing that's supposed to be fixed to the wall only one day it went and fell down right on top of me and almost knocked me out.

I didn't half see stars!

I had to go to the hospital and have a chunk of hair cut off and six stitches, and I had this enormous great lump like a football stuck out the side of my head.

I told Miss Foster I'd slipped on the ice (it was way back last winter and it was really cold). I thought it sounded silly to say a kitchen cabinet had fallen on me.

Like one time when the banister rail broke and I fell down the stairs and twisted my ankle, Miss Foster looked at me like she just couldn't believe people lived in houses where that sort of thing happened. But our house is really old and it crumbles all the time. Just at the moment there was this rotten floor board on the landing. It had got rotted 'cos of rain coming through the roof. Old houses always have leaky roofs; even ones that belong to dukes and duchesses.

I don't know if they have cupboards that come off the walls.

Mum and Dad had a right old row about that cupboard 'cos Mum had been telling Dad for ages it was going to come down.

"We'll fix it for her," said Dad. "Be like a sort of birthday treat."

"But Mum's already had her birthday," I said.

Dad said OK, it would be an *in-between* birthday treat.

"And while I'm about it, I'll knock down that wardrobe and make a shelf for you."

Well, at least we bought the stuff for doing it with. Some things to hold it up and things for fixing it to the wall. I mean, it was a start. It was closer than he'd ever come before.

"I'll do it," said Dad. "You'll see."

I really thought that this time he might, but I wasn't surprised when he didn't. I know my dad! He means well, but he gets very easily sidetracked.

ho.ho! I'll believe that when it happens.

Like on the way back from the D.I.Y. store he wanted to get side-tracked into the betting shop, only I wouldn't let him.

Last time he got sidetracked in the betting shop he put all the housekeeping money on a horse called *Sweet Sandy Star*, on account of Star being my mum's name before she got married. Dad said it was such a terrific coincidence that the horse simply couldn't lose. Only it did. It came in last. Dad's horses always do. So after that he gave me strict instructions: "You're not to let me go into that betting shop ever again. Understand? I'm relying on you, girl!"

It is rather a responsibility, but it made Mum really upset when he lost all the housekeeping money. We had to beg from Nan, and Mum hates doing that.

When he's in a good mood Dad actually thanks me for stopping him. That's what he did that Saturday. He ruffled my hair and said, "Good old Mand! Keeping her dad on the straight and narrow." And then he said was he allowed to just buy a couple of lottery tickets, and I said yes, because you never know, you *could* win a million pounds, it's just that I have to be there with him or he'll start buying scratch cards like there's no tomorrow and that's almost as bad as the horses. The thing is with Dad, he can't help himself. Like Mum can't help doing some of the daffy things she does.

They need me to look after them.

Mum was so pleased when Dad and I got home without spending the housekeeping money! Dad said, "You've got Mand to thank for that. She's my guardian angel, aren't you, poppet?" And then he showed Mum all the stuff that we'd got at the D.I.Y. All the screws and the hinges and things to make holes with and the things to put into the holes once they'd been made, and Mum said, "Oh! You're never going to fix that kitchen cabinet at last?" Dad just grinned and said, "Only if you behave yourself."

He didn't do the cabinet that afternoon because of sport on the telly. Dad's a huge sports fan! He'll watch anything, even snooker. Mum and I don't care for it, so I went into my room to do some more tape for Cat, and Mum went over the road to her friend Deirdre that's just had a new baby.

Sometimes I think that Mum would quite like a new baby herself, but I expect Nan's right and it wouldn't be sensible. I bet I know who'd end up looking after it if she did have one! Not that I'd mind; I think babies are cute. When I grow up I'm going to have at least six. Both sexes. Maybe triplets, then I could get it over with in just two goes.

Of course I would have to find a husband first, and that might not be so easy as at the moment I happen to think that boys are the pits. We have a *lot* at our school.

They are all disgusting. Maybe they get better as they grow older. I can only hope!

When Mum came back from seeing the new baby she said to Dad, "What do you want for your tea?" and Dad said, "Something special," and I saw Mum start to look worried 'cos I knew that all she'd got was fish fingers or egg and chips (which as a matter of fact are two of my all-time favourite meals). Then Dad jumped up and switched off the telly and said, "Let's go out! It's time we treated ourselves."

Mum got as far as saying, "But what about the—"

Gas bill, probably. Or the electricity. A bill of some kind. But when Dad gets an idea in his head there's no stopping him. He simply pulled Mum towards him and planted this huge smacker of a kiss on her lips and roared, "Forget it! Whatever it is. Forget it! I'm tired of counting every penny! I want a good time!"

So Mum went and got dressed up in her best pink skirt and this lovely slinky blouse that has pictures of pop stars all over it, and Dad put on his best denims and his Levi jacket, and slicked his hair back like Elvis, and we went trolling up the road to the Indian restaurant.

I feel really proud of my mum and dad when they get all their gear on! If you didn't know, you'd think probably they were on the telly, or celebrities of some kind. Mum was still going on a bit about the bills (I think Nan scared her when they had to ask for help with the electric) but Dad said —

I can't say what he really said as Cat's mum might not like it! I expect where she lives in Northwood they don't say things like ••••.*

And it was fun, to begin with. It always is, to begin with. I always hope that it will go on being, and sometimes it does and that is wonderful. I mean, that is just absolutely THE BEST.

I kept my fingers crossed that that was how it would be that night.

Just at first, I thought it might. Dad picked

* Note from Cat's mum: I'm afraid they do, but you're quite right, I don't like it.

up the menu and said, "Now, Mand, you can have just whatever you like." So I started off with poppadoms and chutney, and then I had samosas, with mint sauce, and then I had a biryani, and then I had an ice cream, bright green with little coloured bits all over it: only by the time I got to the ice cream, things weren't being such fun any more as Mum and Dad were having one of their rows.

Dad accused Mum of being a misery and a killjoy, and Mum accused Dad of being irresponsible. She said that it was Nan's fault, she said she'd spoilt him, and Dad said, "You leave my mum out of this!" and before I knew it they were at it hammer and tongs.

They say such terrible things when they get angry. Like, "I don't know why I ever married you" and "You're nothing but a millstone round my neck." The sort of things that make me terrified they won't want to go on living together. I couldn't bear it if my mum and dad split up! I know Nan says they're useless, the pair of them, but they're my mum and dad and I love them!

What made things worse was that Mum was drinking too much wine. She's all right if she just has one glass, but if she has more than one it makes her tearful. And if she has more than *two* it makes her tipsy. She doesn't get drunk or throw up or anything horrid like that. She just gets a bit wobbly and out of control and then the wine gets spilt and the glasses get smashed and Dad says she's a liability and that he can't take her anywhere.

I tried to stop her. I said, "Mum, if you have any more you'll only get tipsy," but she wouldn't listen to me. She was going on about the telephone bill and how the telephone people had sent a nasty letter saying they were going to cut us off and how she wasn't going to go to Nan for help, not this time, not ever again, "Because she's so hateful to me, she always seems to think it's my fault!"

Dad said well, it was. He said Mum was the one who was supposed to buy the stamps for the telephone bill; why hadn't she bought them? And Mum poured another glass of wine and started crying and saying how could she buy them when Dad insisted on throwing money away on Indian meals when he could have stayed at home and had fish fingers?

To which Dad snarled that he couldn't stand

another day of Mum's cooking, she couldn't even cook a fish finger without ruining it.

And I knew what was going to happen, so I just took out my pen and some paper, which I always carry with me, and started doing some drawings and tried not to listen.

But you can't not listen as they always drag you into it.

It's always like this. It's very embarrassing, in the middle of a restaurant. Both of them wanting to know that I love them best. I love them equally! I love them both *so much*. I wish they wouldn't fight! I really really do!

It is a good thing that Balji, who owns the restaurant, is used to my mum and dad. When Dad went storming off to the loo and Mum reached out a hand and sent her wine spilling all over the table and just sat there weeping, he came over immediately with a cloth and very calmly began to mop it all up.

I said, "I think we'd better have the bill, now, Balji," and Balji nodded and said, "And a cab?" I said, "Yes, please. And a cab."

He always gets us a cab. Well, I mean, not *always*. Mum and Dad don't *always* have rows in his restaurant. Mum doesn't *always* start weeping. But it has happened quite often. I always pray that it won't, but Mum does worry so about how the bills are going to be paid and Dad does so hate to be nagged. If we just had a bit more money, things would be all right.

By the time we got home Mum had stopped crying and Dad had stopped threatening to walk out and they were both sitting there in front of the telly so I thought it would be safe to leave them. So I went to bed and said my special prayer and I had just about fallen to sleep when I was woken by the horrible voice of old Misery Guts shrieking up the stairs.

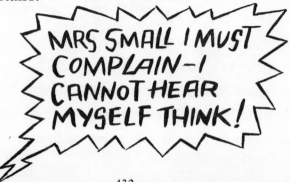

Mum and Dad were at it again. Bickering and bawling at each other in the sitting-room.

I threw back the duvet and went tearing into the sitting-room. I was in such a rush I forgot all about the broken floorboard on the landing. My foot went right through it.

At least it stopped them fighting. So I guess it was worth it.

Cat's mum has typed out the whole of my first tape! She must type incredibly fast. About 100mph, I should think.

Phew! I can't imagine how anyone could move their fingers that quick. And no crossings-out, or anything. It's as neat as neat, just like a real book.

I wonder who will publish it? If anyone! I can't think who would be interested in the life story of someone like me. Cat says, "People who have the same sort of problems, that's who."

What does she mean, problems? I don't have problems! Cat seems to think that Mum and Dad are a problem, but they are not. Only when they quarrel, because that is upsetting, but they have promised they will not do it any more.

They *say* they have turned over a new leaf.

It would be nice if they didn't — quarrel, I mean — but I expect they will. It's when things get on top of them and Dad spends all the money and Mum does something daft. But so long as I am there to keep an eye on them they will always, hopefully, kiss and make up.

oh ho ho!

Cat says it must be a great responsibility for me. She says, "It's a very grown up sort of thing to do, Mandy." Well, so maybe I'm a very grown up sort of person! I don't see what's wrong with that. Cat says what's wrong is that I should be enjoying myself and doing all the things that other kids do. *I* say, suppose I don't want to do the things that other kids do? I can still enjoy myself! It's not a problem for me to keep an eye on my mum and dad. It would only be a problem if we stopped being together as a family. But that is why I say my special prayer every night.

When I tell this to Cat she says, "That's what I mean about people who would be interested in reading about you. You're not the only one who worries about their mum and dad getting divorced. I'm afraid it happens all the time."

I said, "I'm not really worried." Not if I go on saying my prayer. My mum and dad couldn't get divorced! How would one of them manage without me?

All the same, it did make me stop and think. Imagine if there are thousands of other people just like me, all worrying — *really* worrying — and saying their prayers. Perhaps they would read my book and think, "Oh, that girl is just like me. I know just how she feels." And it would be a comfort to them to know that they are not the only ones. That is what Cat says.

So maybe somebody *will* publish it, after all! And then I will be famous and make lots of money, which I will give to Mum and Dad so that we can move to a proper house where the floorboards don't collapse and there is a bathroom all of our own and they will not quarrel any more. That, at least, is my dream. Tracey Bigg will be just so-o-o-o jealous!

Oh! I have just had a thought. Suppose she tries to sue me for that thing that people are always suing the newspapers for? When they say things that aren't true?*

But I am only saying things that *are* true. So sucks to Tracey Bigg!

*Note from Cat's mum: Libel? Yes!

I'm really glad I didn't go on that summer camp. Two weeks with Tracey Bigg! Yeeeeeurgh!!!

Cat asked me the other day if I had any friends at school. I haven't, but who needs them? I've got my mum and dad!

Cat said, "You ought to have friends of your own age, Mandy." I don't see why. I did have a friend, once. She was called Janis and she was really nice. She lived next door and we used to play together. She had to be in a wheelchair 'cos there was something wrong with her legs, and I used to gallop her up and down the street.

One time she fell out, but she didn't mind. She just laughed!

She was ever so sparky, Janis was. Even though she couldn't walk, we still had fun.

Then the Social came and moved her, her and her mum, 'cos they said their accommodation was *sub-standard*, meaning it was like ours, all damp and fungussy and falling to pieces, so now they're on an estate and it's miles away, miles and miles, and I never see her. But she was my friend.

There isn't anyone at school I would want to be friends with. They all think I'm a retard. Tracey Bigg said once that I ought to be in a special unit.

Wait until I've had my book published! Then she'll change her tune.

That'll show her!

Chapter Four

Sunday was one of the best days. We had a really good time on Sunday! A *really* good time. Mum and Dad didn't quarrel once. It was one of those extra special days when just everything goes right.

It started with me and Dad making Mum's breakfast and Dad taking it in to her, all on a tray, all proper, with a tea towel and all.

We did:

Dad said, "Here you are, Moddom! Room service!" Mum sat up in bed in her nightie and went, "Ooh! A Sunday treat!"

Dad said, "We're spoiling you, 'cos we love you. Don't we, Mandy?"

And then, guess what? He went out to the

kitchen and came back with the frying pan, pretending to be Elvis!

He sang Mum's favourite, *Love me Tender*. It made them go all spoony, so I finished off the toast.

After breakfast, we did the washing-up. Together! Me and Dad! Usually Dad won't do the washing-up, he says it's a woman's job. This is because he never had to do it when he was a boy, and why Mum says he's been spoilt. Nan is incredibly old-fashioned. It's  weird because she was around in the Swinging Sixties and so you would think she would be rather swinging herself, but she isn't at all. It would be hard to imagine anyone less swinging than my nan!

I think Grandy might have  been a bit of a swinger, if Nan would have let him.

But Nan keeps a tight rein. That is what Mum says.

Mum says that if she didn't, Grandy would most likely "break out".

But I don't think he could run very far, at his age!

After Dad and I had washed up, I came into my bedroom to do some more tape, leaving Dad in the kitchen surrounded by all his bits and pieces from the D.I.Y. He was going to fix the cabinet at last!

I'd been in here for about ten minutes when there was a knock at the door and Dad peered round. He said, "How much?" I said, "How much for what?" Dad said, "For letting me have a listen! How much'll it take?" I said, "*Da-a-ad,*" and threw one of my pillows at him.

Dad said, "Oh, come on, Mand! None of that prissy missy stuff with me!"

I told him it wasn't prissy, it was PRIVATE. "Like a diary."

"You mean, you can't be bought?" said Dad.

I said, "No, I can't!" and hurled my other pillow at him.

"Spoilsport!" said Dad, as he chucked it back at me.

The next minute I crept over to the door and heard the sound of a drill whizzing in the kitchen, so I knew he'd just been trying it on. All the same, I have found a safe place to keep this tape! This is where I'm keeping it.

I don't think Dad would ever do anything behind my back, but he is *dead* curious to know what I'm saying!

By the time Mum got up to do the dinner, the kitchen cabinet was back on the wall. Mum was ever so pleased! She threw her arms round Dad's neck and gave him the hugest kiss ever.

Dad grinned and said, "Will I get one like that from you, Mandy, when I do your bedroom shelf? Or maybe you'll let me have a listen to that tape, instead…"

Dead curious!

He didn't get around to doing my shelf that afternoon as Mum's friend Deirdre came over with her husband and her baby. The baby's name

443

is Felix. He is really sweet! He has the darlingest smile and these tiny little hands with an amazingly strong grip.

Deirdre said I could hold him if I wanted, so I took him on a guided tour of the room, showing him things and giving them to him to hold, only most of the time he wanted to put them in his mouth!

After we'd been all round the room, I sat with him on my lap, and then I said to Deirdre that I thought maybe his nappy needed changing – it was just this strange feeling that I had! – and so we went into the kitchen and I was right, he'd gone and pooped himself with all the excitement. I suppose to some people it might have seemed a bit yucky and pongy, but he's only a teeny baby, after all, and it is quite natural, so that it didn't bother me one little bit. I even helped Deirdre to change him! When we got back to the sitting-room she said to Mum, "Your Mandy is quite a little mother already."

Mum said, "Yes, I expect she'd like a brother or sister of her own, wouldn't you, Mand?"

Quickly, because *someone* has to be responsible in this family, I said, "Yes, but only when my book is published and I have made a lot of money and we can move into a proper house. I think we ought to wait until then, otherwise where would it sleep?"

Everyone seemed to find this rather amusing, I can't think why, but grown-ups do tend to laugh at the strangest things. Dad said, "Wait until you have a book published? Stone me! We'll be waiting for ever! How do you expect to write a book when you don't ever read any?"

"My tapes," I said. "They're going to be one."

Dad said, "Oh! Your tapes." And then to Deirdre and her husband, whose name is Garry, he said, "She's making these top-secret tapes that I'm not allowed to listen to."

Garry said, "Quite right! How can she slag you off if she knows you're going to be breathing down her neck?"

I said, "I'm not slagging him off! I wouldn't ever slag my dad off." And then I looked at Felix, back in his mum's arms, and I said, "I'm going to have six babies when I grow up."

Everybody laughed – *again* – except Dad, who said, "You're a bit young to be thinking of that sort of thing."

"She can dream," said Garry.

"The only problem is," I said, "finding the right man."

"That's all our problems," said Deirdre.

"Boys are just so *grungy*," I said.

Later in the afternoon we all went down the road to the park, where there was a fair going on. Oliver and his mum were there. Oliver and me waved at each other as we passed. Oliver called out, "Hi, Mandy! I'm having fun!" When we'd gone on a bit Deirdre said, "Who was that strange little chap? He looked like a turnip!"

I said, "That's very unfair to turnips," and everyone laughed, but afterwards I felt mean and wished I hadn't said it. Everyone laughs at Oliver.

Dad had seen a coconut shy. They had all these coconuts wearing politicians' masks and Dad couldn't wait to go and throw things at them!

We were just making our way over there when Garry caught my arm and said, "Hey, look at that, Mand!" and pointed to where there was this notice announcing:

TALENT COMPETITION
chilàren up to
14 years

Mum and Deirdre immediately wanted me to have a go, but I couldn't think what I could do. (I didn't know then that I could put on voices or maybe I'd have been the Queen or someone.)

It was Dad who told me to sing a song. He said, "Go on! What about that one Grandy taught you? One about the dustman?" Garry said, "Yeah! Brilliant!" and he and Dad marched me over to the person that was in charge and got him to write my name down on a list and I just didn't know how to get out of it. I thought perhaps Mum might tell Dad to stop being so daft – I mean *me*, singing! – but she seemed just as keen as he was. She kept saying, "Imagine if you won!"

I was quite nervous when my turn came 'cos lots of the other kids had been really good and nobody had sung a song like Grandy's dustman song. But Deirdre said, "Sock it to 'em, baby!"

and Dad gave me a little push, and before I knew it I was out there, in front of everyone, and this man was introducing me as "Miss Mandy Small, who is going to sing for us."

This is the song that I sang:

"My old man's a dustman
He wears a dustman's hat
He wears cor blimey trousers
And he lives in a council flat.

He looks a proper 'nana
In his great big hobnail boots
He's got such a job to pull them up
He calls them daisy roots."

CLUMP! CLUMP!

And I did this clumping dance to go with it, which made everyone laugh.

I'd never done the dance before. It just, like came to me all of a sudden, and so I did it.

I don't expect it's the sort of song that Cat's mum would approve of* but people clapped and clapped and guess what? I got third prize!!! It was a CD of Oasis, which was a pity in a way as we don't have a CD player but Deirdre does, so I gave it to her to keep for me and she said I could go over and play it whenever I liked. So far I've played it about fifty times!

After the talent competition Oliver came up to us with his mum and said he thought I should have won first prize, not third. He said he was going to tell everyone at school about it only of course he didn't, did he? He forgot. And I couldn't very well go round telling people myself, so Tracey Bigg never got to hear. I'd like to have seen the expression on *her* face if she'd seen me winning a prize!

Anyway, Mum then decided she had to have a go at something so she went to this stall where you had to throw hoops over pegs 'cos there was a teddy bear she was desperate for. She tried and tried, but she couldn't get the hoops anywhere near, so in the end Dad said, "Let me have a go," and he won it for her! A huge great big teddy bear! Mum wanted to give it to me, to make up for the CD that I'd had to give to Deirdre, but

*Note from Cat's mum: Nonsense! It's great fun.

Dad wouldn't let her. He said, "No way, Sand!" He sounded quite hurt about it. He said, "I got it for *you*." So Mum kept it and now it sits on her pillow and she calls it Dumpling. I don't mind about not having it. I'm too old for teddy bears!

We stayed in the park till nearly eight o'clock. We ate burgers and fries and iced donuts, and Garry bought me candy floss, and I saw a girl from school and wondered if she'd heard me singing in the talent competition (which she obviously hadn't or if she had she never mentioned it). Altogether it was a lovely, lovely day and one that I shall remember for ever. When I am old and grey like Nan I will still be telling my grandchildren about it, about me winning third prize and singing *My Old Man's a Dustman*. And maybe I will croak my way through it and do the little dance and they will look at me and think, "Poor old Nan! She's past it." But I won't care! 'Cos I will still have the memory.

When we got home, Deirdre and Garry came in for a cup of coffee and we all sat and watched the telly and I was allowed to stay up till almost midnight. This is something my nan thinks is terrible, a child being allowed to stay up. But Mum and Dad always let me, if anything exciting is going on. They don't really mind what time I go to bed. Dad says, "She's not stupid. She'll go when she's tired." And I do, as a rule, but that night I was having too good a time!

Deirdre wanted to see the floorboard before she left. She knew about it 'cos of my black eye. She said, "You'd better show me. I don't want to go falling through it." But Dad told her it was all right, it was further along the landing, and anyway he'd roped it off.

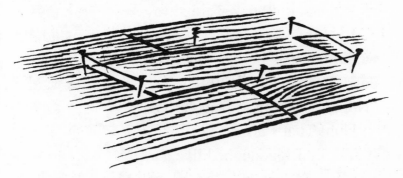

We all stood, gazing at the floorboard.
"Oh, that's really classy, that is," said Garry.
Poor Dad looked quite crestfallen!

Next day was Monday. Ugh! I hate Mondays. Mondays mean *school*.

It was the last week before the summer holidays and I begged and begged Mum to let me stay at home. I looked such a sight!

How could I tell Miss Foster I'd fallen through a floorboard? I'd just be so embarrassed! She'd already heard about the kitchen cabinet falling on me and the banisters breaking. Miss Foster doesn't understand about old houses. She lives in a modern flat. She doesn't realise that old houses are always a bit crumbly.

But anyway I had to go 'cos Mum said it would be breaking the law if I didn't and Mum's dead scared of breaking the law. She said, "Nobody's going to laugh at you."

Huh! That's all she knew.

Tracey Bigg laughed like a *drain*.

Miss Foster said, "Dear me, Mandy! In the wars again? What happened this time?" I told her that I'd fallen down the stairs, and old Tracey, she pulls this face, as if to say, "She would!" and afterwards, when I go into the playground, she's waiting for me with her gang and she's made up another of her stupid rhymes.

She needn't think *I* care.

I've been thinking what sort of house we'll buy when my book is published and we have lots of money.

It's got to be a real house, not just rooms in someone else's. And it's got to have a garden, so that I can grow flowers.

This is the sort of house I think we'll have.

And it won't be in London! It will be somewhere nice, like Croydon. My Uncle Allan and Auntie Liz live in Croydon. They live in Linden Close, and it's really beautiful.

Uncle Allan is Dad's brother. He has done well

for himself, my nan says. He is a manager in Sainsbury's, and that, I think, pays more money than being a window cleaner. But I bet my dad could be a manager in Sainsbury's if he wanted! He just doesn't want, that's all.

When we have our house it will be like Uncle Allan's, in a nice road that is all quiet, with trees and grass. And it will have a name, such as Sky View or The Laurels or Mandalay. Mandalay, I think, is pretty. There is a house near us called Mandalay. When I was little I used to think it said Mandy!

We will definitely have a house; it is the first thing we will get.

Another thing we will have is a car. Everybody has a car. Even Deirdre and Garry have one, though it is what Dad calls a banger, meaning it is clapped out and you can hear it coming from streets away.

We will have a better car than that! A little one because they are sweet, and also they would not use so much petrol.

We are the only people I know who don't have a car (apart from Misery Guts, but she is too old). It is all right for Tracey Bigg going on about the ecology and how cars are poisoning the planet, but her mum has a *whacking* great huge one which she comes and picks her up in after school. It is a real gas guzzler.

Our little baby car will only need a tiny drop.

Anyway, I can't say I've ever noticed Tracey walking home to save the planet being poisoned. She jumps into the car quick enough. She's all mouth, that girl is.

I have made up a rhyme about *her*.

Tracey Bigg goes "Wah-wah-wah"
When she talks it's all blah-blah
She's a stupid steaming nit
Posho loudmouth bighead twit.

If I knew how to spell it I'd chalk it up on one of the lavatory walls.

I will know how to spell it when Cat's mum has typed it out. Ho ho! You just watch it, Tracey Bigg!

Chapter Five

Hi! It's me again. Back on line, doing my life story. I've been working on it for ages, now. Ever since Cat first suggested it, which was way back months ago.

I aim to finish it pretty soon. I asked Cat when she wanted it done by, and she said, "Well, just as soon as you can manage." What she means is, I should get it all down before I go completely fruit and nutty.

I *will* be fruit and nutty, before very long. Just as I think I've got my mum and dad sorted, they go and do something else totally mad and daft and irresponsible. It's like they are both completely *off the wall*.

I hoped after I fell through the floorboard we'd have a bit of peace and quiet in the Small household. I mean, the hot water heater had already blown up, so that couldn't happen again. The floorboard had been roped off, and so had the banisters; I just couldn't see what else there was that could go wrong. But trust my mum and dad! They'll always find something.

First thing that happens, Dad gets out of bed in the early hours of the morning and forgets about the floorboard and goes and treads on one of the nails he's knocked in to stop people falling through. He doesn't half yell!

He yells so loud that even Mum wakes up. Her and me come rushing out, and a door opens somewhere down below and old Misery Guts starts shrieking up the stairs.

Dad's got this big hole in his foot and he's in agony, dancing up and down. Mum bathes it for him but we haven't got any Dettol, only household cleaner, and he won't let her use that. I say what about if I go down to the garden and get some mud, 'cos I've heard that if you put mud on to wounds it helps them heal, but he won't let me do that, either.

He bawls, "What's your game? For crying out loud! I could lose my leg!"

Misery Guts then joins in with "Mr-Small-do-you-mind-I-am-trying-to-get-some-sleep!" to which Dad shouts  something a bit rude and goes limping back to bed, and I lie awake all the rest of the night wondering what we'd do if he really lost his leg and thinking that I've got to finish this book, quick, and get some money in case he can't clean windows any more.

So that's the first crazy thing that happens. The second thing is that I meet Mum at Bunjy's after school and she's dead set on going off to buy some paint that will glow in the dark so's we can paint the floorboard and Dad won't be able to tread on it by mistake any more. So we get this paint, it's bright yellow, and we go rushing home with it all happy, and we have a cup of tea and a bit of a watch of the telly, 'cos there's this programme Mum really likes called *Carrot Tops* (it's for kids, really. But it is quite funny). Then Mum sends me down the road for some fish and chips while she gets on and paints the floorboard.

When I come back Mum's yanked out all Dad's nails and the floorboard's gleaming bright yellow like a fried egg yolk. It hits you the minute you get to the top of the stairs. It kind of YELLS at you.

"Nobody could miss seeing *that*," says Mum, proudly.

But guess what?

You've got it! Dad misses it.

Actually, he goes and puts his foot right in it.

So now we have yellow blobs all along the landing.

My family!

Next thing I know it's morning and I have to go to school again, and I've still got my black eye and Tracey Bigg's still doing her stupid song and dance act, but I don't take any notice. Oliver's in the corner of the playground crying 'cos Billy

Murdo's gang's duffed him up, so I go over and talk to him and try to put a bit of stuffing into him.

I say, "What's the problem?" and he goes, "*Blub – hic – sniffle* – Billy – *blub – hic* – hurt – *sniffle* – me." I feel sorry for him 'cos he's ever so harmless and they just pick on him all the time. They *torment* him. They're real bullies. There just isn't any way poor old Oliver can get back at them. He's just not that sort of person. I mean, if Tracey Bigg and her mob tried to duff me up I'd give them what for, I can tell you. I'd knee them and crunch them and use Kung Fu like on the telly.

I certainly wouldn't go into a corner and blub. But Oliver is ever so pathetic and weedy. I guess he just can't help it.

People that beat up on weeds are despicable.

It's the last day of term and tomorrow everyone except me and Oliver and a couple of others are going off to summer camp so for a treat Cat takes me and Oliver on a special trip, just the two of us.

We get on the tube and go to Mile End, where there's this museum that's a real old Victorian school. Cat says, "It'll show you what it would have been like to be Victorian children."

Oliver and me look at each other and giggle. I don't quite know why we giggle. Maybe it's just the excitement of being out of school, on our own, with Cat. If it was an ordinary school trip I'd be expecting to be a bit bored. I mean, a *museum*. All full of dead stuff, and things from the past. I'm not interested in the past! But as we're with Cat I think maybe it might be fun, 'cos I can't imagine Cat ever doing anything that's boring.

Oliver says to me, "When's Victorian?" and I'm not sure. I say, "Oh! About… a hundred years ago." And I'm right! Cat says that Queen Victoria died in 1901. I know more history than I thought!

The museum isn't a bit like I think it's going to be. I think it's going to be very large and gloomy with glass cases full of dead stuff, but all it is, it's just this old grungy building with nothing in it, except when you go up the stairs you suddenly find yourself in a schoolroom, with all desks and benches, just like it would have been in Victorian times. There's even a teacher, wearing a white frilly blouse and a long black skirt with her hair pulled into a bun. She's standing at a blackboard with this long stick that Cat says is called a pointer.

There's other children there besides us. They're all sitting down, waiting for the class to begin, so me and Oliver sit at the back, next to each other, in this funny sort of desk that's like two desks joined together.

It's really ancient, you can tell. The wood's all worn and stained, and there's loads of names and initials carved into the top.

Cat whispers, "Imagine! Some of these were done by children over a hundred years ago."

It makes me feel a bit shivery when I think about a girl the same age as me sitting where I'm sitting, resting her elbows on the desk lid just like I am, *a hundred years ago*. She'd have sat there never guessing that one day I'd be in her seat, trying to picture what she was like. I look at the names and initials and think that she could have been Eliza, or Jane, or "SW" or Grace. She'd be dead by now, of course. She'd have had her life. I've still got all mine to come!

I think it's good, sometimes, to remember about people from the past and wonder what they would have been like. The answer is – just the same as us, only different!

Not different *inside* themselves; just outside. I expect Eliza or Jane or whatever she was called would have understood about Tracey Bigg and how she gets on my nerves. She might even have had her own Tracey Bigg. Except she probably wouldn't have been called Tracey, because I don't think people were. Not in those days. She'd have been called... Henrietta. Henrietta Bigg! And Eliza Small. And they'd have made up rude and revolting rhymes about each other just like me and Tracey.

Well, that's what I like to imagine.

When everyone's sitting at their desks, the teacher announces that the first lesson is going to begin. Oliver looks at me, and I can see that he's a bit apprehensive. Oliver's not very good at lessons. Nor am I, usually, but today, surprise surprise, I turn out to be THE STAR!

The first lesson's arithmetic. We all have to sit with straight backs and chant our tables, right through to twelve.

I know them all! And my voice is the L.O.U.D.E.S.T!

The next lesson is writing, with pen and ink. The old desks have inkwells with real ink in them, and the teacher gives us all a wooden pen with a funny scratchy nib and a sheet of something called blotting paper. The blotting paper's thick and white and it blots the ink so's it doesn't smudge.

The teacher writes the letters of the alphabet on the board in beautiful curly shapes and we all have to copy them. Cat says the shapes are "copperplate" and they're the way Victorian children had to write.

The idea is to do them without any splotches or mess. I do mine really well! Not a single splotch! When we've copied all the letters off the board we have to write our names in the same sort of writing. This is mine:

Mandy Small

The teacher says mine is the best! She even hands it round for people to look at. And then she gives me a gold star and writes 10/10 in red ink. So I feel really pleased and think that things are looking up, what with me winning a prize in the talent competition and now getting a gold star for writing my name in copperplate. It's a pity Oliver can't get one, too, but his copperplate is all blotched and drippy.

O.liver.

Cat says it doesn't matter. She says the idea was that we should enjoy ourselves, and in any case I don't think Oliver really minds all that much. When Cat asks him if he's had a good time he gives her this big goofy grin and says yes, he'd like to go to a Victorian school every day "and sit next to Mandy in a big desk".

He's so funny, Oliver is. I quite like him really, I suppose. He can't help being a weed.

When we get back to school Cat says she's got something for me, and it's all the pages of my life story that her mum has typed out! She gets me to read bits of it and I'm really surprised at some of the long words I'd used. Without even realising!

The only trouble is, some of them are so long I can't read them. Imagine! Not being able to read your own life story!

I'm really worried about this. I ask Cat if she thinks I'm that *word*. The one her mum said. *Dys-*something. The one that means you get your letters muddled up. But Cat says she doesn't think I am. She says, "Just a bit slow at getting the hang of it." Before I can stop myself I say, "Just a bit *slow*." Cat gets really cross. She does what my nan calls "bristling".

She says, "No, I do *not* mean 'just a bit slow'. You're a bright girl, Mandy. Why do you keep putting yourself down all the time?"

I tell her that I don't *all* of the time. Just some of the time. And I don't want to grow up with everyone still sneering and jeering at me 'cos I can't read!

Cat promises me that this won't happen. She tells me about her brother, who was just like me when he was my age, but one day, quite suddenly, bingo! He discovered he could do it.

"And now he's at college, training to be a teacher."

I don't mean to be rude but I can't help pulling a

face when she says this 'cos a teacher is just about the last thing I'd want to be. Imagine having to teach someone like Tracey Bigg! So Cat asks me what I'd like to be, and I say maybe an actress or someone that does funny voices and makes people laugh. And then I tell her that what I'd really like would be to go to an acting school, if only I had the money. I say, "Maybe after my book's published I will have. Maybe it will make my fortune."

Cat looks a bit anxious when I say this. She explains to me that it is not easy for anyone to get a book published. She says, "It will still be a wonderful achievement whether it's published or not. But I don't want to give you false hopes. I'd hate you to be disappointed."

I won't be disappointed! I can tell the difference between what's real and what's just pretend. It's a game I play. "When my book is published." I know it won't be *really*. Probably not. But I can dream, can't I?

After school's broken up and we've all been set free I go and meet Mum from Bunjy's and show her my copperplate. Mum says the copperplate is beautiful. And then she looks at the blotting paper, which the teacher said I could bring with me, and she takes out her mirror and shows me how you can read the writing that's on it.

Mandy Small (mirror writing)

Like a secret code!

When we get home old Misery's on the prowl. She's found a dob of yellow paint on the hall floor and she wants to know how it got there. Mum says, "Oh, dear, it must have dropped off the brush when I leaned over the banisters," and old Misery does her bits and pieces.

What's her problem??? We've got *loads* of dobs on the upstairs landing! Brightens the place up, if you ask me.

So we get upstairs and go into the kitchen to make a cup of tea, and you'll never believe it, the kitchen cabinet's fallen off the wall again and half the cups and saucers are smashed.

Oh, and the telephone's been cut off. It turns out it's been cut off for days and we never even realised.

As Mum says, trying to look on the bright side, "It just goes to show how much we need it."

This is the story of my life. Tape no 2. To be continued...

Soon I'm going to have filled up another tape. That will be the third one! I can't believe I've found so much to say. I thought at first my life was completely empty, but now I see that quite a lot of things have been going on in it. It's only when you stop and think about it that you realise.

Something I haven't said anything about is when I was little. This is partly because I can't remember very much and partly because I think probably it would be quite boring. I don't want my book to be boring! This is the trouble with some of the books that Miss Foster reads to us at school. Right at the beginning they're a drag because you don't know what's happening or who the people are; and then just as you're starting to get into the story and thinking maybe this book is not so bad after all, you come to another draggy bit that makes you yawn and fidget and feel you never want to go near a book again *ever*, as long as you live.

I am trying very hard not to have draggy bits. That's why I've started my story when I'm old enough to talk and have opinions, and haven't bothered going back to babyhood. Babies are lovely but not very interesting in books, I don't think. What babies are best at is *doing* things.

crawling   kicking

smiling   playing   crying

cuddling

I expect I must have done all those things when I was a baby, but who wants to read about it? Not me!

So all I'm going to say is that I was born in the hospital and that for the first few years of my life we lived with Nan and Grandy in Soper Street, which is just round the corner from where we are now. I don't think Mum liked living with Nan. Nan used to nag her and tell her what to do and what not to do, like for instance whenever I cried she would tell

Mum "Not to go running! Let her get on with it."
But my mum is a big softie. She couldn't bear the
thought of me lying there crying so she didn't
take any notice of Nan. She used to cuddle me all
the time. I think this is right. When I have triplets
— two lots! — I will cuddle them. You bet!

Cuddling is what babies are for.

When I was about three, Nan and Grandy's
house was knocked down. The whole street was
knocked down and all the people, well, most of
the people, were sent to live on this new estate
way out at the end of the tube line. It's called
Arthur's Mill, because once upon a time, before
they went and built houses all over it, it was
owned by a man called Arthur who had a farm

and a windmill. It sounds lovely but in fact it is rather ugly and boring.

Nan likes it because she says it's a step up. From Soper Street, I suppose she means. She reckons it's dead superior, living on a new estate! But it is *grey* and *dreary* and it is UGLY. Not like Linden Close!

Anyway, Mum and Dad came to live in Bundy Street and that is where we have been ever since. And I have been at the same school, which is Spring Street Primary. And that is the story of my life up to the time I started writing this book!

Oh, I almost forgot: when I was five I had the chicken pox and got all covered in spots

some of which I *picked*.

Also there is a photograph of me with my front teeth missing.

Thank goodness I grew some new ones!

Chapter Six

I can't remember where I left off. I think it was the end of term, the day we broke up.

Yes, it was! I've just gone back and listened.

Everyone except me and Oliver had gone off to camp and I was stuck in London. Not that I'd have wanted to go to their rotten camp even if I could. Crammed in a barn with Tracey Bigg for two weeks? Ugh! No, thank you!

Just because it was school holidays didn't mean Mum could stay off work. She still had to go into Bunjy's and sell bread every day, like Dad still had to clean windows.

We discussed what to do about me, and I said that I'd be all right on my own. I don't mind being on my own! I quite like it, as a matter of fact. The one thing I begged Mum not to do was send me to my nan's.

I said, "*Please*, Mum! Please don't make me go away!"

I mean, partly it was 'cos I didn't want to leave Mum and Dad. I just didn't see how they would be able to manage without me. And partly it was 'cos I really really *hate* going to Nan's. I hate the way she picks on me and the way she grumbles all the time about Mum and Dad being rotten parents.

There was only one place I would have liked to go, and that was Croydon, to stay with Uncle Allan and Auntie Liz, but they wouldn't have me any more. I went there once and it was ever so lovely, only something really terrible happened: Auntie Liz sent me home in disgrace. I'd only been there a couple of weeks and she said she didn't want me in the house any more on account of my language. "Language of the gutter," she called it. She said, "We got out of London to avoid all that. I don't want my little Princess being contaminated."

Mum was really hurt and I felt ever so ashamed. *I* didn't know I spoke the language of the gutter. Dad just laughed. He said that Allan and Liz had become "proper toffee-nosed twits" since they'd moved to Croydon.

But when I stopped and thought about it I could see what Auntie Liz meant 'cos it's really

really nice in Linden Close, where they live. There's no mess or rubbish or burnt-out cars. There's no rude words sprayed on the walls. Nobody has punch-ups or gets drunk.

"Dead boring," says my dad. But I don't think it's boring! I think it's lovely. And I can understand why Auntie Liz doesn't want me to contaminate her little Princess.

The little Princess is my cousin Jade. I wish I had a beautiful name like Jade! It's a pity her surname is Small, as Jade Small doesn't sound very good, but maybe when she grows up she will marry a man called something grand such as Fairfax or Winstanley. These, I think, are very aristocratic.

Jade *will* probably marry someone aristocratic as she is extremely pretty, with dark curly hair and bright blue eyes. She is only four at the moment but already I can imagine how she will be when she is grown up.

I know it sounds truly yucky her mum and dad

Jade

Jade grown up

calling her their little Princess, but she is so beautiful that I can forgive them. Normally I wouldn't! Normally I would make vomiting noises.

But Jade is special, and everyone adores her.

I wish I hadn't upset Auntie Liz by using bad language! I mean, it was just, like, stuff we say all the time in the playground. The sort of stuff you don't even think about. But Auntie Liz moved to Croydon to get away from all that.

Blurp Blurp Blurp

I wish she'd give me a second chance! But I don't think she will. Whenever she takes Jade to visit Nan and Grandy she always checks first that I'm not going to be there. She calls me "that child". I've heard her. I was at Nan's once and she rang up and I could hear her voice on the telephone. She said, "We'd like to come and see you next Sunday, Mum, but I wouldn't want to bring Jade if that child was going to be there."

Nan says she's quite right. She thinks I'm a real bad influence. Maybe when my book is published and I've made a lot of money and we can live in a nice house they will change their minds. I do hope so because I really love Jade! She is so funny and clever and sweet, and she's my only cousin in the whole wide world. I would be miserable if they never let me see her again.

But at the moment they don't want me anywhere near her in case I suddenly without thinking say something crude and vulgar, so Mum knew it wouldn't be any use asking if I could go to Croydon to stay. (Dad said he wouldn't let me in any case. "After they insulted us? No way! My Mand's worth a dozen of that little ponced-up miss." My dad always sticks up for me.)

I told Mum that I would be just fine on my own. I said, "I've been on my own before and I didn't burn the house down." Mum is more likely to burn the house down than I am!

Mum said, "Yes, but that was only for a few days."

See, it wasn't as if she just didn't bother. It wasn't like she just walked out and left me. She was really worried. She said, "You'll be here every day, all by yourself. What will you find to do all the time?"

I said that I would get on with my recording

for Cat, and do some wall painting, and clean the flat and do the shopping and the ironing and lay the table ready for Dad's tea.

"And on Saturdays we can have fun 'cos there won't be any work for you to do… I'll have done it all!"

Mum liked that idea. She got quite excited and started planning all the things we could do on Saturday afternoons as a family. She said, "We'll all go to places together. Think of some places where you'd like to go!"

So I made a list, which I have lost now, but these are some of the things that were on it:

• London Dungeon

• The Waxworks

• The Zoo

• Chessington World of Adventure

• Burger King

• Covent Garden

I put Covent Garden because I once heard Tracey Bigg telling Aimee and Leanne that there was some street theatre there and it was fun. She'd seen people walking on stilts! I'd love to walk on stilts. I bet I could, too! I bet I'd be really good at it. I can already walk on my hands and do cartwheels.

Tracey Bigg can't. She tried in the playground and just went flump.

I was really looking forward to doing things as a family, and so was Mum. I don't expect, really, that we'd have been able to afford to do everything that was on my list, but we could have done *some* of them. We could have gone to Covent Garden to see the people on stilts, and we could have had a burger. And then maybe we'd have made a picnic and gone on the tube somewhere to eat it. Somewhere nice and green, like… like the park, or somewhere. We might even have looked at houses all day and chosen which one we'd like to buy when my book is published.

Whatever we would have done, it would have been fun. But the very first day of the holiday, it all went and got ruined.

I was really happy that day! I spent all morning doing wall painting, and then I opened a tin of tomato soup and put a packet of crisps in it (yum yum! Two of my favourites), and then I did a bit of recording, and then I thought perhaps I ought to do some housework, as I'd promised Mum, so I went and got the plastic sacks where she keeps the ironing and I was just setting up the ironing board when there's this ring at the door bell, which makes me jump, 'cos nobody ever rings at our door bell, hardly. And the ironing board goes and folds itself up on one of my fingers and makes me yell.

There's something wrong with the ironing board. Mum bought it second-hand at a boot sale and it's always collapsing. Dad's supposed to have looked at it, but he never has. Anyway, I don't expect he could do anything.

I went kind of slowly down the stairs, sucking at my finger 'cos it really hurt, and old Misery's peering out, all nosey parkering same as usual. She goes, "Who is it? Who are you expecting?" And then she tells me not to take the chain off 'cos it could be a mugger. She's always going on about muggers. She thinks there's a mugger hiding behind every dustbin.

Anyway, I kept the chain on, just to make her happy; I wasn't really expecting it to be a mugger. Afterwards I wished it had been. 'Cos what it was, it was even worse. It was my nan.

She said, "Oh, so you're here! I've been trying to ring you all week."

I explained that the telephone wasn't working, and she said, "You mean it's been cut off, I suppose," and made this cross tutting sound with her tongue. I said, "It wasn't their fault, they forgot to pay the bill. I should have reminded them. They have ever so many things to think about."

Nan said, "Rubbish! They're totally useless, the pair of them." And then she said, "Well! Aren't you going to let me in?"

So I let her in and we went upstairs and she said how she'd been going to ask old Misery Guts what had happened to us.

"I thought you'd all been murdered in your beds or your mother had finally managed to set fire to the place. Either that, or you'd been thrown out. Where is your mother, anyway?"

I said that Mum was at work and Nan nearly hit the roof.

"You mean she's left you here on your own?"

I said, "I'm old enough!" I wasn't going to have Nan slagging my mum off.

Nan said, "Don't be absurd, you're nowhere near old enough. A child of your age!"

I really resented that. I told Nan that in some countries there were people far younger than me out on the streets having to look after themselves. Nan said that didn't make it right and that Mum ought to be ashamed of herself. She said, "It's an absolute disgrace!"

I said, "Why pick on Mum?" It wasn't that I wanted to get my dad into trouble, but I didn't think it was fair, only having a go at Mum.

Nan said, "They're both as bad as each other. And where did you get that black eye?"

I didn't like to tell her I'd gone through the floorboard. She'd only have started on again about Mum and Dad being useless. I said, "I fell over in the playground." Nan made this snorting noise down her nose and said, "Fighting, I suppose."

Indignantly I told her that I didn't fight. "People pick on me."

"Oh, yes?" said Nan. "And what in heaven's name has been going on in here?"

She'd barged her way past me, into the kitchen. I have to admit, it did look a bit of a mess.

I started to explain that I hadn't yet got around to tidying up when there was yet another ring at the front door bell. I couldn't believe it! Twice in one day!

I said, "I'll go!" and went galloping back down the stairs.

Old Misery yelped, "You keep that chain on!" but this time I didn't 'cos I was just about sick of old Misery Guts and the way she kept poking her nose in where it wasn't wanted.

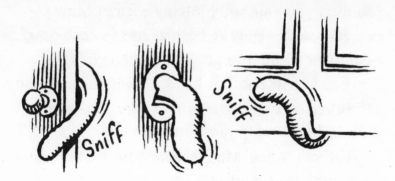

I thought that if it was a mugger I would ask him in and first he could mug Misery Guts and then he could go upstairs and mug my nan. I wouldn't let him mug me, I'd kung fu him!

But I reckoned he'd probably have done enough mugging by then. Anyway, it wasn't a mugger, it was Mum. She giggled and said, "Good thing you're here! I forgot my key." I said,  "Mum," trying to warn her, but she was in one of her bubbly moods and didn't listen. She set off up the stairs, burbling as she went.

"Eh, Mandy, guess what? Guess what old

Sourpuss gave me? A birthday cake! It was for this woman that never come to collect it, so she reckoned I might as well have it. It's got 'Happy Birthday Barny' on it, so I thought what we could do, we could change Barny into Barry and give it your dad and—"

That was when Mum reached the top of the stairs and bumped into Nan.

She said, "Oh! H–hello, Mum." Nan said, "Why has this child been left on her own all day? It's a disgrace!"

And then old Misery Guts' voice came shrieking up the stairs: "That's not the only thing that is!"

"What's she on about?" said Nan. She peered over the banisters and called down. "Who pulled your chain?"

"Ask them, ask them!" yelled Misery Guts. "Rowing and carrying on at all hours! They're not fit to have a child!"

"You just keep your lid on!" shouted Nan. "We don't need you shoving your oar in!"

"She's always having a go at us," said Mum.

"Yes, and not without cause, I'd say." Nan turned to go stomping back into the kitchen. "What's all this?" she said. She'd suddenly noticed the yellow blodges and the fried egg. I said it was paint, and Nan said she could see that, thank you very much.

"What's it doing there?"

So then I had to explain about the floorboard, and Mum told her about the water heater and how the landlord wouldn't do anything, and how the banisters had broken, and the kitchen cabinet wouldn't stay on the wall, and there were holes in the lino and the roof leaked and the whole place was just a tip; and Nan listened to it all with her face growing grimmer and grimmer.

"It's a death trap," said Mum.

"Yes," said Nan, "and you go waltzing off to work and leave this child to cope on her own."

"I can cope!" I said. "And Mum has to go to work 'cos we couldn't pay the bills otherwise."

"Don't you talk to me about paying bills!" snapped Nan; and I knew that I'd gone and said the wrong thing. "Look at this child!" said Nan. "Look at the state of her!"

"It was the floorboard," pleaded Mum.

"What was the floorboard?"

"How she got the black eye!"

"*Oh*?" Nan swung round on me. "What d'you want to go telling me lies for?"

"My Mandy doesn't tell lies!" cried Mum.

"I cannot believe—" Nan's bosoms sort of heaved upwards "— I cannot believe that it has come to this!"

"To w–what?" stammered Mum.

"*This*!" Nan flung out her arms. "I'm sorry, Sandra, but it cannot be allowed to go on. I am not having a grandchild of mine left all day and every day in this – this rubbish dump! That interfering old busybody downstairs is quite right. You're not fit to be parents. Either of you!"

"Mum and Dad can't help it," I said. "It's not their fault the house is falling to pieces, it's—"

"Amanda, will you please BE QUIET!" roared Nan.

My name isn't Amanda. It's Mandy.

"Just go to your room," said Nan. "I want a word in private with your mother."

She took Mum into the sitting-room and slammed the door, and I crept up and tried to listen but I couldn't hear very much, only the sound of Mum crying. And then the door opened and Mum came out and went running straight past me, all blotched and tear-stained, and Nan sailed after, looking like one of those things they have on churches that the water spouts out of.*

Really cross and horrible.

She said, "Right, that's settled. Go and get your bags packed. You're coming to live with me."

Not just stay with her.

Live with her.

It was my worst nightmare come true.

I don't really want to tell this next bit.

I'd rather tell something else.

Like, for instance... the day I went to my friend

*Note from Cat's mum: They're called gargoyles.

Janis's school sports and they had a PHAB race*
and Janis was in her wheel chair and I was
pushing her and we won first prize and had our
pictures in the paper.

That was great, that was! I'd much rather talk
about that than all about what happened next in
my life.

I mean, I don't *have* to talk about what
happened next. If I really don't want to. Nobody
can make me.

Except then perhaps they wouldn't publish it.
They would say, this girl is so boring, she is so
happy all the time with her mum and dad. Why
does nothing bad ever happen to her?

So I suppose I had better do it.

I suppose.

All right! I'll do it.

I shall take a

D
E
E
P
             breath
and open my mouth
            and just
                talk.

*Query from Cat's mum: Does this stand for physically
handicapped-able-bodied? **Yes!**

Chapter Seven

When Nan said I was to go and live with her, my heart just fell right down with a great thunk! on to the floor. I knew it wasn't any use arguing. You can't argue with Nan. Once she's made up her mind, that's it.

But it was awful. It was really awful. Nan was all puckered and pursed, and Mum was just sobbing and sobbing, and then Dad comes home and says, "What's going on?" and Nan tells him what's happened, and how she's taking me away "Until you two get your act together", and Dad just goes mental. I mean, he just goes crashing and banging all about the place, and he's smashing his fist on things and shouting, and Misery Guts is howling up the stairs, and Mum's still sobbing, and Nan's trying to get Dad to calm down and "Listen to a bit of sense, for goodness' sake!" But Dad won't. Not for ages.

When at last he stops crashing and shouting,

he grabs me and pulls me to him and says, "You can't do this! You can't take my Mand!"

To which Nan retorts that if she doesn't take me it's only a matter of time before someone like old Misery Guts calls the Social Services.

"And once they get their hands on her, you can kiss her goodbye. She'll be sent to a children's home or put with foster parents, and that'll be that. And I wouldn't blame them, either! This way, I'm giving you a chance. You get yourselves sorted, I might consider letting you have her back. But I'm not having my grandchild brought up in a pigsty just because her mum and dad are too stupid and irresponsible to look after her properly. So there!"

There was a long silence after Nan said this. Dad went pale and even Mum stopped sobbing. Nan said, "Look at the place! Look at the state of it! You're like children, the pair of you. Just playing at keeping house. Look at this!" She ran a finger along the top of the mantelpiece. "*Filth*!"

I said, "I was going to see to that," but Nan turned on me, really sharp, and snapped, "It's not up to you!" And Dad chimed in with, "That's right.

It's not up to Mandy. It's up to her mum!" He glared at Mum as he said it, and that set Mum off crying again, and to my complete amazement Nan snarled, "Don't you try shifting all the blame on to Sandra! You're no better. Useless great lummock!"

I'd never known Nan turn on Dad before. It's always been Mum she's had a go at. But she was really mad. She kept on about "the Social" and how the shame of it would kill her. She said, "You'd just better pull your fingers out, the pair of you! Get this place cleaned up and start taking a few lessons in elementary house-keeping!"

Dad looked rebellious and started muttering, but Mum wept and said, "We will, we will!"

"Both of you," said Nan. "That means you, lummock!"

And she actually poked a finger right in the middle of Dad's chest.

Dad's jaw dropped way, way down.

I almost would have laughed, it looked so funny! But Mum was still sobbing, and there was my bag standing all packed and ready to go.

And any minute now Nan was going to say, "Right! That's it. Come along, Mandy," and I just couldn't bear it. I felt something hot and prickly happening in my eyes, and at first I couldn't imagine what it was but then it was like seeing everything through a window that rain is dripping down and I knew that I was crying.

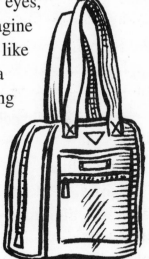

But I don't cry! Not *ever*. I didn't even cry when the kitchen cabinet fell on me and cut my head open. Not even when I had to have stitches. Not even when Tracey Bigg makes up her horrid rhymes about me.

Crying is a sign of weakness. I didn't want to

cry! Nan said, "Come on, then, child. Let's get going," and I raced over to Mum and threw my arms around her and whispered, "I'll be back, Mum! Don't forget to make out shopping lists." If Mum doesn't make out shopping lists, she can't remember what she needs to buy. "And give Dad proper meals, Mum! 'Cos he needs them."

And then I raced over to Dad and hugged *him*, and begged him to be kind to Mum and not fly off the handle.

"Please, Dad! Don't get cross with Mum. I hate it when you do that!"

Next thing I know I'm being pushed down the stairs in front of Nan, and old Misery's there spying as usual, but for once she doesn't say anything, and we're out on the pavement and the front door's shut behind us and all I can think of is Mum sobbing and Dad going round bashing things.

Nan said, "It's the only way. They've got to learn. It's high time they grew up and started to behave like responsible adults."

But I loved my mum and dad just the way they were! I didn't want them to be any different. I hated Nan for taking me away from them. I felt that it was my fault. I felt like I'd let them down.

If only I'd tidied up the place before Nan had come! I could have made it look ever so nice. Really spick and span. Then maybe she wouldn't have got so mad. And I could have told her I wasn't really on my own, I could have told her old Misery was keeping an eye on me, or that I'd been over to Deirdre's, or just *anything*. Anything that would have stopped her having a go at Mum.

That first night when I said my special prayer, I added a bit at the end. After "For ever and ever" ten times, but before "Amen", I added, "And please let me go back to them soon. PLEASE!"

I just couldn't see how they were going to manage without me to keep an eye on them. I kept having these nightmares that Mum would do something daft and ruin Dad's tea and Dad would rise up in a rage and say that that was it, he'd had enough. And then he'd walk out and Mum would be on her own and she wouldn't know what to do, and she'd be so lonely, poor Mum! 'Cos we're the only people she's got in the whole world, me and Dad. And Dad would jump on a ship and go to Australia, which was what he was always threatening to do, and I wouldn't ever see him again.

I wasn't going to see them again for ages and ages, anyway. Nan had said she wanted them both to stay away until they had got themselves sorted. She said, "I want this girl given a fair chance. I don't want you coming round and upsetting her."

And Mum and Dad were ever so meek. They just did whatever Nan told them. She'd gone and scared them by saying how old Misery could go to the Social Services. Even Dad's scared of the Social Services, even if he does call them snooping do-gooders.

That first week at Nan's I said my prayer over and over, not just when I went to bed but when I woke up in the morning and lots of times in the day, as well. Once I was doing it, with my eyes screwed tight shut, when Nan started to say something to me. But I still went on doing it! Nan got angry and said why didn't I listen when she spoke to me? She said, "Are you sulking about something?"

I said, "No. I was thinking." Nan said, "Well, you just stop thinking and pay a bit of attention! It's very rude to go on thinking when someone's talking to you."

I could have told her it was rude to interrupt a person when they had their eyes closed, but you can't argue with Nan. She always likes to have the last word.

Grandy isn't so bad, but he is what Mum calls "under Nan's thumb".

He just likes to come home at tea-time and light his pipe and have a quiet life. During the day he is on guard in a bank, wearing a uniform and keeping an eye open for armed robbers. It is a great responsibility, guarding all that money, and I think Nan ought to let him rest when he comes in instead of keeping on at him the way she does.

What she mostly keeps on about is *me*. At least, that's what she kept on about while I was there. All about my manners and my language and how I hadn't got any decent clothes and look at my hair, it was just a mess, and "How am I supposed to take her anywhere?"

And Grandy just sat there and grunted, and puffed on his pipe, and you could tell he didn't really want to be bothered. Or maybe he didn't think I was quite as bad as Nan made out.

I thought at first I would never survive. I worried all the time about Mum and Dad and how they were managing without me and whether Mum was still crying and whether Dad was flying off the handle. And then at the weekend they telephoned me. I spoke to Mum first. She was still a bit tearful but she also giggled quite a lot as well.

She said, "Guess what? You'll never guess! We've gone back to school! Me and your dad... we're going to parenting lessons. Learning how to be good parents."

She said that Cat had called round, and when she'd heard what had happened she'd arranged for Mum and Dad to take these classes.

"They're ever so good," said Mum. "I'm really learning how to do things properly."

And then Dad came on and said, "How about

that, then? Your mum and dad doing lessons! We'll be different people, Mand, when you come home. You won't recognise us! We'll be model parents, we will."

I told this to Nan and she just sniffed and said, "That'll be the day." But then she added that any improvement had to be better than none.

After that, I began to feel a little less despairing and to believe that perhaps Nan really might let me go back home sometime. I still said my prayer with the special bit added, but now I only said it twice a day, once when I woke up and once before I went to sleep. I thought that if Mum and Dad were learning how to be model parents, perhaps I ought to make a bit of an effort to be a model granddaughter so Nan wouldn't be ashamed of me any more.

So I tried. I really, really tried! But Nan wasn't in the least bit grateful. Like, for instance, when we went shopping I said to her, "I'd better check your shopping list. Make sure you haven't forgotten anything." That's all I said, just trying to look after her, like I do with Mum. She nearly jumped down my throat!

She said, "What do you mean, *check my shopping list*, you bossy little madam? I'll check my own shopping list, thank you very much! I don't need your assistance. I haven't gone senile yet, you know."

Then another time I caught her doing sardines on toast for Grandy's tea. Sardines on toast! At the end of a hard day's work, guarding the bank! I knew I had to warn her. I said, "You really ought to give him a proper man's meal, Nan. They don't like just having bits of stuff on toast."

Whew! If I hadn't have had this really thick skin, her eyes would have bored through me like lasers. I'd have had all holes.

She said, "Are you presuming to tell me how to feed my own husband?"

She really didn't like me trying to help her, so after that I thought I'd help Grandy, instead. But even he didn't seem to appreciate it. Like one Saturday we went into town together and he was going to get some paint for doing the inside of the house and he actually bought *three different colours*. He got this goldy colour for the ceilings and green for the windows and white for making little lines round things. He said that Nan had chosen them.

"She likes the place to look nice."

I was horrified. I said, "But Grandy, it's ever so much more expensive using all those different colours! It's really wasteful. You ought to stick to just one. It works out far cheaper. And if you went down the market you might even find a bargain!"

That's what Dad did last year. He staggered home with simply gallons of paint that nobody wanted on account of it being a strange sort of orangey-browny colour. (A bit like sick, really.) So far he hadn't actually got around to using it, but he reckoned there was enough there to do the whole place with. And the colour wasn't actually too bad. I quite liked it, myself. I thought it was cheerful. Mum agreed. She said it was "eye-catching". But when I told Grandy about it he just chuckled and said, "Yes, I've heard about our Barry's orange paint. Your Nan would have a fit if I came home with something like that."

I said, "But think of the money you'd save!"

Grandy said, "Young lady, if your Nan wants her house painted three different colours, I think that's her business, don't you?"

You can't help people if they don't want to be helped. Another time when we went into town Grandy said he'd just got to nip in and place "a bob or two each way" on a horse. I don't know what a bob is, whether it's a lot of money or a little, but I remembered Dad going into the betting shop and spending all Mum's housekeeping money, and so I grabbed hold of Grandy's arm and said, "Grandy! No!"

Grandy looked at me in surprise. He said, "No what?" I said, "Don't go in there, Grandy! You'll only regret it! You'll spend all the housekeeping!"

Grandy didn't freeze me out like Nan had, but he did sound sort of… irritable. He said, "Good heavens, child! I've been having a little flutter once a month ever since I got married. I'm not going to stop now!"

It's odd that even though Nan and Grandy don't seem in the least bit worried about money, not really, I mean they don't fly into a panic when brown envelopes land on the mat and they've never once had their telephone cut off, they don't ever seem to *do* anything. They'll never suddenly jump up and say, "Let's have fun!" the way we do at home. They're like two stodgy dumplings, sitting in a stew.

One day when Nan was wondering what to give Grandy for his tea – "And kindly don't tell me that he needs a man's meal!" – I said, "P'raps we could go out  somewhere." Nan said, "Out? Out where?" I said, "Anywhere! We could go for an Indian meal."

Nan shuddered and said, "No, thank you! You won't catch me eating that muck." She said that she and Grandy didn't care for Indian food: "It doesn't agree with us."

So then I said, "Chinese?" and Nan said, "Chinese gives me a headache. Besides, you never know what they put in there."

"Burgers?" I said. But Nan said burgers weren't proper food and in any case, what did we want to go out for?

"It's a sheer waste of money. You can eat far better staying at home."

I said, "Yes, but it's not nearly as much fun!"

Nan just snorted and said, "There's more to life than just having fun. That's a lesson we all have to learn."

I didn't actually say it, 'cos I knew she'd tell me it was impertinence, but what I actually thought, inside my head, was, "I hope it's not what Mum and Dad are learning."

Mum and Dad and me always had fun. No matter what. Even if the house was falling down and we hadn't got any money and sometimes Mum cried and sometimes Dad yelled, we always, sooner or later, had a kiss and a cuddle and a bit of a laugh.

I think that is what life is all about.

This next chapter is going to be the very last one! It will be Chapter Number Eight, and I think that is enough for anybody. It must be extremely exhausting for Cat's mum, typing it all out.*

I'm glad Cat's pleased with it, though, 'cos I've worked really hard. *Really* hard. I mean, I've been sat here doing this tape every night, almost, when I could have been watching telly or wall painting or even reading a book. (Ha ha! That'll be the day.) But anything rather than just talk talk talk all the time. It wears you out, talking does.

I wish I could just do everything in pictures!

*Note from Cat's mum: Not at all! I'm quite enjoying it.

Chapter Eight

One day when I had been at Nan's for a fortnight, Grandy came home from work and said, "Guess what? There's a chum of yours staying just across the way."

I couldn't think what he was talking about. I don't have any chums. Not since my friend Janis got moved. I really miss Janis. We used to have ever such fun together.

Grandy said, "Someone who goes to your school," and my stomach fell plop! right down into my shoes.

"If it's Tracey Bigg," I said, "I hate her. She's my worst enemy."

Nan tutted and said, "Hate is a very extravagant word, my girl."

I said, "She deserves it. She's evil."

Nan opened her mouth to start on at me but Grandy got in first. He said, "Well, it's not Tracey Bigg, it's a boy called Oliver Pratt."

I said, "*Oliver*?"

"Now I suppose you'll tell us he's evil," said Nan.

"Oliver's all right," I said. "He's just a bit of a wimp."

"Well, he says you're his friend," said Grandy. "He's staying with his nan, same as you are, while his mum's at work."

It turned out that Oliver's nan lived in Soper Street, just up the road from Nan and Grandy. She'd been moved out to Arthur's Mill same time they had. But just 'cos our nans happened to live on the same horrible estate didn't make us friends!

"I said he could drop by," said Grandy. "Tomorrow morning, after breakfast. That all right?"

It didn't really matter whether it was or not. When grown ups go and arrange things for you, you're expected to just meekly do what they say and not make any sort of fuss. 'Cos if you *do* make a fuss, then heavens! You should hear them carry on.

So that's how I got lumbered with Oliver. Only actually, as it happened, it wasn't so bad.

I wasn't really looking forward to it. I mean, for one thing, Oliver reminded me of school, which is something I'd rather *not* have to think about during holiday time. For another, he's not exactly the brightest. Janis might have been in a wheelchair, but she was really smart. We had fun together! But poor old Oliver, he's – well! Not always quite with it.

So I woke up next morning thinking "*Oh, drear*" and gazing glumly into my cornflakes expecting the worst, and it just goes to show that sometimes things can turn out better than expected.

We spent that first day making up rhymes about Tracey Bigg. I told Oliver my one…

Tracey Bigg goes wah wah wah,
When she talks it's all blah, blah!

and then he said that he'd got one, too. One that he'd made up all by himself.

Tracey Bigg
Is a big fat pig.

I said, "That's great, Oliver! That's really ace."

You have to encourage him. It wouldn't have been kind to point out that a) his rhyme was an insult to pigs and b) not strictly speaking true, since Tracey Bigg is just BIG rather than fat.

Although I hate, loathe and utterly detest her, I think you should be honest about these things.

Here are some of the other rhymes we made up.

2, 4, 6, 8,
Who's the person
that we hate?
T.R.A.C.E.Y.

Oh dear, what
♫ can the matter be? ♪
Tracey Bigg is locked
♪ in the lavatory! ♫
She'll be there from
Monday to Saturday
And nobody jollywell
cares! ♫ ♪

Actually, I sang a word that is ruder than "jolly" but I am thinking of Cat's mum and remembering that she doesn't like bad language and so I am trying to be polite.*

*Note from Cat's mum: Thank you! Very much appreciated!

Here is another one that Oliver made up.

Tracey Bigg's
a great fat cow.
I dont like her
anyhow!

This is another one.

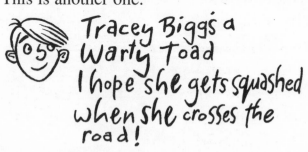

Tracey Bigg's a
Warty Toad
I hope she gets squashed
when she crosses the
road!

He's got this thing about animals. He wanted to do one about her being a hippopotamus but he couldn't think of anything to rhyme with it.

This is one that I did.

Tracey Bigg is a total grot
Picks her nose and eats
her snot
Picks her scabs and chews
them up
Makes you feel like
throwing up.

BLUUUUUUURGHGH!

She does pick her nose and eat it. I've seen her doing it. She's disgusting!

Someone once told me that if you keep picking your nose, your head will cave in.

Ha! That would be something.

Next day I went round to Oliver's place. Well, Oliver's nan's. He'd got something he wanted to show me. It was this bit of garden his nan had given him. Just this little patch right at the end. He'd had it since he was eight years old, and it was all full of flowers, just like my bedroom wall except that these were *real* – and it was Oliver who'd planted them!

What was totally and utterly amazing was that he knew all their names. I'd say, "What's this pink one?" and he'd say, "That's an anemone." And then I'd say, "What's the blue one?" and he'd say, "That's a delphinium."

He probably couldn't spell them (neither can I!) but he knew all there is to know about them, like what sort of soil they grow in and when you have to plant them and whether they're the kind that come up every year or the kind that die out.

Being really interested in flowers myself, because of the garden that I am one day going to have, I learnt as much as I could and tried to store it all inside my head. What I did was I drew pictures of all the flowers that Oliver had grown and put their names by them.

I bet Tracey Bigg doesn't know half as much as Oliver! I bet she doesn't know *any*thing. I think

Animony Delfinum

Oliver's really clever, being able to grow all those flowers and remember their names. Nobody helped him. He did it all on his own. I thought to myself that I would tell Cat about Oliver's flower garden when we went back to school. She'd be dead impressed! It's almost as good as writing a book.

Maybe *as* good. In a different way.

Oliver was only staying with his nan for three weeks. After that, he and his mum and dad were off to Ireland to live in a caravan for a bit. I would love to stay in a caravan! I think it would be really neat.

You would have little beds one on top of the other, and little tables that folded away when you didn't want to use them, and a little stove for cooking on, and a little teeny bathroom with a shower.

Everything would be lovely and warm and cosy and if you met someone you didn't like, such as for example Tracey Bigg, you would simply drive on to somewhere else.

Oliver said that the caravan he and his mum and dad stay in in Ireland isn't the sort that you could drive places in. It is in a caravan park and cemented to the ground.

I don't care. It would still be fun!

I felt a bit miserable when Oliver went off to Ireland. I suppose I'd sort of got used to having him around. He promised he'd send me a postcard with an Irish stamp on it, and he did! It's lovely. On the front there's this picture of a little funny creature that Nan said was called a leprechaun

and on the back he'd written a message:

Dear Mandy
   How are you?
         Love Oliver.

It wasn't much of a message, I suppose, but it gave me a happy feeling, especially as nobody had ever sent me a postcard before. Also I know that it is very difficult for Oliver to pick up a pen and write real words. I expect his mum and dad had to help him. He is a worse speller even than me!

He is also funny – he makes me laugh when he does his Tracey Bigg rhymes! – but a bit pathetic, as well, so from now on I am going to look after him. We have vowed that we will stay together, and when Tracey Bigg or the Murdo gang start their nonsense I will stick up for us. Oliver has said that he will stick up for us, as well, but I don't think it would be wise to rely on him. But that is all right! I can do it for both of us.

I won't mind so much about going back to school now that Oliver and me have decided to be friends. It's not so bad if you have someone to go round with. You can share things and have secrets and tell each other jokes. And we can sit together in class and choose each other for partners. And it won't matter if people jeer and sneer and say we're no-hopers, 'cos there'll be two of us.

Anyway, we're not! Oliver has his flower bed, and I have written a book!

Well, nearly. When I've finished this chapter I will have.

Once a week while I was at Nan's, Mum and Dad rang me to report how they were getting on at their classes. They were ever so excited about it! Mum said, "We're coming along a treat, Mandy! The teacher said that being willing to learn is half the battle."

Dad said, "We'll be reformed characters. You'll see!"

Nan still wouldn't let them come and visit me. She said that they had got to learn how to stand on their own two feet, and that it would only unsettle me. She said, "You're doing very nicely. I don't want them coming and setting you back again."

Wow! It was news to me that I was doing very nicely. I'd thought I was just one big pain in the you-know-what.

Then one day Auntie Liz rang up and I listened at the door while Nan was speaking to her.

I know you're not supposed to eavesdrop but I wanted to hear if Nan talked about me, which she did, so I reckon that made it OK. If people are going to talk about you then I think it's only fair you should be able to listen to what they're saying. That's what I think.

Anyway, this is what I heard Nan say. She said, "As a matter of fact, her manners have improved by leaps and bounds since she's been with us. She's quite a different child, you'd hardly know her."

Next Auntie Liz said something that I couldn't hear, and then Nan said, "I don't think you'd need have any worries. She's

me!

not a bad girl at heart. I'm really quite proud of her."

Help! Faint!

That weekend, Uncle Allan and Auntie Liz came to visit, and they brought Jade with them. Jade remembered me! She was ever so happy to see me, she cried, "Mandy, Mandy!" and came running over for a cuddle. I remembered my manners and talked dead posh, just like the Queen and was as good as good can be. They let me take Jade into the garden and we played skipping games and hopping games and I didn't use gutter language once!

When they went home that evening Auntie Liz said, "Well, Mandy! We'll have to see about getting you down to visit us some time."

I never *ever* thought she'd let me go to Croydon again. It didn't exactly make up for being away from Mum and Dad, but it did give me this lovely warm feeling of being approved of.

Yah boo and sucks to Tracey Bigg! I bet she hasn't got a little cousin like Jade.

I was so grateful to Nan for telling Auntie Liz nice things about me that I thought I really ought to start making more of an effort to be helpful to her, and I racked my brains thinking what I could do. She wouldn't let me check her shopping lists or make suggestions about what to give Grandy for his tea. But there had to be something!

And then I had an idea and thought that as a surprise I would re-organise her kitchen for her while she was upstairs one day having her afternoon nap. I did this for Mum, once, and she was ever so pleased. She said, "Oh, Mandy, that's brilliant!" It was, too. Before I got at it Mum's kitchen had been a proper mess, what with saucepans on the floor and the chip pan under the cooker (once we even found *mouse droppings* in it).

Nan didn't have saucepans on the floor and she didn't have a chip pan at all, 'cos she uses oven-ready, but I could think of all kinds of things I could do that would be an improvement.

First I moved the vegetable rack and put it

where the saucepans were, then I put the saucepans where the waste bin was, and then I put the waste bin by the back door.

Next I re-arranged all the cups on their little hooks, and then I changed the plates and cereal bowls around, and then I put the spice rack over near the cooker and tidied up all the sieves and the ladles and the things for crushing garlic and for chopping eggs and mashing spuds. Nan has a whole load of stuff in her kitchen! Ever so much more than Mum.

It took me a whole hour to get it all worked out. It looked really good! I honestly thought Nan would be pleased with me.

But she wasn't.

She made me put it all back again.

"*Everything…* just the way you found it!"

I said, "But, Nan, it didn't make sense the way you'd got some of this stuff. I mean, you need *saucepans* by the *cooker*. And the *waste* bin—"

Nan said, "I'll have my saucepans where I've always had my saucepans, if you don't mind! *And* my waste bin."

I tried ever so hard to be patient with her. Because, I mean, she is quite old. I explained how she really needed to plan things so she didn't have

to keep walking to and fro all the time. I said,
"You see, Nan, it's a terrible waste of energy.
When people get to your age—"

Nan just exploded. There was, like, steam
coming out of her ears.

She said, "Mandy Small, I have had just about
as much as I can
take of you and
your bossy ways!
I think it's high
time you went
back and bossed
your mum and dad,
instead."

Oh! I was so happy I rushed right across the
kitchen and hugged her.

Me! Hugging Nan! I've never done such a
thing in my life before. Nan just isn't a hugging
sort of person.

But she didn't seem to mind. She said, "I reckon
you'll do. Though whether those parents of yours
will have learnt anything is another matter."

I didn't care whether Mum and Dad had learnt
anything or not. I just wanted to get back to them!

The day I came home was the VERY BEST
DAY OF MY LIFE. Mum threw her arms round

me and I threw my arms round Mum and Dad threw his arms round both of us and we laughed and cried until we couldn't laugh or cry any more.

Mum and Dad wanted to tell me all about their classes they'd been having.

"We've learnt a thing or two, Mand!"

"We're going to be model parents from now on!"

Then Dad wanted to show me all the things he'd done around the place while I'd been away.

"See? I've put up that shelf in your bedroom at long last."

He had, too! He'd chopped up Nan's horrible old wardrobe and now I had the shelf that I'd always wanted. (I didn't ask where my clothes were going to go 'cos that might have upset them. At the moment they were all in piles on the floor, but I thought probably we'd be able to find a rail or something at a boot sale. Anyway, who cares

about clothes! My shelf was more important.)

Mum said that she'd been round the second-hand shops finding little ornaments to go on it.

"Little cats and dogs... I knew you'd like those."

As well as Dad doing things the Council had got on to the landlord and now we had a brand new water heater that worked first time without blowing the place up.

The floorboards had been fixed, and so had the roof.

And Dad had used up all his orangey-browny paint! He'd painted everything – the landing, the kitchen, the sitting-room, his and mum's bedroom, my bedroom, even the ceilings. They were all orangey-browny!

"Doesn't it look beautiful?" said Mum.

It did! It looked beautiful. Not really like sick at all.

"See, we've turned over a new leaf," said Mum. "We're going to keep the place nice from now on."

"That's right," said Dad. "Keep it in good nick."

"No more black eyes. No more broken heads."

"No more accidents of any kind. Come and have a look at this!"

Dad grabbed me by the hand and whizzed me into the kitchen. "See that?" He pointed, ever so proudly, at the kitchen cabinet. It was back on the wall. "There for good, this time," said Dad. "That won't be coming down again in a hurry!"

After I'd been shown all the wonderful things that had happened while I was away, Mum suddenly said, "Oh, I almost forgot! Miss Daley called about an hour ago. There's something she wants to tell you. She said it was important. You'd better ring her."

Me, ring Cat?

"I haven't got her number," I said.

"I have," said Mum. She sounded really pleased with herself. "Look! I wrote it down. See?"

"Does she really want me to ring her?" I said. I don't know why, but for some reason I suddenly felt nervous. I mean... *me*? Ring Cat?

"Yes, go on!" said Mum. "I'll dial it for you."

I just couldn't believe it when Cat told me the news. She said that "some bits of my book" – what she called "extracts" – were going to be put on display at the Town Hall! She said it was an exhibition of "creative activity" in the borough and that I'd been chosen out of hundreds of others.* What we had to do was get together and decide which bits we wanted to use. Not, *unfortunately*, the bits about Tracey Bigg! Cat said, "Some of the bits with the drawings. How about that?"

Fine by me! The drawings are what I like best. So now, yippee, I'm a Real Author!

"Of course, you do realise," said Cat, and she sounded sort of anxious, "there won't be any money attached to it?"

I knew that! I've known all along that I wouldn't really make my fortune. That was just a game I played. Pretending. I was just happy that everyone was going to see my name!

Mum and Dad were really thrilled.

"Get that!" chuckled Dad. "Our Mand's going to be a celebrity!"

"Yes," I said, "and I've drawn pictures of you and Mum, so you'll be celebrities as well. And I won't give any secrets away," I added, just in case he was still bothered.

*Note from Cat's mum: Well done!

But Dad was too proud and excited to care about secrets.

"This calls for a celebration!" he cried; and he decided that we would all go up the road to the Indian restaurant.

So that was what we did. And it was a really perfect evening. It started off being happy and it ended up even happier. Mum didn't cry, and nothing got spilt, and as we walked home Dad sang some of his Elvis songs while me and Mum swung hands.

I love my mum and dad! They'd tried so hard while I'd been away. They'd done so much. But I couldn't help giving this little secret smile as I looked at that kitchen cabinet. I thought to myself, "I bet it won't still be up there this time next week…"

kerrash!!!

I was right.
It wasn't!

Fruit and nut case, here I come!